ART QUARRY

Welcome to Purgatory

Zombies & Dragons #1

Copyright © 2023 by Art Quarry

All rights reserved. No part of this publication may be reproduced, stored or transmitted in any form or by any means, electronic, mechanical, photocopying, recording, scanning, or otherwise without written permission from the publisher. It is illegal to copy this book, post it to a website, or distribute it by any other means without permission.

This novel is entirely a work of fiction. The names, characters and incidents portrayed in it are the work of the author's imagination. Any resemblance to actual persons, living or dead, events or localities is entirely coincidental.

Art Quarry asserts the moral right to be identified as the author of this work.

Designations used by companies to distinguish their products are often claimed as trademarks. All brand names and product names used in this book and on its cover are trade names, service marks, trademarks and registered trademarks of their respective owners. The publishers and the book are not associated with any product or vendor mentioned in this book. None of the companies referenced within the book have endorsed the book.

First edition

This book was professionally typeset on Reedsy.
Find out more at reedsy.com

True words are often unpleasant, pleasant words are often untrue.

Lao Tzu

Acknowledgement

First and foremost, my family – you have always believed in me, even in the face of my faults and failures. Your unwavering support has been my source of courage and resilience. Without you, this book would not have been possible.

To my friends, thank you for not just accepting but embracing my unique brand of weirdness. Your acceptance of my quirks and eccentricities has allowed my creativity to flourish.

I owe a debt of gratitude to the writers who have inspired my love for the written word. As a child, I devoured the works of R.L. Stine, Stephen King, and Christopher Pike, which kindled my passion for the horror genre. Chuck Palahniuk and Kurt Vonnegut, you empowered me to appreciate and harness my unconventional thinking. Lastly, Daniel Kahneman and Morgan Housel, your insights into human cognition have helped me recognize and appreciate all the absurdity in the world to which I belong.

Dylan Garity, your meticulous editing and sharp attention to detail added a polished sheen to what was once an awkward manuscript.

Stewart Williams, your captivating cover design provided these words with a face.

And finally, to readers everywhere, I extend my heartfelt thanks. Keep on reading. Your support is the lifeblood of literature.

I

Perpetual Demise

1

Xane's Second Death

Xane awoke after his first death. His head felt woozy as he opened his eyes. Was it a dream?

His vision was still clearing when he heard the voice. "Welcome to Purgatory," it said. The voice sounded vaguely foreign, though without any recognizable origin.

Another few blinks, and Xane found himself naked on an empty cement floor in a room he didn't recognize. It was shaped like a cube, about eight feet on every side. It felt like a prison cell, but there were no bars, only four barren walls. Xane had been to prison before but never one like this. The wall directly in front of him was a giant video screen, and it seemed to be the source of the voice.

"You're probably wondering if you're dead. The answer is yes." Xane pinched himself and felt a tinge of pain. In the center of the video wall was a strange creature. Its skin was slime green, and atop its head lay sprawling, patchy black hair. The creature wore an off-white tunic underneath a brown belted smock. Huge, white-feathered wings rose above its wide shoulders.

"The next question you have—is this heaven?" The creature smirked. "Nope." Xane's mind raced as he scanned his surroundings. "You must be in hell then, you're thinking?" The creature paused a moment. "Well . . . it's complicated. You are in the city of Gaulcel. That's also my name. The city is named after me. That's because this city belongs to me. Now you belong to me, too."

Xane searched his memory. He recalled looking down and seeing the blood, remembered thinking how it was strange that he didn't feel any pain. If he hadn't seen it with his own eyes, he wouldn't have even realized that the bullet had pierced his chest. That was his last memory before waking up in this room.

He felt for the bullet wound. It wasn't there.

"We call this world Purgatory." Gaulcel said. "Everyone here had their first death on some other world. I see you came here from . . ." The audio stuttered a moment. "Earth."

Xane looked at Gaulcel's mouth. It was moving, but the movement did not match the sound he was hearing. It was dubbed. It reminded Xane of a kung fu movie he'd watched with his uncle as a kid. He looked at the giant screen with Gaulcel and realized that the whole video was pre-recorded. How many people had been shown this?

"Not everyone in Gaulcel is from your world." Gaulcel said. "And those that are, well, most of them are from a different time. You will be hard pressed to find anyone who speaks your language. That means you will need to learn this world's common tongue, but don't worry you will have plenty of time to do so." Gaulcel smirked again. The monster's teeth were hideous. "You're here forever."

The magnitude of everything the creature said was beginning to sink in for Xane. He felt so overwhelmed, he spoke his thoughts aloud. "I'm dead. I'm dead!" he repeated. No one could hear him. He was alone.

Xane had heard of panic attacks, but he'd never known what one felt like. His heart seemed like it would burst through his chest. He wanted to scream, but his voice refused him. He gasped for air in a rapid staccato rhythm. No matter how hard he tried, it seemed no breath would come. Anger overtook the anxiety, and he punched the video wall. It too was made of cement. Xane immediately felt the pain in his fist. He focused on his knuckles and his wrist, concentrating on their throbbing ache. Gradually, his breath returned.

"Before you go any further, I need to show you something." Gaulcel said.

Just then, as though it were on a timer, a conical hose, small and black, jutted down from a vent in the ceiling. Xane smelled gas and heard a click. In a flash, the entire room was engulfed in flames.

* * *

Xane's head felt woozy as he opened his eyes. Was the fire real? The pain felt real. His vision was still clearing when he heard Gaulcel's voice.

"Welcome back. You see, there are some things that are easier to demonstrate than explain. If you are wondering if you died again, the answer is yes. It won't be the last time."

Xane saw that he was in the same cubic cement room—nothing looked different. He could have sworn he'd broken a bone when he punched the wall, but his hand felt fine. The video wall was still showing the same ugly monster.

"Every time you die, you'll wake up right back here twenty-four hours later. This is your quarters. It's empty at the moment, but you're free to fill it with whatever you like. If you fight well, you can earn money in the tournaments and buy all sorts of things. There are tournaments every day. Participation is mandatory," Gaulcel said.

What kind of tournaments was he talking about? Xane remembered winning a Golden Gloves tournament as a teenager—that may have been the last time he ever felt pride. Xane's coach used to tell him that he was gifted as a boxer. It was Coach Clark who came up with Xane's ring name: Reaper. Coach Clark used to tell Xane that if he applied himself, he could have made the Olympic team.

If only Xane had listened to him more. Boxing may have been the only thing he was ever good at.

Xane couldn't help but ruminate on the past. His life was over, or at least the one on Earth anyway. He would never be able to show Coach Clark that he'd made something of himself. Coach Clark could have led him through a promising boxing career, but instead, Xane had started working for the mob. He'd always believed he would go straight eventually, but now there would be no more opportunities to turn his life around. His family, his bosses, his teachers, and his friends had all thought he was a lost cause. They may have never said it aloud, but Xane believed that everyone in his life thought he would never amount to anything. Even when he was at his worst, he still wished he could prove them wrong. Now, he had to take it as fact that that would never happen.

Gaulcel was still talking, and Xane realized he hadn't been paying attention. "The newbie tournament starts in five minutes, but there's one more thing I need to tell you" the creature said.

Xane looked at the vent in the ceiling again, jerking back in fear, but the black hose didn't appear this time.

"I have a special power. I hold a chain over your mind. It lets me read your thoughts whenever I feel like it. I can take control of your body. I hold the same chain over everyone in Purgatory. As you've already seen, I also have the power to kill you whenever I feel like it. I can kill you in whatever way I feel like. My point is, you have to do what I say—or else I can and will torture you to death as many times as I want. You may be thinking that sounds an awful lot like slavery. Well . . . if the shoe fits."

The video faded out as the ugly monster laughed.

2

The Woman with the Plan

He's arrived, she thought. Someone who fit the mold had finally arrived. Maribel had been living outside the gates of the city for what seemed like a century. She had spent all of that time planning, and the sign she was waiting for had finally come.

If all went according to plan, the city could soon be free. Upon learning the news, she felt both excited and nervous. Despite these intense feelings, she maintained her poker face for the elven trader who told her the news.

"Ma'am, I've provided you the requested information—that'll be 100,000 moneta please," Comerciam said. He spoke the words in the common tongue, though his first language was Elven. Comerciam had dealt with more humans in his time than he could ever think to count, and every one of them had been an open book. To the eyes of the elves, humans were notoriously emotional. Usually, talking to them was a terrible chore. Human faces continually and silently screamed with the wearer's emotions. A slight crease in an eyebrow came off like uncontrollable sobbing. A little flair in a nostril like a child having a temper tantrum. Comerciam had learned from his frequent dealings with humans that they couldn't help but express themselves this intensely.

This human was different, though. She seemed stone-faced and unfeeling. If it weren't for her ears, her hair, and her skin, Comerciam might have believed her to be an elf.

Maribel handed the elven trader a nondescript burlap bag of coin. "It's all there," she said. "Count it." She couldn't think of anything that would be more valuable to her than the information she had just learned.

"I'm going to have to take you up on that." Comerciam said. He could feel the weight of the bag, and it was substantial. "Please don't be offended, but we elves don't typically deal with this much in material coin. We prefer to transfer moneta by fingerprint scan, especially with large amounts." Comerciam usually knew whether a human was lying to him, but with this one, he wasn't sure. He reached into the bag and pulled out one stack of a hundred coins bound together with twine. Counting aloud, he made sure the woman could hear him. "One hundred, two hundred . . ." This was going to take a while.

Maribel stood in silence and listened as the elven trader counted the moneta. She had been a kind of lawyer in her first life, during a time when female lawyers were rare. When she aced the intelligence test, the men around her were astounded. Even so, she was treated like she was inferior for most of her career. Eventually, her colleagues learned to respect her, out of necessity. One thing Maribel had never been short of was confidence. She'd lived a long first life and was celebrated for her achievements.

Maribel had been in Purgatory for quite some time. The memories of her first life had started to fade, though she remembered only good things from that time. Her time in Purgatory had been almost all bad, but she had a plan to make things better—not just for herself but for everyone. It was a good plan, and deep down she believed it would work. Waiting for the right circumstances was agonizing, but it still beat her time in the city. Now, the waiting was over. He had come, someone who fit the mold, the exact type of person she needed to put her plan in motion.

Comerciam had given her two valuable pieces of information. First, a person with all the right characteristics had just arrived in the city. His name was Xane, she'd learned. A strange name to her. She wondered how names had changed on Earth since she died. Maybe in the present, Xane was as common as Harold or Clifford had been during her time. It made her miss Earth more acutely than usual.

Xane's name wasn't actually important to her plan. She just needed someone who spoke her language, and someone with a background like Xane's. He sounded like someone she could use.

The second fact the elf had provided was the last piece of information she needed to get Gaulcel. She knew the layout of the city as well as anyone, knew most of Gaulcel's daily routine and that he was almost never alone. Almost. What she hadn't known was how to get to him alone. Now, she did. Gaulcel would be on his own for only a short window of time, but it would be enough. Everything was falling into place.

"Ninety-nine thousand, nine hundred. One hundred thousand. That's the last one. It's all there, just like you said." The elven trader put the coins back into the burlap sack and closed it by pulling on the drawstring. "Thank you very much, Miss. Please let me know if you need anything else."

"No thank you," Maribel said. She needed to get to her quarters, and there was one way back that was quicker than any other. "I'll see you again in the city, and I may need another favor."

Then Maribel pulled out the small dagger tucked into her waist and slit her throat. Soon, she would wake.

3

Victory in the Pit

The bare cement walls of Xane's quarters felt like they were closing in on him. Again, he found himself wondering what the creature had meant by tournaments.

Not long after the wall video screen shut off, a hidden door slid open. A bearded man with broad shoulders, carrying a scythe, stood in the doorway and grunted some kind of order at Xane in a strange language.

"Garum ga ba didi gum!" the man bellowed. He stood well over six feet and wore oddly contoured clothes spun from silver-colored cloth. An image of a wolf's face was imprinted on the garment over the heart, and a wolf tattoo covered the length of his right forearm. A silver ring, displaying a matching wolf face to his clothing, adorned his right hand. "Garum ga ba didi gum!" He yelled it louder this time as he handed Xane a sort of white tunic.

Xane put the garment on. It stretched down below his knees. The bearded man motioned for Xane to follow him.

As he stepped through the doorway, he found himself in an even smaller room. The man with the wolf decorations garbled something Xane couldn't understand, and the hidden door shut behind him. Then the man garbled something else, and the room began to move. It was an elevator. Xane felt the room move down for what felt like a few floors. Then it started going sideways. This was not a normal elevator. After several minutes, the door opened.

Xane stepped out into yet another cement room, but this one was much larger. It was crowded too. It reminded him of being near the stage of a big rock concert. The wolf-obsessed man pushed Xane forward through the crowd. A sea of unfamiliar faces watched as he went past. Many belonged to creatures unlike anything he had seen in his life. They all stood on two legs, but most of the crowd was clearly not human.

After being marched for several feet, he found himself staring down into a pit. It was circular, dropping about ten feet below him, with a sand floor. The people and creatures were all gathered around the edge, looking down into it.

Then the wolf obsessed man pushed him without warning, and Xane fell forward.

He landed on his right shoulder at the bottom of the pit. Before standing, Xane looked around at the crowd watching him from above. *This is what a circus elephant must feel like before they go on a rampage,* he thought.

Above the main floor, Xane noticed a balcony. He could barely make out nine individuals sitting in chairs, but he was able to tell that each of them had on a different animal mask. One of the masks appeared to be the same wolf-face symbol he'd seen on the man who pushed him into the pit.

Xane heard a thud. Looking in the direction of the sound, he saw that the wolf-covered man had jumped down into the pit with him, still holding his scythe. The man pointed at his left wrist. "Didi gum gumple ba," he said. Xane instinctively raised his wrist. The man pulled a small metal chain from his pocket; a flat black trinket was attached to one side, covered in strange symbols. He placed the chain around Xane's wrist like a handcuff. "Piffum pa doku," the man said, and pointed at a black metal plaque on the pit wall. Xane could only look at him with confusion. "Piffum," he said again, pointing to the plaque. Then he took Xane's hand and pressed the black trinket on Xane's wrist chain against the plaque on the pit wall.

"You are in one of my tournament hollows." The voice seemed to come from nowhere, but Xane recognized it immediately. It was Gaulcel. He looked around for the creature, but there was no one else with him besides the man in the wolf attire. "The rules of the tournaments are simple. You will have five minutes to incapacitate your opponent. You may kill them if you wish, but it is not required. The fight ends when one of the combatants is unable to continue fighting."

The voice was coming from inside his head.

"If, after five minutes, no combatant has been incapacitated, the winner will be determined by the judges. In the balcony above you there are nine citizens of Gaulcel. Each is a high-ranking member from one of the nine clans. There's no need to explain the clans now, just know that it is in your interest to impress them." Xane looked again at the nine masked men. "Each tournament has sixteen combatants. The winner of each contest receives a small amount of moneta, the currency of Purgatory. A loss means you are eliminated from the tournament, but don't worry—there's another tournament tomorrow, and your participation is mandatory. If a combatant wins four straight contests, they win the tournament. The winner receives a more substantial cash prize, as well as a unique item."

Xane looked at the man in the pit with him, who shook his head and pointed up to the edge of the pit. He watched as a lizard-like creature fell from above, clearly having been pushed just as Xane had. The creature fell face-first into the sand, then angrily lifted itself onto two legs, each as wide as a tree trunk. Xane couldn't help but notice the creature's size—its head nearly reached over the edge of the pit. It had to have close to a hundred pounds on him.

The man with the wolf tattoo grabbed the lizard creature's wrist and wrapped a small chain around it, one that looked just like Xane's. He pulled the creature over to the plaque that the man with the scythe had called "piffum"—or at least Xane thought that was what had happened. He watched as the creature reacted to Gaulcel's voice in his head. It seemed the creature was hearing the exact same message that he just heard. Then the lizard looked at Xane.

The man with the wolf tattoo pointed to a light bulb hanging above their heads in the center of the pit. In a flash, it came on and shined bright red. A buzzer sounded. The man with the wolf tattoo pointed at Xane, then at the creature. Standing between them, he brought his hands together and took a step back. The fight had begun.

The lizard creature didn't waste any time. It began moving toward Xane with transparently bad intentions.

Xane couldn't help but think of his time with Coach Clark. His boxing training took over, and he sized the creature up. It was right-handed, and from the way it moved toward him, it was clear that the creature was no experienced fighter. Xane knew exactly what it would do first.

The right hand swung wildly toward his head. Xane dodged it easily and jabbed his left fist straight into the center of the thing's face. Its head snapped back from the blow. On instinct, Xane sent a right uppercut straight to its scaly lizard chin, following that up with a left hook to the temple, putting his full weight behind the last punch. It was a combination he'd practiced thousands of times. Coach Clark always used to say he had a left hook like Joe Frazier.

The lizard creature fell stiff to the sandy floor, knocked out cold.

The men and creatures surrounding the pit roared their enthusiasm as the man with the scythe raised Xane's hand. He didn't even bother to check on Xane's opponent. The fight was over.

4

Death in any Language

After the fight, a rope ladder unfurled from the edge of the pit. The man with the scythe pointed at the ladder, gesturing for Xane to climb out, which he did. He was back on the cement floor, surrounded by other men and creatures. Several of them patted him on the back, muttering in languages Xane had never heard before. He could tell, though, that they were meant to sound encouraging.

One of the creatures pointed to a little fenced-in area on the opposite side of the pit. There were fourteen combatants inside, and it looked a bit like a dugout at a baseball field. A viewing deck. Xane walked over to it, and another man dressed in wolf garb opened the gate and ushered him inside.

Turning, he looked back down into the pit. The lizard creature he'd knocked out moments earlier had begun to stir. The man with the scythe nudged it with his foot until it stood up and exited via the same rope ladder Xane had.

The man at the gate pointed to two of the combatants in the dugout with Xane. One of them was human, skinny and frail. The other was a short and stout creature with a prominent face. Not human, but similar. It had a long, red beard and brawny shoulders.

When the frail man realized he would have to fight next, he started shaking his head. "Non, non, non. See teh play, jen voo plah." Xane recognized the language and accent as French but didn't understand what he was saying. There was fear in the Frenchman's eyes. The usher who had opened the gate for Xane now grabbed the man and dragged him out of the dugout. Despite the man's protests, the usher threw him down into the pit. The Frenchman landed in the sand with a thud.

In contrast, the red-bearded creature stood up and casually strolled to the rope ladder. It was only about four and half feet tall, but its body was almost that wide. The creature carried its weight on thick, boxy legs. *A dwarf,* Xane thought. The dwarf climbed down with a slow, eerie calmness. His eyes were focused on the human. Xane recognized that facial expression—he'd worn it himself every time he stepped into a boxing ring. The dwarf meant business.

Both combatants were given wristbands and made to listen to the spiel from Gaulcel. Then the light turned red. The Frenchman pleaded with the dwarf, holding his hands up and speaking rapidly in French. Xane didn't understand the words, but the meaning was clear regardless. He was begging the creature not to hurt him.

The dwarf was unfazed. He motioned to the Frenchman, yelling in yet another language Xane could not understand. He was inviting the Frenchman to make the first move. In response, the Frenchman started tapping his shoulder rapidly. Tapping out, trying to tell the dwarf that he quit. His opponent either didn't understand the gesture or didn't care. He dashed at the Frenchman with his head lowered, planting his burly shoulder straight into his knees. The frail man fell face-first into the sand and lay there, motionless.

The dwarf grabbed the Frenchman by the right leg, snapped it toward his head, and kicked him behind the knee. The Frenchman rolled over, yelping with pain. He had been pretending to be knocked out so the fight would be over, but the dwarf wasn't done yet. He stomped on the man's groin with his full weight. The Frenchman grunted and moved his hands down to protect the tender area, but the dwarf was quick. While the Frenchman's hands were down, he stomped again, this time on the Frenchman's neck. The man gasped for air, and the squat, bearded creature kicked him in the chin. Blood spurted from his mouth. The dwarf put a knee into his throat and held it there.

"See teh play, juh new pas respirer." The Frenchman's voice was hoarse and low. His eyelids drooped. Minutes passed before a buzzer sounded.

The man with the scythe came over and patted the dwarf's shoulder to tell him the fight was over. The creature stood up confidently, and the crowd cheered him. The man with the scythe pointed toward the nine masked men in the balcony. The judges. Each held up a card in their right hand with a symbol Xane could not recognize. The decision was unanimous. The man with the scythe raised the dwarf's right hand.

Even after the judges gave their decision, the Frenchman continued to lie in the sand of the pit, not moving at all. The man with the scythe nudged him with his foot—still no movement. Xane realized that he was dead. The crowd didn't seem to care; clearly, this wasn't the first time they'd seen someone die in the pit. The wolf-obsessed referee picked up the Frenchman's corpse, tossed it over his shoulder, and carried it to the wall, where he pulled open what looked like a laundry chute. Then he chucked the body down the conveyor. The Frenchman would wake up again tomorrow, Xane realized. Then he would have to do another tournament. The thought gave him chills.

The next fight also lasted the full five minutes, though the other combatants were winded after one. They were human, and they pretty much just slapped at each other until time ran out. The judges split six to three. This tournament was every combatant's first, Xane recognized. They all must have just woken up in this place around the same time that he had.

That contest was followed by a fight between two catlike creatures. Their bodies were thin and sinewy, and whiskers jutted from pink noses on their fur-covered faces. One of the cat creatures was clearly the superior fighter, though it wasn't as sadistic as the dwarf had been. After wrestling for a minute or so, it managed to pin its opponent. It was clear the weaker cat was unable to escape. Ten seconds passed, and it looked at the man with the scythe as if to say this should be over. There was no reason to wait until time expired. He nodded, then begrudgingly raised the cat creature's arm. Its hands looked like paws, but they had opposable thumbs.

As the tournament went on, Xane watched carefully. He sized up each of the other combatants the same way he had done with his opponents during his boxing career. Best to be as prepared as he could. He watched the way that each fought and developed a plan for how he would face them, taking mental notes of their strengths and weaknesses.

His second fight went just as the first had. His human opponent opened with a big, sweeping right that missed. Xane countered with a combination of punches punctuated by his left hook. Another knockout.

The dwarf also won his next fight. Xane noted that he was a grappler. He liked to fight in close and hold his opponents. The dwarf's lack of height and low center of gravity made this hard to defend against, and he was also surprisingly strong. The dwarf lifted his human opponent over its head and slammed him into the sand, headfirst, instantly knocking him unconscious. Even though the fight was over, the man with the scythe had to pull the dwarf away from the human to stop him from continuing the beating.

Xane's next contest was against the cat creature. It had claws on its hands, or paws, or whatever those were at the end of its arms. It was fast, too—he would need to find a weakness. From watching its previous bouts, Xane had noticed how the cat creature never left its stomach area unguarded. Its midsection looked thin and puny. Xane decided that would have to be his target. He was right—more right than he meant to be. When his fist connected with the cat creature's ribs, he heard a snap. He'd broken one.

The sound of the breaking rib brought out Xane's conscience. The adrenaline of the tournament had allowed him to block out reality. Now, having broken this creature's rib, it hit him like a ton of bricks. He felt terrible. What was he doing? It was his first day in Purgatory, and he had already been turned into a prize-fighting slave. This whole world was deranged. Xane was mad at Gaulcel, but even more so, he was mad at himself. He knew the cat creature was feeling severe pain, and it was his fault.

Xane didn't want to fight anymore after that, but his opponent wasn't done. Apparently, the adrenaline coursing through its veins wouldn't allow the reality of the broken rib to manifest yet. Coughing up blood, the feline beast managed to catch Xane's right cheek with its claws. At first, it felt like just a slap. Xane moved to the side and pushed the cat creature to the ground. Finally, the cat creature realized it wasn't getting back up. The man with the scythe stepped in between them and raised Xane's hand.

He didn't care that he had won the fight. He could only think of the creature that was still writhing in agony.

"I'm sorry," Xane said aloud. "I just wanted to defend myself." He knew the other fighter wouldn't understand him, but he needed to say it anyway. The broken rib could heal, Xane thought, but it would take months. For months, it would hurt just to breathe. The man with the scythe grunted and motioned for Xane to move aside.

He suddenly realized what the scythe was for.

The man laid the weapon's blade in the sand next to the cat creature. He pointed to the blade, then dragged his finger over his neck sideways—the universal symbol for death. The scythe started glowing a bright white. In a rapid motion he pulled the scythe toward the cat-creature, who died instantly. It was a mercy killing. In this world, where death was temporary, the creature would wake up tomorrow with its ribcage intact.

Xane was shocked. His eyes widened to the size of quarters, and tears started to flow. It wasn't until that moment that he realized his right cheek was bleeding. The cut from those claws had been deep. It would leave a scar. *Good,* Xane thought. He felt like he deserved it. He wanted the scar to always remind him of what he had done. In fact, he decided he needed to stay alive as long as he could so that the scar never went away.

He had to figure out a way to escape this city—or save it from its evil ruler. The crowd's reaction to the death was mixed. There were cheers, but many of the men and creatures remained silent. The silence was somehow audible. The mood had changed. They'd stopped being spectators, remembering that they too were slaves.

Xane's win over the cat-creature put him in the finals of the tournament. The sadistic dwarf was his opponent. The creature's small stature meant that Xane would have to punch low. His boxing training hadn't given him any experience with kicking, and Xane knew better than to try it now. The last thing he'd want to do against this dwarf would be to lose his balance.

In his prior fights, the dwarf's stamina had never really been tested. Carrying all that heavy muscle in a fight for five minutes required a lot of endurance. Xane was banking on the dwarf being unable to keep up its level of aggression. There was a saying in boxing—"hit and don't get hit." Xane had always been more of a defensive fighter. He relied on his speed to make opponents miss. Then he would counterpunch while their guard was down. As an opponent got tired, they'd grow careless, and when that happened, Xane would come out swinging. This fight with the dwarf would follow the same plot, or so he hoped.

As expected, the dwarf rushed Xane's legs as soon as the fight started. The creature kept his head and shoulders low, knowing that Xane would have to reach far down to land a punch. If he tried to kick, the dwarf was prepared to grab his leg and take him down. Instead, Xane dodged to the right side like a matador avoiding a charging bull. As he did so, he was able to reach down and land a stiff left jab above the dwarf's left eye.

His opponent shook off the punch as though it were from a fly swatter. Xane backed up, and the dwarf charged him again. The results were the same. Xane's second jab landed in precisely the same spot as the first. His punches weren't doing any real damage, but the dwarf wasn't doing anything to Xane at all. Hopefully, that would be enough to carry the judges.

The dance continued. The dwarf rushed Xane three more times before catching on that he needed to change strategy. The cumulative effect of Xane's jabs had caused the dwarf's left eye to swell up, and a small cut had opened there . Xane heard the dwarf breathing heavy. He was moving slower. The strategy was working.

The dwarf feigned like he was about to rush Xane again, but at the last second stepped to the side and kicked at Xane's kneecaps. He dodged the kick easily. All of the dwarf's weight was now on one foot, his reaction time slowed from fatigue. This was Xane's opportunity. Instead of a jab, he crouched down and shot up with a left uppercut. The punch landed under the dwarf's beard, directly on the chin. The creature fell flat on its back from the force.

Xane had an opportunity to take advantage of his opponent's prone position, but he chose not to take it.

The dwarf got up quickly and rushed Xane again, hoping to catch him off guard, but Xane dodged and jabbed just like he had before. The dwarf's eye was closing from the swelling. Instead of rushing again, he took a step back., motioning for Xane to come forward. Xane moved toward the dwarf, who brought his hands up to cover the injured eye. Xane crouched down and stuck his head forward to give the creature a target. It took the bait, throwing a hard looping left hand in the direction of Xane's jaw, leaving an opening.

Xane blocked the punch with his right hand while his left hook came around like lightning, landing on the dwarf's face with a smacking sound. He could see the lights go out. The dwarf face planted in the sand. It was over. Xane would not need to rely on the judges after all.

When the tournament ended, there was no ceremony. The man with the scythe produced a heavy black punching bag, seemingly out of nowhere, the kind that would hang from a ceiling on a chain. It had four unrecognizable silver symbols in the center, and the wolf image that Xane had seen all over the man's clothing was embroidered on the opposite side.

It was his prize for winning the tournament, he realized. He hoisted it on his shoulders. Then the next tournament, with all new combatants, began.

5

Moneta

Xane woke up. His vision was hazy, his head woozy. He was trying to figure out whether he was hungover or if he'd died. He touched his face. The scar was still there.

"Thank god" he said under his breath before recognizing the irony. He had an eerie suspicion that there might be someone listening.

As it did every morning, the video screen came on unprompted. "Time for the morning announcements," Gaulcel said. It was his real voice, in the common tongue, and Xane was beginning to understand it. A few weeks ago, some spray-paint had appeared on one of the Gaulcel posters in the marketplace. Every day since then, the poor guy they say had done it was killed in an awful and unique way. The worst part was that the guy would do it to himself, on screen for everybody—the whole thing was meant to be a demonstration of Gaulcel's mind control powers.

"Today, Mr. Merit will die from death by a thousand cuts," Gaulcel said. Every day, the monster would mention that Merit was being punished for vandalism, but they never described the words he had supposedly spraypainted. The graffiti that had appeared in the marketplace was written in the common language. From a passerby, Xane had learned that it said, "Vote for Gundarce." The words were sprayed on the poster in a line that went right through Gaulcel's face. Xane did not know who or what

Gundarce was, and neither did the passerby.

Gaulcel continued with his spiel. "His only tool for this task—a piece of paper. So I guess I should say its death by a thousand *papercuts*."

It could happen to me—that was what Gaulcel wanted them to think, but Xane was not going to let that monster mess with his head. He tuned out what was happening to poor Mr. Merit. Merit was a sahuajin, which was the common word for the lizard-like creature Xane had encountered for the first time in the pit. There were more sahuajin in the city of Gaulcel than any other sentient species.

Xane had stopped watching the morning torture sessions. He knew Gaulcel wanted the whole city to watch, so ignoring it was his small act of rebellion. The video wall could not be turned off, but Xane could turn away. He took the time to work out with the heavy bag.

There were so many creatures in this city, Xane almost never saw the same one twice. He'd been kept in the same building, only able to go where the elevator could take him. In all the months he'd been there, Xane had never even seen a window. The city was a prison, and Gaulcel was its warden. But Xane knew there was life outside of the building. There were traders who came in and out, bringing all kinds of goods. That was another thing Xane wanted to learn more about. Any little piece of information could be just the thing he needed to take Gaulcel out.

After that first day, Xane had decided to put all his focus into taking him down. He knew himself well enough to know that he had to focus on something. One thing Xane was never short of was anger. Without somewhere to focus it, anger became self-destructive. Xane's mind worked best when it had an opponent, and Gaulcel fit the bill.

Anger needed an enemy—that was a lesson Xane had learned the hard way. Losing focus was what had led him away from boxing, led him to drugs. He started spending all his time with people he didn't know or care about, people who didn't know or care about him either. In his first life, Xane got into debt and started doing things he wasn't proud of, the same things that ultimately got him killed. He wasn't going to let that happen again.

Xane wasn't sure how he was going to take out the cruel creature yet, but he knew the first step: he had to learn the ins and outs of the city. Then, maybe he could find a weakness and exploit it. For as much as Xane hated this world, he was well suited for it. In the months he'd been in Gaulcel so far, he never lost a fight. Every day, he went to the pit and afterward had a unique prize to bring back to his quarters, as well as more moneta.. For the unaffiliated fighters, one win in the pit was worth five moneta. A tournament win earned you fifty. Moneta could come in physical coins, apparently, but Xane had never seen one. All his cash was only accessible to him by a fingerprint scanner, making it impossible to steal.

There were only two ways to get moneta in Purgatory—win in the pit or get it from somebody who won in the pit. A robust economy had formed around labor in the city, but all the money flowed down from fighters. Anyone who could not fight well had to make themselves useful or starve.

Plenty of citizens starved. Over and over again.

A day's worth of the cheapest food cost about five moneta, the same as one win in the pit. Early on, Xane had tried to give money away to the hungry, but there just wasn't enough. There were too many who needed it, too many desperate. Any chance for free food would bring a swarm of starving creatures. As hard as it was to turn them away, Xane had to do it. He couldn't take on Gaulcel if he became one of them.

Some of the clan fighters had set up a food bank. There wasn't enough to take care of everyone, but there was a lottery system—more fair than first come, first serve. Xane donated most of his winnings every day, but he was also careful to save some up in case he hit a slump.

The big money was in the tournaments of the nine clans. Xane would not become eligible to join a clan until he had been in Purgatory for one year, and the clan would have to recruit him. Any resident who was not in a clan was considered unaffiliated. Clans only recruited the best fighters.

The Wolf Clan had taken notice of Xane after his first tournament, and some of the others were starting to follow suit. Clan members acted as Gaulcel's henchmen, and Gaulcel rewarded them for their service. Xane figured he would have to join a clan to get near the tyrant. It was probably the only way to gain an opportunity.

The morning torture still wasn't over; Xane would be called down for a tournament as soon as it was. It went on for an unusually long time that morning, but Xane kept his focus on hitting the heavy bag. It was imbued with some kind of power so that no matter how hard or how many times Xane punched it, his fists never hurt. Every tournament prize was different, but they all had some kind of power like that. The merchants paid well for tournament prizes, and Xane sold most of what he won. He'd only kept the heavy bag, a pair of padded finger gloves that made his hands faster, and a falchion-style sword. Xane didn't know what the sword did.

There were no hard rules in the pit. All kinds of weapons were allowed. Most fighters chose not to use a weapon, though, because if they did, their opponent might use one too. Xane had been fortunate not to encounter any opponents who did so. He had seen a few of those fights, though, and wanted to be ready if he ever ended up in one. Xane brought the sword with him to the tournament every day, but before the fight started, he threw it in the sand. He didn't know what the sword's power was, and he didn't want to find out. The blade was adorned with strange symbols, different than the ones on the heavy bag. Xane had no clue what they meant.

He was also learning to kick, finally. He'd have to face tougher and tougher opponents if he kept winning, and he wanted to shore up every potential weakness. Guff, from the Wolf Clan, was helping him perfect his balance. He felt confident enough to use kicks in the pit now.

Xane's foot thudded against the heavy bag, drowning out the sound of Gaulcel and Merit's screams. The chain he'd bought to hang it from the ceiling shook violently. It wasn't strong enough to hold the heavy bag forever, but it worked for now. The three symbols glowed with each strike. Xane had learned that they stood for four words in Common. The motto of the Wolf Clan. It roughly translated to, "strong pack, strong wolves." He'd also asked Guff about the symbols on the sword, but Guff wasn't able to translate.

The workout had Xane breathing heavy. He grabbed a cup from under the water cooler that he'd recently installed. The liquid felt cold on his teeth. He swirled it around between his cheeks before swallowing, a ritual to get him into a fighter's mindset. If he lost today, it wasn't going to be for lack of preparation.

"Looks like Mr. Merit couldn't quite make it to a thousand cuts. He survived nine hundred and thirty-eight. I guess he'll have to try again tomorrow," Gaulcel said jovially. The video screen on the wall shut off.

Xane's wrist chain started to blink. That meant it was time to go to that morning's tournament. If he didn't leave immediately, one of the clans would pay him a visit. Xane said "open" in Common. The door obliged, and Xane got on the elevator.

6

Learning the Language

Every day after the tournament, Guff, from the Wolf Clan, would come tutor Xane in the common tongue. Guff always brought his scythe to Xane's quarters, just as he had that first day. It was a tournament prize that the other man had won years ago. It had the power to kill without causing any pain.

Guff was a lieutenant in the Wolf Clan. His job was to referee the tournaments the Wolf Clan produced, and his scythe helped with the job. Each clan sponsored their own tournaments. The unaffiliated fought first in the morning, and then there would be a tournament for Wolf Clan members. Xane had seen Guff fight a few times. He was on a different level, as were all the clan members. Hundreds of years of experience fighting everyday would do that to you.

From what Xane could tell from the descriptions, Guff had come from Earth and died sometime during the Viking age. He had been in Purgatory for close to a thousand years. Whatever language he spoke before he died the first time, he had long since forgotten it. Hearing it now, he probably wouldn't even recognize it.

"Congratulations on your win today." Guff said.

"Thank you," Xane replied in Common. The words had gotten easier to say.

LEARNING THE LANGUAGE

The tutoring sessions consisted mostly of Guff talking at Xane about the city. There were no grammar lessons. Guff had probably never learned the difference between a noun and a verb in his time, let alone past, present, and future tense. He brought a textbook with him but never even looked at it. Xane would skim through it on occasion, but it was all written in Common. Xane had never been very good with grammar in his own language, anyway.

Even so, he was beginning to pick up the common language the same way a child would, through immersion. He was forced to use it every day in the marketplace. Merchants frequently tried to cheat him. When caught, they would play it off as a miscommunication. And despite Guff's imperfect teaching style, his visits were helping. Xane could understand most of what the man said now.

He had been holding on to one question for a long time and finally felt confident enough in his speaking ability that he might get an answer. "Where are all the women?" he asked.

Guff cupped his hands above his chest to symbolize breasts. "Women, eh?" His face wore an amused expression.

"Yes, women," Xane said. "Are there any women in this place?"

"Oh yes . . . if you get into Wolf, there are stores that sell pictures. Videos are very expensive."

"I'm not talking about pictures. I mean live women. Are there any here? Any women I can talk to or see face-to-face."

"Some unaffiliated will pretend to be woman, for a price."

"I'm not talking about sex. I mean female. Opposite gender. No penis. Any people like that in all of Purgatory." Xane desperately wanted Guff to understand what he was asking.

The man furrowed his brow and thought for a full minute before responding. "Yes," he said. "But they exist in different building."

It was the first time that Xane had heard about other buildings in this world. The first time he really knew for sure that he was in a building at all. There were no windows anywhere, and he had never even seen the outside. "Is there any way I can meet them or talk to them?" Xane asked. "Can I leave the building?"

Guff's response was long, and Xane only understood about half of it. From what he got, the location of building exits were secret, and if you managed to find one, it would be guarded. The citizens of Gaulcel were only allowed to leave on special permission from the most elite clansmen or the ruler himself. Guff had never left the building. If the desire to leave had ever occurred to him, he had long since blocked it out.

There were other buildings somewhere, buildings that only quartered women. Some of the most elite clansmen were permitted to meet with actual women and even take wives, but Guff was not high enough in the Wolf Clan hierarchy to be one. Xane learned there were no kids either. He could see why no one would want to have a baby in this godforsaken place.

Apparently, there were legends about rare babies born in Purgatory. The common belief was that their spirits were toxic. If they were discovered, they were disposed of immediately—same with pregnant mothers. Guff believed that individuals born in Purgatory would not respawn. According to Guff, the mothers would, but without the pregnancy. He also said he hadn't seen a child, pregnant woman, or any woman at all for the matter, in his entire time in Gaulcel.

Xane had to stop Guff's monologue so he could digest what he'd just learned. "Practice kick," Xane said.

"Okay." Even though it'd been close to a thousand years, Guff still understood what Xane was going through. It wasn't easy for anyone to adjust to this world. He moved over to hold the heavy bag.

Xane kicked the bag low to start. First with his left foot, then with his right. He was right-footed, but he wanted to make sure both legs were strong. He began low, kicking the bottom of the bag, where Gaulcel's knees would be. Then he went back and forth, alternating left and right kicks, landing each blow with the sweet spot at the broad part of his foot.

Soon, he was warmed up. He tried kicking a little higher, where Gaulcel's chest would be. Left. Right. After another twenty or so kicks, he tried kicking even higher. It was still hard for him to stretch that high, but he was determined. The height where Gaulcel's face would be. Xane started jumping as he kicked. His feet were landing hard against the bag with thud after thud, but his balance was still a little shaky on the landing.

If Xane ever had an opportunity to fight Gaulcel, it wouldn't be a fair fight. He had seen the tyrant's mind control powers during the morning announcements. He would have to hit him hard and catch him by surprise, knock him out with the first blow. If Gaulcel was asleep, he couldn't control anyone's mind—Xane hoped. He didn't like to sucker punch people, but he would have to in this instance. *Or sucker kick,* he thought, and chuckled to himself.

"Let's get some water," Guff said. Xane nodded, ready for a break. He stopped kicking and walked to the water cooler in his quarters.

"Can people get old here?" he asked.

"Yes," Guff said. "Aging same, but old people don't last long."

"What happens when they die?" Xane realized the answer to his own question right after he asked it.

"Respawn." Guff said. "When human comes back, in same physical condition as about twenty-five years old, Earth time."

"What about the nonhumans?"

"Rectus quod," Guff said. "No say nonhuman. Offended."

"Sorry, what about the rectus quod?"

"I don't know their aging. Invunt live longer than humans before old."

"Invunt?" Xane said.

"You know this. Short. Wide. Beard." Guff said. He meant dwarves, Xane realized.

"Okay. Punch," Xane told Guff. They went back to the bag, where Xane practiced his combinations. He had done these drills since he was a kid, since long before he died. There were different starting punches, but the combination wasn't over until he threw a left hook. Jab. Straight. Hook. Each punch landed with precision. Jab. Straight. Hook. The left landed with a thud; Guff held the bag steady. Jab. Straight. Hook. The repetitions sharpened Xane's mind, and he needed to be sharp to beat Gaulcel.

"Can Gaulcel die?" Xane asked.

"Everyone dies. The last time I died was about six years ago."

"But what about Gaulcel?" he asked again.

"City died last about sixty years ago."

"Not city. Rectus quod. The leader. From the morning announcements." Xane really wanted Guff to understand him.

"City died last about sixty years ago. Offended," Guff said. "You're too dense to join Wolf. You best wise up before you hit year."

It was not out of character for Guff to rib at Xane, or even call him dense. "What do you mean the city died?"

"About sixty years ago. Happened fast. City respawned before anyone knew it was dead. Like nothing happened. Enough talk of this. Offended."

Xane was starting to understand how tough this world was going to be. There had to be someone else listening to them train.

"When respawn, still have memory from all the lives lived here," Guff said.

7

Gaulcel's Horde

Xane still felt disoriented at times, but he'd learned a lot since his first day in Purgatory. It made him sick to his stomach when he thought about what happened after that first tournament.

Xane's building in Gaulcel was several miles wide and several miles long. One of the floors close to the first floor was the goppidum, or marketplace. It reminded Xane of the food court in an airport mall, except that it seemed to go on endlessly. Shuttle trains made continuous loops, stopping in the busy areas. It could take lifetimes for Xane to visit every shop and eatery in the goppidum. Most places served dishes Xane had never heard of, from worlds he hadn't heard of either. Guff had brought all the newbies to the goppidum after the first tournament. Then he left them there.

Xane and the other thirteen newbies who'd survived the tournament got lost almost immediately. They followed Guff because they didn't know what else to do. It seemed like the former Viking was trying to give them a tour, but at that time, none of them understood anything he said. The only thing Xane understood was the locations of some bathrooms. Then Guff disappeared into the crowd, leaving them all to fend for themselves.

Xane wandered the marketplace with the group for hours after Guff abandoned them, not sure where to go. He had no idea how to get back to his quarters. He'd allowed Guff to carry the punching bag that he had just won in the tournament, and when Guff disappeared, Xane thought he might have stolen it. The other combatants from the tournament followed Xane as if he were their leader. None of them spoke his language. None of them seemed to understand where they were.

The dwarf Xane had beat in the finale acted different now that the fighting was over. Not only was he not sadistic, he actually tried to be helpful. The stout creature was the first to notice a "piffum" plaque outside the shuttle. This one had a little video screen on the wall next to it. When activated, the screen showed a map of the goppidum. There were hundreds of shuttle stops spread out in the three major regions: a food court called the karbero, an industrial section called kopus, and an area with different kinds of shops called the korum. The group was currently in the middle of the karbero.

A few of them motioned for Xane to scan his wristband to the piffum first. Then they took turns until they all had the map explained to them in their own language. The dwarf looked at Xane and rubbed his gut. He was hungry. The whole group was hungry. They walked by several eateries, but customers were segregated. There were places for the lizard creatures, places for the cat creatures, places for the dwarves, and places for humans. Xane thought it best to keep the group together.

Eventually, he found a place selling something called kabloaf. There was a mix of all types of creatures eating the stuff. Xane figured it was the best chance to please everybody. He pointed to the place because he couldn't read the sign, which was written in Common. One small space in the endless mall, the eatery's store front was surrounded by fencing that jutted out into the karbero walkway. Within the fence lay small tables and chairs filled with every kind of creature eating kabloaf. Two guards from the Viper Clan stood outside the lone entrance.

Xane approached. The guards grabbed his hand and scanned his thumb. A light on the scanner turned green. It showed the guards that Xane had moneta. For the first time, he saw how much he had. The number appeared in his mind at the same time his thumb was scanned, and the guards waved him through.

The dwarf walked in next, followed by a few more of Xane's fellow tournament combatants. As each of them stepped through, the guards scanned their thumbs. The cat creature that had lost in the first round was stopped by the guards on the way in its scanner turned red. The guards would not let it through. Earlier that same day, it had been outclassed in the pit by the other cat creature Xane had killed. The losers of the first round earned no moneta, so they could not have food. This was truly a cruel world.

Xane motioned to the guard to let the cat creature through. He would have gladly paid for all the fighters in his group that came up short that day. The guards didn't respond, and at first Xane thought they just didn't understand. So Xane grabbed the cat creature, looked at the guard, held up his thumb, and pointed to the creature. The guard, another human, pushed Xane back and barked something at him in Common. Then he pushed the cat creature back.

The guard was wearing a scimitar sheathed on his waist, and he put his hand on it. Six members of their motley group were not being allowed into the place. It would have been eight if not for the Frenchman killed by the dwarf and the cat creature Xane had killed. He motioned for all six of them to wait.

The fence contained an enclosure with about twelve tables, all of them occupied. Some creatures were eating their kabloaf while standing. Every creature with the dish was at least three feet away from the fence. Behind the eating area was a counter, where a single lizard creature served the patrons. The creature scooped the kabloaf out of a trough protected by a sneeze guard. No other kind of food was available.

The line was about ten creatures long. Xane got in line, and the portion of his group that had made it beyond the fence followed in behind him. Payment was made by thumb scan. The cost for the kabloaf was one moneta. Xane saw it deducted in his head when his thumb was scanned. The prize for winning the tournament was fifty moneta, so Xane was able to pay for the whole group.

After the lizard creature handed Xane his kabloaf, he held up two fingers to indicate that he wanted a second serving. The creature shook its head.

"Can I have a second one if I finish this one?" Xane asked. The lizard creature just looked at him, clearly not understanding. Xane decided to try anyway. He went and stood at one of the tables, intending to wolf the meal down as quickly as possible.

Now, Xane saw the kabloaf up close. His plate held a cube-shaped, gelatinous white blob. It looked awful, and it smelled awful. Xane closed his eyes and began shoveling the kabloaf into his face bare-handed. The first bite made him gag a little, but he held it in. The dish was warm and mushy, with the consistency of mayonnaise. As hungry as Xane was, it was still the nastiest thing he'd ever tasted.. Torture for his taste buds. For a brief moment, Xane seriously considered cutting out his tongue. Instead, he kept on shoveling. He just wanted it to be over with.

Before long, Xane had cleared his plate. He was proud of himself for enduring his disgust. The pride only lasted a moment though, as Xane realized the kabloaf was going to come back up.

He ran to the fence surrounding the tables, bent over the side, and emptied his stomach's contents onto the floor. That was the first time he learned of the horde—a huge mob made up of the starving citizens of Gaulcel. Immediately, the horde swarmed toward the unguarded mess like a flock of pigeons. Their ribs poked out over their distended stomachs. When Xane looked up, his eyes were watery, and the inside of his nose was burning. There was already pushing and shoving as the starving creatures tried to get what sustenance they could. Within a matter of seconds, the crowd had grown exponentially. Soon, there was nothing left from Xane's mess. The horde, in unison, then stormed the front entrance to the eatery. The two guards didn't stand a chance.

Hundreds, maybe thousands, of creatures breached the entrance, filling the enclosure until the only way anyone inside could move was to push against someone else. The swell of the crowd pressed Xane against the fence hard. He felt the metal slam into his hip, and he thought he might throw up again. Outside the eatery, he was able to see another group that looked like police. They wore animal insignias from the various clans and bore riot shields and billy clubs. The clan police charged at the horde en masse, swatting at their heads with the clubs.

Another group of clan police, behind the first wave, singled out individuals in the horde, throwing them to the floor and binding their wrists. As the starving creatures became aware of their presence, more and more of them stopped trying to get to the kabloaf behind the counter and instead started to flee. Because the entrance was blocked, the only way out was over the fence—the same fence Xane was pressed against. A group of the horde pushed him, and he flipped over the waist-high enclosure, landing on his shoulder. From the ground, he watched as hundreds of horde feet flew over him, landing next to his head. Xane narrowly avoided being trampled. He was still recovering from having vomited moments before.

Xane managed to crawl a few feet to where the crowd had dissipated a little. He found a wall to sit against and get some air, from which he watched the chaotic scene. The clan police perp-walked the few individuals they'd arrested away from the area.

What does prison inside a prison look like? Xane thought. Hundreds more managed to escape. A few creatures were trampled to death, their bodies strewn about. He watched as guards dragged them to the incinerator chutes. The entire riot only lasted a few minutes. Then the guards at the entrance reassumed their post, and another line of customers formed.

All of Xane's tournament companions were lost in the commotion. Xane never saw any of them again. They were all still somewhere in the city, but Gaulcel was too big and crowded to randomly run into them. Not long after the riot, Xane found Bill's pizza place. Bill sold him some pizza and helped him get to his quarters, where Xane went to sleep. It had been a long first day.

8

Bill's Pizza Place

After his nap, Xane wandered aimlessly around for a few hours, in search of food that was familiar to him. In a nearly deserted area of the building he just happened to walk by a sign with the familiar image of a pizza. It was like an oasis in the desert. Xane didn't believe it was real. He was still recovering from the riot his puke had caused, still recovering from having killed an opponent hours before—and from dying himself. Everything felt like a dream.

The layout of the pizza place was the same as that of the place that sold kabloaf. Every eatery in the karbero had the same layout, but this place was mostly empty inside, Xane stood staring inside the fence for a full minute. He smelled the cheese and marinara sauce and started drooling like a dog.

Behind the serving station stood one human man. He had a short, graying black beard, olive-colored skin and deep-set Mediterranean eyes. Xane watched entranced while the man sprinkled cheese over a pie on its way into an oven. There was no line. Xane was reluctant to enter because he was afraid of shattering the illusion. Finally, he approached the guards. They scanned his thumb and waved him through. He trudged to the counter, mouthwatering and dumbfounded.

The man behind the counter said something to Xane in Common that he didn't understand. Xane made a face to signal his confusion, which he had perfected over the course of the day.

"You must be new here," the man said. The words washed over Xane at first. His brain was in such a slog that he failed to see the significance in someone speaking to him in his own language.

"Yep," Xane said hardly lifting his head. His eyes were trained on the slices behind the counter.

"Well, all we have here is pizza. You can have any topping you like, as long as its cheese," the man cracked. His smile had a mischievous quality. He looked to be in his late forties, but he made Xane feel like a child. The fact that Xane could understand what Bill was saying hit him all at once. He thought of Gaulcel speaking in those weird videos.

"Wait, what did you say?" Xane asked, flabbergasted.

"Just a stupid joke. We can't get toppings because of . . . you know . . . where we are."

"That's really pizza. You can talk. Is that really pizza? We can talk to each other. Can I have some pizza?" The words all just kind of fell out of Xane's mouth.

"I'm Bill," the man said. "Have a slice on the house." He made the "shh" gesture, with a finger over his lips, and handed Xane a fresh slice.

He ended up eating a whole pie.

Xane returned to see Bill twice every day after that. Once for lunch after his daily tournament and then again for dinner. There were rarely more than a few customers, and Bill and Xane were able to talk for hours. It felt good for Xane to talk to someone in his own language. He had a sense that it felt good for Bill, too. The man had been born and raised in Philadelphia, and died there as well. He had been a boxing fan during his time on Earth, but Xane didn't want to tell him he'd been a boxer. The thoughts of what might have been hurt too much to think about. When he'd died, only the most devout boxing fans would have heard of Xane, and they'd probably forgotten about him anyway.

Bill's knowledge on the sport was vast, though. They talked about their favorite fighters and their favorite fights. They bitched about the corrupt fight promoters, mused about ones they thought had been fixed, and fantasized about those they never got to see.

The man explained to Xane that he was horrible in the pit. He lost almost every day. Bill said he would be part of the horde if not for the pizza shop. It was owned by a Wolf Clan fighter. Whatever meager profits the shop made went to the owner, but at least Bill got to eat for free. He'd worked in pizza places for practically his whole life on Earth—it was what he loved to do. He even opened his own shop a few years before he died. It had been doing very well, and he'd made plans to open a second location, but he never got to see that come to fruition.

Even though he never said it, Xane could tell that Bill's shop in Gaulcel was not doing that well. The man was clearly worried about what would happen if the owner decided to pull the plug. Bill treated this business like it was his own. The owner, other than stopping in for free pizza himself sometimes, was completely hands off. There weren't too many creatures in Gaulcel that knew what pizza was.

Bill and Xane rarely talked about Gaulcel—neither the city nor its ruler. Their conversations about boxing were a chance to escape, at least in their minds. Xane needed Bill to keep him grounded. He could see how easy it would be for someone to lose their mind on this world—many of the creatures around him clearly had. But Xane needed his sanity, if for nothing else than to take out the city's evil leader.

One time, Xane asked how the shop got its supplies. Bill admitted he was able to communicate with suppliers from outside the city who brought him the ingredients for dough and marinara. He didn't want to say much about those outside suppliers, though. Xane understood that there were some secrets Bill would get tortured for disclosing. The ingredients of the pizza were never exactly right, but they were as close as the man could get on this world. There was only one cheese maker, and the milk he used definitely didn't come from a cow. Even so, the pizza was pretty good.

Xane got the feeling that Gaulcel's spies were everywhere, even though he'd never seen any hard evidence of it. The spies' existence was probably another secret someone could get tortured for disclosing. The evidence was in the way that folks acted, their constant fear. Everyone knew what happened every morning. They saw fellow citizens tortured, and that was all they needed to know. No one really knew all the details of the city because they didn't dare find out. There was only one real law in Gaulcel: don't do something that could piss off the leader. Folks could only guess at how to follow it.

As Xane kept winning in the tournaments, Bill's customer base increased. Clan members stopped into the shop to talk to Xane, working on recruiting him. Their presence made moneta for Bill's shop, but it also made Bill uncomfortable.

Over time, Bill and Xane's talks got shorter, and Xane missed them terribly.

9

A Prison in a Prison

"Our glorious city is a utopia, but this utopia has laws. Break the law, and go to the prison. Believe me, you don't want to be there. Let me show you what happens to Gaulcel's undesirables." Gaulcel was speaking matter-of-factly. "Today is a special day for the morning announcements. Today, we're going on a tour." He was talking directly into the camera. The cameraman's instructions were to follow him wherever he went.

"To our right is death row. To our left is also death row. Every row is death row!" Gaulcel let go of his straightforward demeanor and giggled to himself. This was funny to him. "The penalty for every offense is death. The question is what kind of death, and how many times." His laugh, muffled through closed lips, sounded like a wet fart. "This is . . . what's his name?" Gaulcel asked the cameraman offscreen. "This is Kevin."

The camera swiveled to a sickly figure chained to a wall. It was clear he wasn't going anywhere even if he hadn't been chained. His arms and legs had withered to sticks, and his ribs were visible through a thin sheet of skin. Kevin's belly looked like a balloon filled with slowly failing organs. "Kevin here stole food," Gaulcel said. "His punishment is death by starvation . . . for five lifetimes." He chuckled.

A sight like Kevin used to sicken Eleris, the cameraman Gaulcel was speaking to. Lifetimes in the city, however, had desensitized him. With the things he had seen, the things he had done, he could no longer allow himself feelings. Eleris hated Gaulcel with every fiber of his being. Despite this, he was his right-hand man. Gaulcel was able to read Eleris's mind. *He must know that I hate him,* Eleris thought. *He must know that everyone hates him.*

Eleris was gifted, even compared to other elves. At over six feet, he was exceptionally tall for his species. He had a thin frame comprised of lean muscles with arms that stretched more than eighty inches. His sturdy legs extended like trunks from a young tree. Eleris was not only exceptionally strong and athletic, but he also had a brilliant mind. Before his first death, he had been a famous writer on his native elven world. All the elves in Gaulcel knew of Eleris from their first life. His literary works were still well known even thousands of years after his first death. Eleris had a special aptitude for language. Upon first arriving in Purgatory, several thousand years ago, he'd taught himself the common tongue in just a few days. Over his lifetimes, he had learned almost every other language spoken in Gaulcel.

Sometime had passed since Gaulcel last assumed control of Eleris' mind. They had spent enough time together that Eleris could tell what Gaulcel was thinking. He could tell what he wanted. At some point, Eleris decided it would be better to do what the ruler wanted than to become powerless again. The feeling of losing control of his own body, having to watch Gaulcel control him like marionette—nothing was worse than that.

Gaulcel made him do terrible things, so to avoid being controlled, Eleris did his bidding without hesitation. Gaulcel didn't need to take his mind anymore to control him. Eleris was thoroughly broken.

"Don't let his calm demeanor fool you. Kevin here only appears calm because he has no energy. He's actually in unimaginable pain. Isn't that right, Kevin?" Gaulcel asked.

It was true. Kevin couldn't move his limbs even if he wanted to do. His body was completely drained of life. He barely heard Gaulcel's question. Even so, Kevin decided he had to respond. He mustered up every ounce of energy he had left. He wanted to scream his response, but it came out as a faint whisper. "Suck my dick," Kevin said.

In that moment, Eleris was filled with admiration for the prisoner.

Moments like this were rare. Someone had stood up to Gaulcel, and Eleris wanted to revel in it. Instead, he kicked Kevin in the teeth. He did it with no noticeable hesitation. "Show some respect!" he said in the common tongue.

Kevin was laid motionless. He was so weak, the blow had killed him. "This death doesn't count toward his sentence," Gaulcel said. Eleris knew the entire exchange would be edited and removed from the morning announcements, which they always filmed in advance, though Gaulcel was careful to make it appear that they were happening live. The fact they were filmed the night before was a secret. Were Eleris to even say it aloud to the few other guards who already knew, he would be forced to suffer some horrible death, probably several times.

Eleris's position as the leader of the noble guard made him privy to many of the city's secrets. He knew where the exits were. He knew about the settlements outside the city—a civilization of free people. Gaulcel depended on the outsiders for most of its resources. Most of the city's food came from the farms there. All of the raw building materials—the wood, the metals, and the oils the city needs to build and repair itself—came from miners and loggers. There were merchants and traders who brought these materials to the city. They were met at the moat but never allowed to enter, just as the residents of Gaulcel were never allowed to leave.

The city was built on a lake, and thanks to some mysterious force, that lake's water supply was endless. The infrastructure was sorely lacking, however. Access points to the water supply were scarcer than they could have been, and they weren't always functioning. When they did function, they never ran dry. Water was the one resource that Gaulcel did not regularly run out of.

All the resources replenished themselves, Eleris had long ago realized. Otherwise, they would have become exhausted. Whatever magic keeps the citizens of Purgatory from dying permanently must also have prevented the world's resources from being depleted. If Gaulcel had any semblance of leadership skill, there would have been plenty of food for everyone in the city. But the city was corrupt. Clan members hoarded more than they could use or consume. Meanwhile, the horde starved.

Eleris understood the hierarchy of the city better than any other resident. The best fighters were selected to join the clans. Only the most elite among the clans became a guard. Only one member from each clan guard could attain a position in the noble guard. There was only one leader of the noble guard and only one creature above them—Gaulcel himself. When Gaulcel died from old age, Eleris would become the leader of the city. Until Gaulcel came back the next day, of course.

If anyone managed to get even a little bit of power, they soon acquired an insatiable lust for more power. Every creature had an instinct for self-preservation. Even in a place where death was temporary, this instinct never faded. Death was agony. Clan members and guards knew the true law of the land: Don't anger Gaulcel or anyone else above them in the hierarchy. There were no repercussions for stealing from the unaffiliated. There was no penalty for killing or exploiting those below. For most clan members and guards, all they cared about was moving up the ranks. They saw the lower rungs of the society as merely a means to meet that end. Power begat power.

Eleris used to think that way too. He was more ambitious than anyone—until he got to the top of the ladder. It wasn't often that a new leader of the royal guard was anointed. Eleris kept the rank for over a thousand years, much to his chagrin. The last creature to hold his position had disappeared without a trace.

When Eleris was told to take the position, he was elated. He didn't realize the job required him to come face-to-face with unimaginable evil every day. He didn't realize being one rung below the ruler meant spending lifetimes as a lackey and plaything. Eleris had no actual power or autonomy whatsoever. His belief that he'd ever had those things in this city had only been an illusion.

Eleris's position did come with some perks, though. Unlike most residents, he did not face poverty or starvation on a regular basis. He employed servants and had more material wealth than any other resident except Gaulcel himself. Members of the noble guard were even allowed a spouse. Yet none of this made up for the tragedy of his role in the city. Everything could be taken away at Gaulcel's mere whim. Eleris would gladly have lost it all if it meant he could get away from Gaulcel.

Everything the ruler did to Eleris was meant to break his spirit. He wanted Eleris to lose his will, to accept as truth that the only purpose for his endless lifetimes was to serve Gaulcel's every desire. Eleris knew exactly what the monster was doing, but it didn't matter—he was powerless to stop it. Gaulcel had broken creatures before, and he was good at it. He took control of Eleris his first day as leader of the noble guard, used him for his personal pleasure, abused him in traumatic ways that still haunted Eleris. Though Eleris was powerless all the times Gaulcel took control, he still inhabited his own body. He saw it all through his own eyes. Heard it. Smelled it. Tasted it. Felt it with his own skin. In some ways what Gaulcel did to Eleris was worse than the torture he inflicted on the city's prisoners. Gaulcel had succeeded. Eleris was thoroughly broken.

* * *

"Let's go to the dissenters wing." Gaulcel said now to the camera, continuing the tour of the prison. Eleris could already smell the blow torches and hear the screams. The clan members tasked with torturing the prisoners would be especially active, believing this an opportunity to impress their ruler. Eleris pointed the camera at Gaulcel's back shoulder as they made the short walk down another cement hallway. "Rest assured, any scum that even thinks of disturbing the order in this city only does it once," Gaulcel said, opening one of his wings slightly. He communicated with Eleris telepathically. *"Keep the camera shot mostly covered by my left wing, then I'll fold it in to reveal the mangled body of one of the prisoners."* Eleris knew the shot Gaulcel wanted even before he told him.

Gaulcel had arranged Eleris's marriage. At the start, it was mostly for show, another perk intended to inspire loyalty through envy. Guards and clan members heard all about Eleris's wife, the beautiful Ciessa, though Eleris hadn't seen her in decades. She was a guard in the Panther Clan.

Their relationship had lasted several hundred years. In part out of necessity, but in part because Eleris loved her. Eleris and Ciessa were going through a rocky patch. They had gone through many rocky patches, and they both knew it was only a matter of time until this one ended just as the others had.

The last time Eleris had seen his wife was the last time Gaulcel died, sixty-three years earlier. He had grown old again; the body only lasted so long. Dying of old age was a luxury in this city, afforded to almost no one except its ruler. His body would go once every two hundred years or so.

It was Eleris's only opportunity for a day off. Gaulcel knew when his death was coming long before it happened. As per usual, he had all the city's exits buried and closed so no one could escape while he was dead. When he came back, it took several days to dig them out again. Food from the outside couldn't get in during that time.

The last time Eleris had seen Ciessa, they spent half the day making love and the other half in conversation. The conversation, of course, devolved into argument. Neither wanted to hurt the other, but they couldn't help it. Ciessa was the only creature Eleris could be himself with. They were both frustrated and angry with the state of their lives, and that frustration's only opportunity to come out was when they were together. Deep down, they both understood why they were fighting. Neither was actually upset with the other, but strong emotions often could not be controlled, even by elves.

They'd ended the day on bad terms. As soon as Ciessa was out of sight, Eleris regretted the things he'd said and the way he'd spoken to her. But it was too late. He hated the thought of her angry with him, but he knew they would make up the next time they saw one another.

* * *

Eleris and Gaulcel had reached the prison building's dissenters wing. It was the largest section of the prison, going on for miles. Gaulcel lowered his wing and revealed a prisoner, just as they'd planned. This one was already dead, a burnt torso with its legs removed below the knee. The guard who'd performed the torture was standing next to the corpse with a shit-eating grin on his face. He believed his ruthlessness would impress Gaulcel and Eleris. Instead, Eleris was disgusted. This guard no doubt wanted a promotion—he wanted Eleris' job. *If he only knew.*

"How long did this one stay alive?" Gaulcel asked the guard.

"He just passed. I kept him alive for three full days," the guard said proudly.

"When you start in on him tomorrow, try to make it last four," Gaulcel said.

"Yes, sir." The reply was too eager.

Eleris got the full exchange on camera. Given the time, this guard was now aware that the morning announcements were not live. Gaulcel would want him watched carefully, and Eleris would have to assign another guard to do the watching. *Let's hope he doesn't say anything*, Eleris thought. *He'll be in the same role as the prisoner he tortured if he does.*

If Gaulcel's mind-control powers had limits, Eleris didn't know what they were. During the Tremendous War, Gaulcel had controlled an entire army all at once. Before Eleris became leader of the noble guard, the city of Gaulcel had gone to war with the city of Gundarce. Gaulcel called it the Tremendous War because he claimed it was a tremendous victory for his city. Those who lived through it, however, knew the real reason it ended was because the leaders on both sides got bored. Nobody won anything. War was hell, especially when death was temporary. Another thing folks were scared to talk about. If anyone even mentioned the war, they only spoke of a tremendous victory. All lies.

Eleris didn't know anything about the city of Gundarce, except that it was not controlled by Gaulcel. They had their own army, and presumably a leader just as awful. Nobody really knew where the intangible moneta came from. Eleris wasn't sure whether Gaulcel himself knew. He was not the source for tournament winnings, that was for sure. Funds seemed to magically manifest after a fight in the account of the winner. A mine for tangible moneta existed outside the city, but it was defended by an ignertia. There was an old legend about a royal city called Moneta where the true king of Purgatory sat, but Eleris didn't believe it. Faith and hope had been taken from him eons ago.

Gaulcel decided to end the tour of the prison on a wide shot of the mile-long hallway of the dissenters wing. "This hallway goes on as long as it needs to, in order to contain every insolent ungrateful subject that chooses to rebel against my leadership. Rest easy, my citizens—there will be no challenges to my rule. Those of you that know how lucky you are to have me, you will never have to be disturbed by these uncivil few. These men will be rehabilitated, extensively. They will die over and over again in excruciating pain. Their sentence does not end until they learn to respect our great city. Our dissenters wing has no recidivism. That is all for today. Good luck in the pits."

Eleris turned off the camera.

II

Escape from Gaulcel

10

Contraband

"How'd it go today?" Bill asked.

"I won again." Xane said. "I had to face a centaur this time—it was crazy, but I managed."

"Congrats. They're called arbanequus here, by the way. You don't run into them often, but when you do, watch out. They're strong as hell." Bill was spreading dough on an old metal pan. "How'd you do it?"

"Kicked the kneecaps," Xane said. "Their legs are powerful, but if you take those out, they can't do much without them."

"You say that as though its easy." Bill smirked.

An invunt from the Mammoth Clan waiting behind Xane became frustrated with the wait. They were in Bill's pizza shop, and it was crowded. The invunt pushed Xane aside. The force was gentle but deliberate. Xane knew better than to retaliate. He stepped aside to allow the line to move. Then he leaned against the glass cover next to Bill's serving area so he could continue the conversation.

"The arbanequus was a challenge, but it was nothing compared with this spider thing I had to fight the other day."

"An arak?" Bill said.

"Right, a spider thing, whatever it's called. It had eight legs and about two feet on me height wise." Xane knew he was bragging, but he also knew Bill appreciated the stories. "These things don't really have any weaknesses. All I noticed was that it takes a lot for them to turn around. So the fight starts, and the thing starts coming at me, slashing at me with its two front legs. The first thing I do is roll underneath it. I did a full-on somersault under all eight legs and stood up right behind it." It was out of character for Xane to talk this much, but he understood that Bill was worried to add to the conversation. The only thing Xane had to look forward to every day was talking to his friend. He wasn't going to let Bill's fear get in the way.

"Then he starts shooting white stuff out of his butt. Webbing. It was so sticky, I just barely managed to keep it out of my eyes. It was like I was handcuffed. I had to roll back between its legs to keep from getting shot at. So, anyway, I was able to dodge all eight limbs until I broke my hands free. And get this—I punched it right in the butt. Right where that stupid webbing came from. It couldn't shoot at me again the rest of the fight. From there, I was always able to get behind it, so I kept hitting it in the legs. Eventually, the back two buckled. The spider thing was just dragging itself around for the last two minutes."

He shrugged. "The judges ended up giving me the decision, seven to two. I don't know what those other two judges were thinking, the thing never landed a clean shot. I know if it had, I might not have survived, but it didn't. How can you give a decision to a creature that never lands a single shot." Xane had to pause to take a breath.

"I hear that," Bill said. It felt good for him to be allowed the luxury of an opinion.

After countless fights in the pit, Xane was still undefeated. His confidence was off the charts. Recruiters from the nine followed him everywhere. He so missed having real conversations with Bill, but this was better than nothing. He wasn't going to allow Gaulcel's henchman to ruin that.

One day, all the clan members got up from their seats and walked out of the eatery at the same time. They needed to talk, and it was about Xane. Bill took the opportunity.

"They're going to make you go somewhere to do something impossible," Bill said. "Do me a favor—don't go and say you did." Suddenly, his face became serious. From a pocket in his apron, Bill produced a book and handed it to Xane. He kept it low for the handoff. Xane knew instinctively not to look down as soon as he felt it. The book hit his hand like a brick. In a single stealthy motion, he slipped the book into his front pocket.

They continued the conversation as though nothing had happened. Xane told another story. Clan members gradually slipped back into Bill's pizza place, and Bill offered one sentence responses to Xane every thirty seconds or so to help keep his story going. When Xane finished his boastful tale, he said goodbye and went back to his quarters. *I hope they didn't see the exchange,* Xane thought. Whatever was in his pocket could very well be the thing he needed to get to Gaulcel. He needed every ounce of willpower that he had to hide his emotions.

When the clan members saw that he was leaving, several of them followed behind Xane. They stayed pretty far back, but he recognized them easily. Lately, he always had clan members tailing him.

Recruitment to the clans was a strange process. Because he kept winning, Xane had nine clan liaisons, one from each clan. All of them were human, and none of them were the same ones that followed him everywhere. Those creatures never formerly identified themselves. The clan liaisons would always just happen to show up wherever Xane went. At least they would say hi, but each one wore the same fake smile. They would offer to help Xane with anything he needed. He would take the opportunity to improve his fluency with Common. Mostly, he asked questions. In this world, knowledge was hard to come by.

Marid, the liaison from the Viper Clan, saw Xane shortly after he left Bill's. He waved at him and approached as though it were a chance encounter. Marid was a stalky man with perfectly coiffed jet-black hair and beady brown eyes. His chin jutted from his clean-shaven face like a barracuda's. "Hey big guy," Marid said jovially. "I was just on my way to pick up some dinner, where are you off to?"

"Just ate," Xane said. "Heading back home."

"Oh, do you mind if I walk you there? I've been meaning to talk to you about something."

"Free country." Xane said in Common. It was an expression Xane had used often in his first life. He realized it no longer applied. Even if it had, the word for "free" in Common only meant you didn't have to pay for something. If there was a word for "freedom," Xane did not know what it was. He did mind that Marid was walking with him. He wanted to be alone so that he could figure out what to do with the book in his pocket that Bill gave him. No one could know that he had it, especially anyone from one of the clans.

Marid nodded, though it was clear he didn't really understand what Xane meant. He chalked it up to a translation error. "Great," Marid said. "So, the Vipers are deciding who we're going to give a bid to next month." He paused. "I noticed you'll be eligible by then, so I've been talking you up to the folks at the top. I think they are pretty impressed with your string of victories. You just gotta keep it up."

"That's the plan," Xane said. He was walking very fast now.

"If it were up to me, I'd definitely want you in, but there's a whole bunch of us that get a vote. I think if you stay undefeated though, you've got a real good shot of becoming a Viper," said Marid.

"Okay."

"You know, joining the Vipers changed my life. This emblem—" Marid held up the viper figure on his necklace. "It commands respect all over the city. Clan tournaments pay ten times as much as the unaffiliated ones. I've got a bunch of folks that work for me now, get me whatever I want whenever I want it. I've got brothers everywhere too. You know, we look out for each other." Marid grabbed Xane's shoulder.

He had to slow his pace. They were nearing the shuttle now. "Well, this is me. I'll catch up with you later," Xane said, wishing Marid would just leave him alone.

"There's a whole section of the city where only Vipers are allowed. We've got the best gym you've ever seen, with pools and trainers and anything else you can think of. You should see our library, it's huge."

"Library?" Xane said.

"You bet," Marid said. "Vipers are not just the greatest fighters in the city, we also have a rich intellectual history that we've been putting together for a hundred thousand years. Anything you want to know about this city, you can read about it there."

The shuttle stopped, and the doors opened. Xane stood back to let passengers get off. Then the entranceway cleared. "Cool. Have a good one." He hopped on to the little train, hoping Marid would not follow him.

"Hey Xane," Marid yelled from the platform, "you let me know if you need anything. Seriously, anything. I'll see you again soon."

The doors closed, and the shuttle began moving. Xane took a deep breath. He put his hand into his pocket to make sure the book was still there. Even though he couldn't look at it yet, the feel of its worn binding comforted him.

Osso, the liaison from the Bear Clan, looked up from one of the shuttle seats. "Hey big guy, where you headed?" he asked.

Xane was frustrated that Osso was waiting for him on the shuttle but not surprised. He nodded at him, acknowledging his presence, but did not reply.

Osso looked at the dwarf in the seat next to him, flashed his bear pendant, and then motioned for the dwarf to move. The dwarf exited his seat obediently. "Sit," Osso said to Xane. "I've been meaning to talk to you about something."

Xane sighed and mentally prepared to have the same conversation all over again.

Every clan used an animal as an emblem. The symbols were strewn all over the city of Gaulcel—the viper, the bear, the crocodile, the panther, the mantis, the mammoth, the ox, the shark and of course the wolf. Xane had been suffering through small talk with liaisons from each of the clans for months. He didn't know which clan he would join, but he knew he had to join one to have any chance at bringing Gaulcel down.

Each new day in the city brought fresh anger at its evil ruler. There was so much tragedy here and everyone ignored it. Their disregard was out of necessity, Xane knew. He also knew to hide his own feelings. If he were to get visibly upset at the never-ending horrors residents were subjected to, he could be labeled a dissenter. He would have to face Gaulcel's wrath himself and lose any chance at removing him from power. The clans offered Xane a chance to move up and gain knowledge of the city's inner workings. Even so, he was dreading the day he became eligible. He was dreading having to choose.

No doubt politics would come into play once he made his choice. Xane didn't know the substance of clan politics, but he knew there was politics. He could tell by the way clan members acted. They exuded a sort of tension that could only come from those jockeying for power. Xane's choice would be difficult only because he had no idea what he was choosing. From what Xane could tell, there was no difference between the clans. They all operated pretty much the same way, just wearing a different animal emblem. *They're all weasels,* Xane thought. He pictured each of the clan liaisons with a weasel pendant around their necks. The thought made him chuckle.

The only liaison Xane didn't outright despise was from the Wolf Clan. The Wolves' liaison was Guff, whom Xane had known since his first day in Purgatory. Guff was still helping him learn the common language, still helping him train. Xane had to admit to himself that Guff's help was one of the main reasons he kept winning in the pit. And it was the main reason Xane was able to navigate this city without getting into trouble. The other eight liaisons acted like salesmen, but Guff couldn't be a salesman if he tried. He was too straightforward and too dull. Guff didn't have the same agenda or the same level of ambition as the others. He always seemed content just to hang out. Being a referee in the pit was Guff's real job. They probably only let him be liaison because they already knew each other, Xane assumed. Guff rarely spoke of the Wolf Clan, and when he did, it was usually an afterthought.

Maybe it was all a ruse from the start. Maybe Guff acted that way as a recruitment tactic to make him come across as more trustworthy. If that was the case, it was working.

The shuttle ride with Osso went exactly as Xane thought it would, and he was glad when it was over. He boarded the elevator to his quarters half expecting another liaison to be inside waiting for him. Xane was relieved to find the elevator empty. He reached into his shirt pocket to make sure the book was still there. His shirt was just baggy and wrinkly enough to hide the tome's outline.

Xane pulled the corner of the book from his pocket and looked down at it. He had to know it was real. Then he quickly slid it back inside in case anyone else got on the elevator.

From his brief glimpse, Xane could tell that the book was old—very old. The pale green color of the creased binding was deeply faded. The only other book Xane had come across in all of Gaulcel was the grammar book that Guff gave him. That was full of grammar lessons in the common language, but Xane had hardly looked at it, since he could not read Common. He didn't recognize the letters, let alone the words. The book in his shirt pocket had to be different. He knew because of the way Bill gave it to him that he needed to keep it a secret—it was contraband.

When Xane got off the elevator, he was surprised to see Guff waiting outside his quarters. Typically, Guff came in the morning after a tournament ended. It was unusual for Xane to see him in the evening.

"Hey big guy," Guff said. "I thought we could get in a little night training if that's all right with you. Besides, I've been meaning to talk to you about something." Guff stumbled through the words like he was reading a script that had been given to him just minutes before.

"Oh no, not you too," Xane said aloud, and smiled.

Guff looked like his feelings were hurt. "It's okay. I can come back tomorrow if you're busy." He lowered his eyes and started toward the exit.

"No, I'm just kidding you, it's fine," Xane said. "What's on your mind?"

"It's just . . . the Wolves are deciding who we're going to give a bid to next month, and I noticed you'll be eligible. I've been talking you up to the folks at the top." The words sounded strange coming from Guff's mouth. He normally had a self-assured disposition. That was gone now. It was clear there were some things Guff had been told he had to say.

"Does the Wolf Clan have libraries?" Xane blurted out.

"What?" Guff said, thrown off from his script.

"Libraries?" Xane repeated.

"Like the kind with books?" Guff seemed startled.

"Yeah," Xane said.

Guff let the question sink in. "Oh yeah, we got one of those. Can't say I've spent much time there, though."

Xane knew without asking that Guff could not read. He didn't want to make him say it out loud. "Well, that's cool. Tell me what else the Wolves get." He was giving the man a chance to go back to his scripted remarks.

Guff didn't follow. "We've got about sixteen books total, but there are a whole bunch of copies. There are some real nice couches in the library, I remember."

Sixteen books. Xane wondered how truthful Marid had been when he talked about the Vipers' rich intellectual history. Maybe there were some differences in the clans. On the other hand, Marid might just be full of shit. "Cool," he said aloud.

Guff clearly wanted this awkward exchange to be over with, same as Xane. "So, I think the folks at the top are pretty impressed with your string of victories. You just gotta keep it up. If it were up to me, I'd definitely want you in, but there's a whole bunch of us that get a vote. If you stay undefeated though, you've got a real good shot at becoming a Wolf," Guff recited.

Xane pointed at his punching bag, and Guff immediately understood the gesture. Though neither could say it aloud, they both accepted that the conversation was a charade. Xane practiced his punches and kicks while Guff went through the rest of the spiel. As a sign of good faith, Xane occasionally nodded or offered a word of reassurance.

Guff finally got through all the bits he needed to say. "You let me know if you need anything. Seriously, anything." He looked Xane in the eye. "I mean that."

"Will do," Xane said. "Right now, though, I think I need to call it a night."

"Me too," Guff said. Their unspoken understanding had left them closer as friends.

Xane decided to give the heavy bag one more kick for good measure. The force of the kick jostled the book in Xane's shirt pocket. He felt its corners slip out but quickly brought his hand around and shoved it back in. The whole incident lasted a millisecond, but there was still a chance that Guff had noticed. Xane played it down and hoped for the best. "Good night,

Guff," Xane said.

"Good night." Guff turned toward the elevator and left. Xane was finally alone.

11

Another Day in the Pit

Everywhere he went in Gaulcel, Xane had concerns about cameras or microphones recording his words and actions. He'd never seen direct evidence of this, but the way all the citizenry here acted conveyed a fear that they were constantly being watched. Not knowing whether the cameras existed also meant not knowing where they were if they did. Xane had to assume a camera was always recording him in his quarters, though, and from all angles. He had no privacy.

Those quarters were mostly unchanged from the day he arrived. The four cement walls remained bare. Xane had spent the first several weeks sleeping on the cement floor until Guff insisted he buy a bed. Xane settled on the cheapest one available, a foldable, military-style cot. It was his only piece of furniture, not counting the heavy bag he'd won in his first tournament and the water cooler. There was nowhere to hide.

The cot came with a thin black blanket. Now, Xane slipped into bed and pulled the cover over himself. Then he pretended to masturbate. Xane figured the guards wouldn't have time to respond every time someone masturbated, nor would they want to. It made a good cover story to explain why he was hiding. Something no one would even bat an eye at, he hoped. He continued the charade for several minutes, then shifted his knees so that the blanket was away from most of his body.

Xane could finally open the book, and the blanket was just thin enough to allow light to seep through. He held it in both hands and scanned the cover. The pale green binding was blank. It was the type of book that would typically have come with a dust jacket, which must have been lost. The cover contained no title or author, no identifying information whatsoever. Perhaps that was intentional, though—easier to disguise the contents.

When Xane flipped to the first page, his great fear was realized. The book was written in Common. Xane couldn't read it. He had been learning to speak the language but had no real concept of how to read or write. Day-to-day life in Gaulcel had taught Xane how to recognize the symbol for bathroom, but that was pretty much the extent of his knowledge. Worse yet, he had no idea how he could learn to read Common. Guff had taught him to speak it, but the man couldn't read himself. Even if Xane were able to find someone willing and able to teach him to read, he would have to trust them enough to let on that he had this contraband. The book was useless.

Still, he wouldn't allow himself to give up. Xane flipped through every page, scanning for anything that might have meaning to him. The pages were loose, and some had detached from the book's binding. Xane was careful to ensure that each page stayed in place and in the same order. On some pages, the ink was completely faded, and some sections of the book were missing all together. One section contained sketches of various creatures Xane recognized from his time in Gaulcel. From context, he learned to recognize the symbol for each of the kinds. The book appeared to be about how the creatures interacted with one another.

Xane tried to absorb as much as he could. He recognized the symbols that repeated most often and committed them to memory. Then his eyelids grew heavy, and he soon fell asleep.

The next day, Xane slept through the morning announcements. He woke up when his wristband started blinking, letting him know he needed to get to the pit for that morning's tournament. The book was still open on his chest. If there was a camera in his quarters as he suspected, anyone watching would be able to see. Xane shot out of the cot and slid the book back under the covers.

He hopped on the elevator, which took him to another one of the countless cement rooms that held tournaments. They all looked the same, except some had more spectators. Xane took his place in the dugout and began to check out that morning's competitors.

Lately, there was always one opponent who was far superior to the others. The tournament was structured so that Xane and this opponent would meet in the final round. Xane didn't know who was responsible for choosing the combatants or their order of entry for each tournament. However it worked, he was being put in the pit with combatants who were increasingly skilled. His current class of opponents was far superior to the newbies he'd fought on his first day. Xane had heard a rumor about a leaderboard somewhere, but he didn't know how to access it or what his position on it might be. Whatever it was, he could only be moving up, and his adversaries reflected that fact.

That morning, Xane could tell right away who his competition in the finals was supposed to be: a gigantic barool. Xane had seen barools around the city but had never faced one in the pit. The creatures looked like bipedal hogs and were as big as bears. This particular barool was especially large. He had grayish-pink fur, and long tusks extended down below his snout. Xane tried to stay inconspicuous. The barool was probably trying to figure out his opponent, just as he was. He hid his sword at his feet where he sat. Without it, there was nothing that made Xane stick out as a skilled fighter.

The referee for that day climbed down into the pit. It was Druaq, Xane's liaison from the Mantis Clan. There was no way for Xane to know whether that was planned or just a coincidence, but he suspected the former. Either way, Druaq would not acknowledge that he knew Xane while the tournament was ongoing.

Combatants almost never spoke to each other in the dugout, like in a crowded elevator—there was no rule against talking, but for some reason people didn't do it. Despite Xane's efforts, the barool was able to finger him as the planned finalist before the first fight. Its hog eyes looked tiny on its giant head. They glared at Xane menacingly. Xane met the glare with his own, and they both nodded.

As had become the norm, Xane was first up in the pit. His opponent was a lizard creature, which Xane now knew to call sahuajin. Just like his first day, he knew exactly what the creature was going to do. Xane threw down his sword. The sahuajin lurched forward and threw a big sweeping right hand at Xane's head, which he dodged easily. Xane countered with a three-punch combination that landed flush. His opponent stumbled but stayed upright. It came back with two more big sweeping rights, the second of which almost made contact. This sahuajin was quick for its species. Unlike others Xane had faced, it had the foresight to keep its left hand up in front of its head, effectively blocking Xane's target.

Xane attacked from an angle and was able to land more punches, but the creature took them in stride. It was tough, too. The fight continued like that, with Xane struggling but landing occasional shots and the creature missing. When the buzzer sounded, the judges gave Xane a 9-0 decision, but he was dissatisfied with his performance. He should have been able to knock the creature out, or at least knock it down.

The next fight had the barool against another sahuajin. This time, the sahuajin was the smaller of the two. It stepped back and waited for the barool to come, and the barool was happy to oblige. It took one step forward so that the sahuajin was in range, then brought its three-fingered fist straight down on the sahuajin's head, landing with a skull-crushing thud. The sahuajin fell into the sand and did not move. Druaq waved the fight off, but it was too late. The barool stomped on the lizard's head with its full weight, ending its life.

Druaq dragged the body to the side and called in the next two combatants.

Xane's next fight was against one of the cat creatures, known in Purgatory as khajjine. He threw down his sword, and the khajjine was on him instantly. Three blows struck Xane's face before he knew what hit him. This khajjine had lightning speed, faster than any opponent Xane could remember facing. He stepped back and collected himself.

When the khajjine came in again, Xane was ready. He took two blows but managed to land one of his own, his signature left hook. His opponent wobbled from the impact, then Xane kicked it on the side of the leg, knocking it to the sand. The khajjine got back up and stormed at Xane, but anger made it reckless. The next punch was more powerful than the previous barrages, but the larger motion gave Xane plenty of warning. He dodged left, and the creature's paw flew past Xane's face. Xane took advantage of the extended arm to land a straight right. Before it could recover, Xane moved in for the finish. A series of uppercuts from both hands knocked the khajjine down.

This time, it didn't get back up. Druaq raised Xane's hand, declaring him the victor.

The barool dispatched its next two opponents almost as easily as it had its first one. A second sahuajin was able to land several blows on the hog creature, but they proved to be ineffective. A sahuajin's strength was extraordinary compared with most, but not as extraordinary as the barool's toughness. Nothing even fazed the creature. Thirty seconds in, it picked up the sahuajin with one hand and threw it against the side of the pit, ending their contest. After that, the barool's third opponent was a human who ran away for the first few minutes. The barool let the man get tired enough to slow down a step, then grabbed him in a bearhug and knocked him cold with one pounding headbutt.

Xane's third fight in that day's tournament, meanwhile, was against a grappling invunt. It was going well for him until the dwarf got ahold of a leg and took him down to the sand. Xane hated fighting prone. The invunt climbed on top of him and started throwing elbows. Xane defended well, but one got through and did some real damage. His right eye had already been struck several times in the fight with the khajjine, and now it was starting to swell.

He pulled his knees up to his chest to keep the invunt off him, then swung hard with his right hand. The invunt took the blow on the shoulder, but it was hard enough to knock him off, allowing Xane to get back to his feet. From there, Xane stayed outside the invunt's range and peppered his face with stiff jabs until the buzzer sounded. The judges split. Three found for the dwarf, and the other six went for Xane. It was a narrow victory, and the struggle would cost him some of his sight in the next contest.

As expected, Xane and the barool met in the final round. Xane quickly formulated a strategy. While he was no match for the monster's power, he was far more agile, and he'd have to use that to prevail. He even considered using his sword this time. After all, there was no rule against it, and as far as he knew, the barool didn't have a weapon. Its whole huge body was all the weapon it needed. The falchion blade was just an equalizer.

The light turned red, and the buzzer sounded. The fight had begun.

Xane threw his sword into the sand behind him. He'd never used it before, and he'd never lost a fight in the pit. "If it ain't broke, don't fix it," Coach Clark used to say. Xane decided he could find a way to win without the weapon. It was an almost superstitious belief.

He ran at the barool and threw his shoulder, with all of his weight behind it, straight into the creature's right knee. Each of the barool's legs had the same circumference as Xane's torso. His chop block didn't even cause it to shift its weight. Xane's momentum spun him around until he stumbled backward, losing his footing and falling on his back. Xane barely rolled out of the way as the barool tried to stomp on him with its massive left leg. He jumped back to his feet but had to duck to avoid the barool's forearm as it swung over the top of his head.

For a creature of such size, it had remarkable stamina. Its arms kept swinging at Xane and scarcely missing. He could feel the wind in his hair. Shuffling right, he planted a roundhouse kick into the back of the barool's knee. Again, the hog monster didn't react to the strike. It squared up with Xane and started firing more rights and lefts. In some ways, the creature's height was a disadvantage, because Xane could duck under its punches without too much effort. He bobbed and weaved for what seemed like an eternity, hoping the barool would eventually tire. Occasionally, he landed a well-timed jab in the monster's gut, though it had no effect.

Xane knew if the beast managed to land a single punch, it would end his undefeated streak. The vision in his right eye was diminished from the previous fights, and his opponent was aware. The barool kept moving to Xane's right. As the fight went on, it started feinting and juking to mislead

Xane. Eventually, the creature would catch him with a punch he couldn't see coming, and Xane couldn't let that happen.

He jumped up and grabbed the creature by the tusk, pulling its head down while lifting his knee. It rammed into the barool's snout—hard. The creature wasn't seriously hurt, just mad. As Xane continued backing up, the barool eyed his sword in the sand. The creature reached down and grasped the weapon with a three-fingered hand. It was going to use Xane's own blade against him.

The sword extended the barool's reach considerably, making it even harder for Xane to avoid getting hit. And if he was going to ensure his victory, he would need to land more blows of his own. As the blade whizzed by, Xane twisted his body, trying to form the smallest target he could. The barool chased him all around the pit, but Xane didn't let himself be cornered. The monster started another swing of the sword, and Xane saw an opening. At least he thought he did.

Xane brought his trademarked left hook around and connected solidly with the barool's jaw, but the hog didn't swing the sword like Xane was expecting. It only pretended to, as bait. Xane had been set up. He didn't see the barool's right fist coming in until the last second. Xane moved but it was too late to avoid the blow entirely. The beast got enough of the blow to put him on his ass.

Xane got back to his feet, dazed yet determined, but the buzzer rang. Druaq stepped between them. The fight was over.

That's it. The judges are going to give it to the barool. I'm going to lose, Xane thought. Druaq pointed to the judges' balcony. It was a unanimous decision. All nine judges decided Xane was the winner. The barool threw down Xane's sword in disgust. Using a weapon against an unarmed opponent must look bad in a competition, Xane realized. Druaq raised Xane's hand. It was just another day at the office to him.

Xane touched his face, feeling his scar. It would remain another day.

* * *

That day's prize was a pair of eyeglasses bearing a Mantis insignia. Xane planned to sell them, but until he could get to the merchant section of the city, he decided he'd wear the glasses to cover up his swollen right eye.

As Xane got on the elevator, Druaq emerged from the crowd and entered with him.

"Hey big guy . . ." Druaq started.

They must literally give them a script, Xane thought.

"Nice job today. Where you headed?" He cut Xane off before he could answer. "Why don't we go get you some ice for that eye and then I'll show you what you can do with those glasses." Druaq was a wiry blond man, tall and skinny with long arms and legs.

"I'll get ice later. I'm going to go see what these will fetch at the market," Xane said.

"Before you do, let me at least show you what they're for. They're reading glasses."

"That's okay," Xane said. "Not much to read around here anyway. He hesitated for a moment. "I don't even know how to read Common script."

Druaq let out a fake laugh. "That's it—I'm taking you to a bookstore right now." The man recited coordinates into the elevator's speaker.

Xane was frustrated but also curious. A bookstore? "All right."

A few moments later, Xane and Druaq stepped off the elevator into a section of the korum where Xane had never been. He'd been forced to listen to the typical liaison spiel from Druaq on the way over, but at least that was finished now.

"Here it is," Druaq said. They stepped inside a small, three-walled room. A single bookshelf stood against one of the walls. The clerk was a diminutive, chubby elf with a long white beard threaded into a single braid.

"Good morning, gentlemen," the elf said. Based on his name tag, he was Lastoya. "I hope you fared well in today's tournaments."

Druaq ignored the clerk and spoke directly to Xane. "Okay, take the glasses off and then walk over to that bookshelf."

Xane did as he was instructed. The bookshelf was six rows high. Each row contained four or five copies of the same book. There were only six different books to choose from, and the titles were written in Common. Xane recognized the text on the bottom shelf as the grammar book Guff had given him. The other five shelves were filled with five different volumes, each displaying a different picture of Gaulcel on the cover. In one picture, the creature looked studious and serious, posing with thick-framed glasses. In another, he wore what appeared to be a military uniform. He posed to appear strong and self-assured.

The images made Xane sick. "Is this your entire selection?" Xane asked the clerk.

"We just got a fresh printing of all six books," Lastoya replied.

"These are the only books allowed in the public areas of the city," Druaq told Xane. "Now put on the glasses."

Xane brought the glasses up to his face. As the lenses covered his eyes, the symbols on the book covers changed. Instead of impenetrable Common, the words in the titles appeared in Xane's own language. He could read them easily. The top shelf was titled *An Unabridged History of Our Glorious Leader Gaulcel: Part I*. The shelf beneath that: *An Unabridged History of Our Glorious Leader Gaulcel: Part II*. Xane slid the glasses off, and the letters shifted back to unrecognizable symbols.

"Those glasses make it so you can read in any language. Pretty cool, right?" Druaq said.

Xane instantly thought of Bill's book sitting under the covers in his quarters. The coincidence seemed too good to be true. Had Bill known he would win this today?

"Here, read it." Druaq picked up Part I and handed it over. Xane opened the book; unsurprisingly, it was written in Common, but as soon as he put the glasses back on the symbols turned into familiar letters. Xane didn't need to look past the first page to know the volume he held was nothing but propaganda. Even so, he could read again, and he was happier for it. Soon, he would learn the contents of the book Bill had given him. Maybe it would hold a secret that could help him get to Gaulcel. Xane decided to buy a copy of Part I for the dust jacket.

"How much is this?" Xane asked the clerk.

ANOTHER DAY IN THE PIT

The price the elf cited was outrageous. It was more than Xane had made for every tournament he'd won combined.

"Let me get this for you," Druaq said. He turned to the clerk. "Put it on the Mantis tab."

"Okay, thanks," Xane said.

12

The Book

When Xane got back to his quarters, he went straight to his cot. He was carrying the expensive volume about Gaulcel under his arm, but he had no plan to ever read it. It was all lies; Xane knew that without reading a word.

Climbing into the cot, he was relieved to find that the book Bill had given him the previous day was still right where he'd left it that morning. Xane removed the dust cover from the Gaulcel book and slipped it onto the one Bill gave him. Now he could read Bill's book without worrying if someone was watching him. The eyeglasses he'd won that day were tucked into his shirt. He opened the first page and put them on.

Just as before, the symbols on the page changed into recognizable words. Xane read the title of Bill's book for the first time: *Success in Hand-to-Hand Combat*. It was written by someone named Acherona and published by Purgatory Publishing Company. His eyes, now able to read the words, hungrily devoured page after page.

It was a textbook meant to teach fighting skills, but Acherona had written it for elves. Much of the material was stuff Xane already knew from his first life and his training with Coach Clark. Some wasn't applicable because Xane didn't have an elf's senses and their bodies don't work in the same way. There were some points that seemed like they could prove useful in the pit, though.

The last section had a lot of helpful detail about the different creatures of Purgatory:

Fighting Styles of the Sentient Species of Purgatory

There are ten known sentient species that inhabit purgatory. Each has distinctive advantages and disadvantages when engaged in hand-to-hand combat.

Invunt

At its core, all of invunt culture boils down to one concept: a fair day's work for a fair day's pay. Invunt take work very seriously. Once an invunt accepts a task, it becomes their main purpose in life, and they seldom think of anything else until they've completed the task satisfactorily. The same is true even if that task is fighting. Invunt find pleasure in the work itself and rarely involve themselves with hobby or vice. When they do, however, they devote themselves entirely. For instance, a drunk invunt spends no time sober—they drink until they are either incapacitated or no drinks are available.

Invunt also take the concept of money very seriously. Under no circumstances will an invunt work for free. They never give money away, either, no matter the merits of the charity. To an invunt, receiving anything they did not earn is a grave insult. For this reason, they never give or accept gifts of any kind. To do so would be a source of great shame. Invunt thieves are virtually nonexistent. However, they are hoarders of material things and tend to accumulate vast wealth over the course of their many lifetimes.

An invunt's strength in hand-to-hand combat comes primarily from its legs. An average invunt can squat five or six times its own weight. For this reason, they tend to grapple with opponents, using their leg strength to lift and throw them. The stout creatures are built low to the ground. Because of their short stature, they can be difficult to keep out of arm's reach, and once they have taken hold of an opponent, they can be dangerous. Additionally, invunt are sturdy. Their low center of gravity makes it difficult to cause an invunt to lose their footing. The most effective strategy for fighting an invunt is to keep the creature outside of range with quick strikes and fast feet.

Sahuajin

The most common of the sentient creatures in Purgatory, sahuajin are impulsive and foolhardy. They are barely sentient and behave on almost pure instinct. Nearly without exception, sahuajin do not think ahead. They do not make plans. They see that kind of intelligence as a weakness. Their language is rudimentary. It does not have a future tense, and it lacks words for abstract concepts like emotions.

Once a sahuajin desires something, they will attempt to obtain it immediately. If they do not satiate that desire, they give up just as quickly. Sahuajin are large compared with most of the other sentient species in Purgatory. They are typically two to three feet taller than an average elf, and their limbs are long and strong. Their green, sandpapery skin is rough but thin and has a thick layer of muscle underneath.

Sahuajin use their density to strike at opponents with great effectiveness. They are also known to bite at opponents. Sahuajin fight in short bursts, using all their energy at once. While they are in attack mode, they are the most precarious. A single blow from a sahuajin, when landed, often ends a fight.

Despite their immense size, they are also surprisingly fast. They tire quickly, however, and once they do, they will avoid combat until they regain their stamina. During this respite, they tend to have good defense, blocking incoming blows with their long limbs. It can be difficult to predict when a short burst of strikes will occur, as sahuajin do not plan. The best time to attack one is during their first burst of offense. They do not defend themselves while attacking. Also, if a fight is not going a sahuajin's way, they are known to give up quickly.

Khajjine

Khajjine are furry creatures with pointy ears and whiskers. The color of their fur varies, but they always have yellow eyes. They are highly adaptable and have good survival instincts, but this can be offset by their high confidence and dominant temperament. Quick to anger, they tend to be rash in decision-making but are unable to admit when they have made a mistake. They are typically incapable of accepting defeat.

As fighters, khajjine are aggressive and tenacious. They use their superior quickness to set up strikes with their sharp claws. Khajjine can also jump exceptionally high and tend to be skilled at tackling and pinning opponents. Like sahuajin, their attacks often come in quick bursts, but khajjine are not quick to tire. Their main weakness is their midsection, which is frail and thin. Targeted blows to this area will take the wind from their lungs and slow a khajjine down.

Arbanequus

Arbanequus are uncommon in purgatory. They have the torso of a man and the body of a horse. Sometimes, males grow horns like bulls. It is rare for an arbanequus to learn more than the basics in the common tongue, and practically no other creatures are able to understand the arbanequus language. For these reasons, little is known about the world they come from. They tend to be stubborn and set in their ways. Arbanequus are deliberative and slow to act, but once they have decided on a course of action, they are diligent and persistent. They have the longest lifespan of all the creatures in Purgatory. If they are fortunate enough to survive to old age, a single lifetime can last eight hundred years or more.

It is rare for an arbanequus to engage in hand-to-hand combat outside of the forced tournaments in cities. Should one decide to attack, however, they are formidable opponents. When fighting an arbanequus, it is imperative to avoid their powerful front and rear legs, which can knock down even a barool with a single kick. One cannot overlook their humanlike arms either, which can be quite strong in their own right. Fortunately, they have trouble turning their long bodies. The most effective strategy is to attack from varying angles to either side and accumulate strikes at their legs behind the kneecaps. Some have attempted to mount the horse section of the body to grab the torso from behind and put the creature into a chokehold. This is inadvisable, however, as arbanequus are quite skilled at bucking riders, and should one fall from their back, the creatures are known to trample opponents.

Arak

Many believe that arak are uncommon like arbanequus, though in reality they are nearly as prevalent as sahuajin. This mistaken belief occurs because it is rare for an arak to reach its full size. These creatures have the body and legs of a spider with the upper torso of an acolyte. They have large, poisonous fangs that are the length of their head. They also have spinnerets in the rear portion of their abdomen that shoot a sticky kind of webbing. When they respawn after death, they are about the size of a common house spider, and they are typically killed by another creature before they are able to grow much larger. Most arak, even at full size, do not grow larger than a small dog. However, the largest among them can grow to be as big as an arbanequus. While they are not known to cooperate with other species, arak are culturally collaborative with one another. The arak language is comprised of movement instead of sound. They excel at repetitive menial tasks, making the architecture within an arak hive very impressive.

When it comes to combat, arak are extremely aggressive. They attack smaller creatures on sight, eating them as though they were prey. However, they will not voluntarily attack a creature larger than themselves. Every arak attacks in the same way. They shoot and incapacitate their opponent with webbing, then lift them with their front two legs and bite them with poisonous fangs. When delivered in a large enough dose, the poison paralyzes the opponent instantly. Should this attack succeed, the result is certain death, as the arak then devours the opponent. Despite their frightening appearance, these creatures are easy for any skilled elf to defeat because of their predictability. Simply avoid their webbing and fangs. Arak legs are fast but thin, and a strong attack against them will cause the creature to buckle.

Barool

Barool are both the largest and most rare of all species in purgatory. They are taller than sahuajin and stouter than invunt, with the snout and tusk of a hog. Their defining characteristic is ugliness. Barool are selfish and hedonistic creatures who seek pleasure above all else. They are given to excess, especially when it comes to food. Individuals have no regard for others, even within their own species. They possess great intelligence and cunning and are known to scheme and deceive others to achieve their selfish aims.

It is best to avoid hand-to-hand combat with a barool altogether. A barool's toughness is nothing short of miraculous, and elves are frankly not strong enough to hurt a barool without the use of a weapon.

Additionally, barool possess a great deal of stamina. Fortunately, their immense size makes them rather slow, and it is easy enough to run away. If one is unable to circumvent combat with a barool, the creature's weakest point is the genitals, which are quite large. A strong blow to the area may slow the creature down for a brief time but will not stop it entirely.

Humans

Of all the sentient species in purgatory, humans have the greatest variance among individuals. They are the most similar to elves when compared with the other sentient species on this list. On average, they are slightly taller and larger, though this can vary significantly. Like khajjine, humans often have strong emotions, though some can remain in relative control of themselves. They are dreamers and planners, constantly seeking to impress one another and acquire power over others. They can form strong bonds when collaborating with other humans that share a common goal. They can be cooperative with other species as well but tend to be distrustful. Human culture is unique in that humans rarely adapt to their environment but instead try to change their environments to suit them. They are unlikely to accept their place in a hierarchy or civilization, always seeking to improve their individual circumstances. Unsatisfied with the present, they often think of the future. To a human, insignificance is intolerable.

Most humans are poor fighters. They lack the natural attributes of other species. The skilled fighters among them rely on training and strategy for success. Moreover, some humans possess a great deal of resolve. Through sheer strength of will, they sometimes persevere against adversity. Because of the differences among individuals, there is no one strategy effective against all humans. That said, repeated strikes to the head will knock them unconscious.

Elves

We elves possess agility and intelligence superior to all other species in Purgatory. We are logical thinkers, strong in the areas of language and mathematics. Additionally, we have a keen ability to focus and absorb knowledge. Like some other species, elves have strong emotions, but unlike others they do not allow emotion to affect their actions. Elves are keenly aware of their feelings, so much so that they are able to disregard emotion while making decisions. They rely solely on reason. Elven bodies are as agile as their minds are sharp, with exceptional balance and dexterity.

Elves are skilled at recognizing their opponent's thoughts from their facial expression. They use this ability to predict their opponent's next move. Elves are also known to use this ability on one another. For this reason, when facing a fellow elf, one should keep the chin tucked and the face hidden as best as possible so as not to reveal one's thoughts. Occasionally, elves get wrapped up in calculating their next moves, which can cause reticence and missed opportunities. One can take advantage of this by overwhelming the elf with choices or acting illogically. This may cause an elf to freeze for a moment, during which they are vulnerable.

Acolytes

Acolytes are incredibly dangerous and should be avoided at all cost. These creatures can take control of their opponent's mind and body. Once this happens, any chance of victory is lost. They can control numerous individuals simultaneously this way, so they should not be accosted even with a large group. Further, acolytes are known to be quite sadistic. Elves who encounter them typically end up becoming a kind of slave. For this reason, knowledge of acolytes is limited, acquired only from the few who have managed to escape. They are known to molt, shedding their skin once every few years. They rarely sleep. It has been said that an acolyte can go decades without a full night's rest.

Despite their immense power, acolytes live in a state of pure and constant fear. They arrange their living situation to avoid any potential harm, whether physical or emotional. Each acolyte in Purgatory uses their mind control abilities to instill fear in any creature they encounter. This effectively insulates the acolyte from any threats, real or perceived. Acolytes are wary of humans and steadfastly choose to avoid them. All my research has not revealed the reason for this, though the prevailing theory is . . .

The ink on the last few paragraphs was smeared and illegible, and the next few pages of the book were missing. It appeared as though someone ripped them out. Xane felt frustrated. It was probably the most useful part of the entire book, and he couldn't read it.

All of this left Xane with more questions than answers. What was the tenth sentient creature? Why did acolytes avoid humans? Most importantly, how could he defeat Gaulcel? Xane realized he had never faced an elf in the pit—in fact he'd never even seen one participate in a tournament. Elves weren't that common in Purgatory, so it had to just be the odds.

Just then, Xane heard Gaulcel's voice. The morning announcements had come on. He had been up all night reading, and he needed to get ready for that day's tournament.

13

The Bid

Maribel came into the city in the dead of night. She hated coming back, but she wouldn't be staying long. Maribel chose the secret entrance right by the creature's quarters. It was muddy getting in, but it was the only way to be sure she would avoid detection. Maribel liked to be sure. She knew she had only a small window of time to get to him. If she missed the window or she was discovered, all would be lost.

* * *

"Fortunately, I've got the pizza place," Bill said. "I couldn't fight for shit, and I got sick of dying every day."

He was at Xane's apartment—the first time he had ever been there. Xane had been pleasantly surprised to see him at the door, and even more so when he saw that the man had a pizza with him. The only other visitor Xane saw regularly was Guff, and he was a little thrown off by someone new, but he welcomed Bill in. In Xane's first life, his apartments were always a mess, but that wasn't the case now. Here, Xane didn't have enough things to make a mess with.

After the door closed behind him, Bill hugged Xane. Another first. It felt good for both men. In the world they lived in, physical touch only seemed to ever happen out of aggression. They began discussing the pits as usual, but this time, Bill was dominating the conversation. His voice somehow sounded both rapid and relaxed.

"My pizza place saved me in more ways than one," Bill was saying. "The Wolf Clan helped me get it set up. They take all the profits, of course, but it gave me a daily meal and a purpose, which is more than most people here get." Bill spoke with a kind of candor Xane had never heard. "The fights between those of us at the bottom of the unaffiliated leaderboard are often to the death. Folks go in thinking they must win or die. It's better to die and wake up tomorrow than it is to go a day without food, you know?"

"I hear that." Xane suddenly wondered how Bill had gotten the pizza here, past the horde. "Man, it's really good to see you, but I've got to ask . . . what are you doing here?"

"Tomorrow is your one-year anniversary in Purgatory. In the morning, you're clan eligible. I thought we could celebrate," Bill said.

"Being stuck in this place for eternity isn't really cause for celebration," Xane said. "But I do appreciate it. Thank you for the pizza."

"Tomorrow is a big day for a lot of reasons—some you don't understand yet." Bill said. "If you get into a clan, it'll change everything for you."

"If . . ." Xane replied. "Come on, they're all recruiting me. I've never lost a fight. If I don't join a clan, it'll be because I choose not to."

"Confidence is good. Cockiness is not. Nothing is certain," Bill said with a stern expression, but then his face relaxed. "Naw, who am I kidding. You'll probably get a bid from all nine of them. Any idea which one you'll join?"

"I don't know. They all seem so phony to me."

"You're not wrong. This place instills phoniness, especially among clan members. But the benefits are worth it. If you turn it down, I'm worried you may regret it."

Xane thought about getting to Gaulcel. He needed to be able to get close if he was going to take him out. "Maybe the Wolves," Xane told Bill. "At least I kind of know Guff, and they helped you with the pizza place."

"Good choice. Hell, from what I know about the clans, they're all pretty much the same. It sounds like you've got some good reasons, though."

"The least of the nine evils." Xane sighed. "Anyway, let's eat this before it gets cold." He pointed to the pizza. There was no table in Xane's apartment, nor chairs. The only piece of furniture was his cot. Both men sat on the floor and ate the pizza, talking about their days before Purgatory. There was nothing to do but enjoy each other's company. Hours passed quickly. It seemed the conversation would never run its course, but at some point, they both silently agreed it was important to sleep.

Bill stood up. "Come by the pizza place tomorrow and let me know what happens."

"Will do," Xane said while reluctantly walking him to the door. "See you then."

* * *

Xane was still a bit groggy when the morning announcements came on the next day. A year had passed, and he had only watched them a handful of times. Instinctively, he started his daily routine. He went through all of his usual combos of punches and kicks on the heavy bag before he heard a knock at the door. He opened it, and Guff stood by himself in the entrance.

Guff held a small wolf emblem with two hands at chest level. "This is your bid for entry into the Wolf Clan." The emblem appeared to be made of pewter. It was a dullish gray with no luster. The thing was wolflike in shape only, with no color or fine detail. "I cannot give this to you now. The offer is contingent upon you winning today's tournament. If you lose, we will withdraw your bid, and you will not be eligible again until a year from now."

After showing Xane the emblem and explaining the bid and conditions, Guff just walked away. Xane never said a word in response. He stood with the door open for a bit before he even appreciated what had happened.

Then he went back to his combos, mulling over the conditions of the bid. He was surprised that he didn't just get in with no strings. The whole situation felt wrong to him, and he began to rethink whether he should even join the Wolf Clan. Xane figured another clan would come and offer him a bid any minute, but none did. His wristband began to blink. It was time for that morning's tournament.

As Xane entered the dugout by the pit, he noticed two elves already in the dugout. It took Xane aback because it was the first time he'd ever encountered elves in the tournament. He would see them around the karbero occasionally, but never in the pits. Elves were fairly uncommon in Purgatory, so he figured it was just a strange coincidence.

The second thing Xane noticed was Bill, seated behind the two elves. The memory of last night was fresh in his mind. The man looked tentative, out of place in the tournament room. Xane hadn't thought much about how Bill had to fight every day too. Occasionally, Xane had gone to his pizza shop to find Bill absent. He wondered if it was because the man had died in the pit that day. They often talked about Xane's fights, but Bill never brought up his own.

When Bill noticed Xane in the dugout with him, and a smile came to his face. He waved him over, and Xane sat down next to him behind the two elves. Xane smiled back and the men embraced. He didn't care who saw.

"Did you manage to get any sleep last night?" Bill asked.

"I passed out hard right after you left. Come over again later—we can pick up where we left off."

"I'll do that." There was something off in his voice. From its intonation, Xane got the impression that Bill might be lying. He realized there was a chance they might have to fight today.

"Hey man, I want you to know—if we face each other I'm going to try to win. We've become close since you got to Purgatory. Honestly, you're my best friend. You're like a son to me, but I am still going to try and win and if we fight, I'm going to try to beat you. I hope you can respect that," Bill said.

"Of course." Xane was grateful that Bill had said it first so he wouldn't have to. "Just know, I'm the same way. I'm not going to go easy on you just cause we're friends."

The two man shook hands.

"So, how many bids did you get this morning?" Bill asked. He sounded more jovial with that out of the way.

"Just one," Xane replied. "Well, I guess technically none. I'm not in unless I win."

"I guess you better hope we don't face off." Bill laughed as he spoke and raised his fists, kidding with Xane.

"I'm wondering if maybe I'll get another one later today."

"From what I've heard, all the clans give out their bids in the morning, right after the announcements. I don't know, maybe I'm wrong though. I never got one. Who's the lucky clan?"

"Wolf."

"Well, at least that's who you wanted, right?"

"Yeah, I'm a little pissed there are strings attached, though." Xane was looking down into the pit. "I feel like nothing I did this year mattered. What have I gotta do to get some respect?"

"Keep winning," Bill said. "You gotta look at it from their perspective. They see you as a guy with promise, but you've never faced anyone in their league. Nothing you did before matters until you've shown what you can do there."

Xane noticed the elves in front of him speaking in their own language. He had no idea what they were saying, but the sound of it was beautiful. It had a musical quality, almost like they were singing. The elves' voices seemed to be both high- and low-pitched at the same time. Every word was a three-part harmony

"You ever seen an elf in the pit before?" Xane asked Bill.

"Yeah, they're good. Way out of my league. I've never seen one lose."

Just as Bill finished speaking, the referee appeared outside the swinging door of the dugout. He was a big man from the Panther Clan. He pointed to the two elves and motioned for them to enter the pit. The tournament had started.

The elves obliged the referee. With impressive agility, they hopped the bar of the dugout and landed in the sand of the pit, ten feet below. One of the elves was about an inch taller than the other. He had cobalt-colored hair down to his shoulders, which were uncharacteristically broad for his race. The taller elf stood on the balls of his feet, assuming a tight defensive stance. He nodded to the second elf, who nodded back.

The light bulb turned red. The shorter elf launched forward with a jump kick high enough to hit the taller elf in his head. The taller elf dodged, but his adversary landed on his feet. The speed of the fight was astounding. It was like watching a kung fu movie on fast-forward. Both combatants had speed, agility, and reflexes greater than those of any fighter Xane had ever faced. The elf with the cobalt hair had a clear advantage, though. Despite his opponent's speed, the other elf couldn't connect. The fight ended when the more skilled one swept the other's legs, knocking him toward the ground. Somehow, as the shorter elf fell, the one with cobalt hair was able to bring his other foot around, kicking him in the head while he fell. The blow knocked the shorter elf unconscious. The ref from the Panther Clan raised the taller elf's hand.

The winning elf introduced himself to Xane after his fight. He was all smiles, but Xane recognized the tactic. He wasn't being nice—he was trying to intimidate him.

"I'm Comerciam," the elf said.

"Xane."

"Good luck in there," Comerciam said while visibly sizing Xane up. The expression that the elf wore told Xane *I'm going to beat you so bad, you'll be embarrassed.*

Next up in the pit, the referee pointed to Bill and a sahuajin that Xane hadn't noticed. Bill assumed a fighting stance that reminded Xane of Bernard Hopkins and the Philly shell defense. It was clear that Bill had been a fan of boxing, as they'd discussed, but it was also clear he was just a fan. His stance was a little off in some important ways that could make a difference against a skilled opponent.

The red light came on. Bill's sahuajin opponent wasn't especially skilled but had above-average strength. The sahuajin immediately threw a right hook at Bill's head, which connected cleanly. Bill's feet left the ground momentarily before his body fell into the sand with a thud. He was out cold. The referee raised the sahuajin's hand.

Bill came to a few seconds after the fight ended. He found a place to watch the rest of the tournament on the viewing deck. When his eyes met Xane's, he gave a little shrug, and Xane shrugged back. They were too far away from each other, and the room was too loud for any conversation. Xane felt appreciative that Bill was going to stick around to watch the rest of the tournament, though. He turned his focus toward Comerciam.

Anyone who watched the first round of the tournament knew the two fighters that would make it to the final. Xane and Comerciam outclassed the other combatants in every way.

Xane beat his opponents soundly, but Comerciam obliterated his. His second fight was over in seconds. In the final fight, Comerciam deliberately took his time. It was against a Khajjine. The elf knew everything the creature was going to do before it did it. This wasn't a fight; it was a demonstration. Comerciam was showing Xane what he would do to him in the final. He was trying to get into Xane's head and scare him. He was stoking doubt, and it was working. For the first time in as long as he could remember, Xane questioned himself.

In all three of the elf's fights, none of Comerciam's opponents landed a single blow. The elf was untouched the entire tournament. Untouchable. Xane had learned to block the feeling of doubt when he started his boxing career, internalizing the belief that doubt was weakness. For as long as he'd fought, he refused to allow himself to ever feel doubt, but as he watched Comerciam's skill and ability, it snuck through. Xane missed Coach Clark.

After Comerciam's performance against the khajjine, Guff made an appearance in the pit. He shook hands with the elf and then called Xane down to join them.

Xane entered the pit and stared intensely at his opponent. The elf stared back with the same intensity. Xane was so focused on Comerciam that he hardly acknowledged that Guff was in the pit with them instead of the

Panther Clan referee who had worked the rest of the tournament. Guff was holding a megaphone-like device. He held it to his mouth and pointed it toward the viewing deck.

"The prize for winning the tournament today is this emblem." Guff spoke into the megaphone. He produced the wolf emblem he'd shown Xane at his apartment that morning. "This emblem constitutes an official bid to become an initiate in the Wolf Clan. To my right is the human, Xane 'Reaper' Bridges, and to my left, the elf Comerciam, from the Evergreen flock. Both of these creatures are unbeaten in the tournaments over the past year. They have earned their right to compete for the honor of Wolf Clan membership, but only one of them can receive a bid. Please give them a round of applause, and may the best fighter win."

When Guff finished speaking the crowd clapped and yelled with enthusiasm. Xane was just able to make out Bill's voice cheering him on.

The level of the elf's intensity toward Xane suddenly made sense. He needed to win just as badly—the stakes were the same for them both. The winner would get to join the Wolf Clan, while the loser had to wait a year for another shot. Xane thought about what clan membership meant and decided he didn't really care about being a member. Clan members were suck-ups, all deeply entrenched in the cruel authoritarian systems of this city. But Xane knew he had to join a clan. Someone had to take out this city's cruel dictator, and that would be easier from inside the system. He needed to win this fight.

Xane remembered what he'd learned from the book Bill had given him. He covered his face. It was a gamble, because it would limit his sight, but if Comerciam was able to predict his moves, he would have no chance. The small light bulb turned red.

When the fight started, Comerciam ran toward Xane. Then he jumped nearly seven feet off the ground and did a backflip. While flipping, he stuck his right foot out from the rest of his body, launching sand. His foot whizzed by Xane's face, but the air and sand that followed the kick irritated Xane's eyes, forcing him to close them. Even so, the kick missed. Maybe he was beatable after all.

After the backflip kick, Comerciam landed steady on his feet. It was one of the few times that day he had missed with a strike, though his face wore no frustration. Comerciam feigned a front kick, and Xane took the bait. He shuffled backward as a dodge. Then the elf took a step forward and spun while extending his left arm. He was staying on the outside, Xane realized, trying to build momentum and knock him out with one blow.

Xane ducked under Comerciam's spinning backfist. The successful dodge brought out his confidence—Comerciam's miss had set him up perfectly. Now the elf was standing right in front of Xane. With his arms extended, he wouldn't be able to block. Xane was in the perfect position for his signature combination.

Comerciam moved his head backward at the left jab, narrowly avoiding contact. Xane's right uppercut also failed to land on its target, but it was closer. When Xane brought the left hook around, Comerciam wasn't expecting it. The tactic of hiding his face had worked. Comerciam's face still managed to turn with the punch, though, which barely grazed his left cheek. Xane had missed all three blows, but not by much.

Xane was still planning his next move when he saw something that surprised him. Comerciam was face-down in the sand. He wasn't moving. Xane couldn't believe it. He hadn't landed a single punch, at least not flush. The crowd roared like nothing Xane had ever heard. The sound of their excitement reverberated through Xane's body. The ref raised Xane's hand. He had won.

But he hadn't won. Comerciam was faking it. He'd fallen on purpose, he had to have, but why? Nothing made sense. Xane looked again at the elf. Comerciam's cobalt hair was covering his face. The elf had been playing mind games since the tournament started. Was he faking that too? Xane desperately wanted to make eye contact, to understand what caused the elf to throw the fight.

Before he could lock eyes with Comerciam again, though, Guff came under his legs, and Xane found himself on his friend's shoulders. Guff walked Xane around the edges of the pit for the crowd to gawk at. It seemed like everyone in the viewing deck was going ballistic. Xane spotted Bill, who reached down for a high five. Xane slapped his hand. Comerciam's fraudulent fall must have looked real to the audience. They all thought he'd really won. Life in this city was not known for having inspirational moments, and the crowd was reveling in the opportunity to bask in one.

Xane couldn't enjoy the moment himself. He thought back to his boxing career. He wished he'd won a gold medal, wished he'd won a championship. He would never have a chance now.

Guff knelt so that Xane could get back to his feet. "Congratulations," he said in Common. "The last time a human beat an elf was over a hundred years ago. I'll be honest, no one thought you could do it, but I was pulling for you." Guff handed Xane the crude wolf emblem. "This is yours, Initiate. Now, come with me." He escorted Xane past the screaming fans and out of the tournament room through a side door. Guff had to scan his wristband for the door to open.

14

A Pack of Wolves

Once they were clear of the screaming crowd, Xane turned to Guff. "Did you call me Initiate?"

"That might as well be your name for the time being. You'll get a primer on our rules, but I may as well tell you some things now. You will be an initiate until you've proven yourself worthy for the next rank, and from now on, you must refer to all superiors as 'Leader.'"

"Guff, what are you talking about?"

The man slapped Xane in the face, hard. "You will address me as Leader Guff, Initiate."

Xane was so stunned by the blow he didn't even think to retaliate. He stared, stone-faced, at his former friend. This was his reward for victory?

"Put the emblem on—you must wear it at all times to show your rank," Guff said.

Xane felt a small chain attached to the back of the emblem. He reluctantly pulled the chain out and put it over his head, wearing the emblem as a choker.

Guff walked Xane through a long corridor ending in a chamber with nine doors; each had an animal emblem hung above the door frame. "It's time for your tour." Guff waved his wristband to open the door with the wolf emblem. They entered an elevator that let out into a warehouse-sized room filled with exercise equipment. In the center lay an Olympic-size swimming pool. "This is one of our gyms. Any kind of exercise equipment you can think of is in here," Guff said.

"I never learned to swim."

"We'll teach you. There's a lot of things you won't know how to use at first. Other worlds use different equipment than you're used to, but don't worry—you'll get an orientation on all of it."

The tour of just the gym took almost an hour. Guff showed Xane several sparring rooms where creatures trained in different kinds of combat. "We host intra-clan tournaments here. Sometimes we travel to other gyms to face off against other clans, and on special occasions, we fight in the pits. You still have to participate in tournaments, though not every day like before."

Weapons also had their own large room. Each individual weapon had a wolf insignia. Xane noticed that one section of the wall was covered in falchion-style swords that looked identical to his own.

After the gym, their next stop was what Guff called a luxury emporium. There were shops full of clothes, furniture, jewelry, and even electronics. Xane noticed a radio and wondered what kind of programming there might be in Gaulcel. Every single item had a wolf symbol on it. "You can have any of these things with wolf credits," Guff told him. "You get wolf credits by doing jobs for your fellow clan members. For instance, the guy who'll teach you to swim will get paid in wolf credits. A lot of guys employ the unaffiliated because they work cheap. Anyway, we'll give you ten thousand credits to start. It's enough to get you most anything here, but we don't have time to shop today. Also, we took the liberty of furnishing your quarters with the standard Wolf initiate set up."

Xane and Guff then went to a recreation area. It had ping pong and foosball and skateboarding ramps and countless other types of recreation. One room was an arcade with loads of different video games. There was also a simulated indoor park with benches and foliage and butterflies flying around. One landed on Xane's finger. He still hadn't seen what Purgatory looked like outside of this building, and the experience was transcendent.

They spent the full day touring the other Wolf Clan amenities—there was a special cafeteria, a temple, a bar, and an adult bookstore, which didn't sell any books.

The last stop of the tour was the library. It was much smaller than the other rooms. "We share this with the other clans," Guff said. So all of the clan recruiters had lied, Xane realized. Most of the shelves were stocked with the same four books about Gaulcel that he had already seen in the bookstore. The only other section was for "How To" books. Guff handed Xane a pale green book written in Common. Xane recognized it as the same book that Bill had needed to sneak him earlier. He flipped to the end and saw that the same pages were missing. "I've heard this book can help a lot with the tournaments." Xane suddenly remembered Comerciam taking a dive. So much had happened that day, it seemed like it was weeks ago instead of that morning.

"What'd you think of the tour?" Guff asked.

Xane shrugged. He wasn't in the moment. He was in his head, thinking about everything that was happening.

Guff either didn't notice or pretended not to. "Now, it's time for your first assignment." He led Xane to a kind of conference room but with cement walls. A large map hung on one of them, and a lanky, turquoise-haired elf sat at a round table in the center of the room. "This is Superior Leader Talona. He represents the Wolf Clan in the noble guard."

"I trust Guff gave you quite a lot to take in, so I will be brief," the elf said. "As you've seen, the rewards of being a Wolf are unparalleled, but they are only available to those in good standing. If you go against the Clan, your punishment will be swift—and worse than anything you've ever experienced. It's my job to keep an eye on Guff here, and Guff keeps an eye on you for me. That's how our organization works. Guff is reporting back on everything you do, and I will be looking in on you myself from time to time."

Xane didn't respond, though he knew the elf could see his anger. The amenities Guff had shown him were impressive, but he could tell he was being sold to. It made him skeptical. Xane had never been very accepting of authority in life, especially when it was unearned. This Talona had not shown Xane that he was worthy of his respect.

"I can tell you are reticent of our ways. My recommendation to you is to acquiesce until that feeling passes. In time, you will come to accept your place, as we all have. Just as I am Guff's leader, I have a leader to answer to—Eleris, the Leader of the noble guard, and even he must report to Gaulcel himself. One day, you may even have your own initiate that calls you Leader," Talona said.

Xane continued to remain silent but refused to hide his face. They were expecting him to be overjoyed after seeing all the Wolf Clan amenities. He wanted the elf to see that their sales pitch hadn't worked. He wanted Talona to see his unbridled rage.

"Guff will give you assignments every so often that you must complete. As today is your first day as a Wolf, I'm going to give you the assignment myself." The elf allowed a deliberate smile to form on his face. "You must clear out a mine outside of the city. A creature called an ignertia has taken residence there. We need to you to kill it so we can access the mine's resources. Guff will accompany you, but you must kill the creature yourself. The assignment begins tomorrow. Now you're excused, Initiate."

Guff hastily grabbed Xane's arm and walked him out of the room. They took the elevator to the karbero. "That's all for today," Guff said. He hadn't lost his authoritative demeanor since the end of the tournament. This was not the Guff that Xane was used to, and Xane hoped the change wasn't permanent. "Go get dinner. I know you'll want to see your friend with the pizza place." Guff had never mentioned Bill before. "Then get some sleep. I'll see you right after the announcements. Don't ignore the announcements tomorrow—we know how you like to do that." Guff was intentionally letting Xane know they'd been watching him, even inside his own quarters.

Guff left in the elevator, leaving Xane by himself for the first time that day. Guff was right that he needed to see Bill. It occurred to Xane that no one had ever asked whether he wanted to join the Wolf Clan.

* * *

The terrible scream startled Eleris. Gaulcel was alone in the next room, and the elf was on guard duty. Gaulcel was almost never alone, but tonight was an exception.

The scream was the most feminine sound he'd heard in recent memory. It reminded him of a young girl seeing a spider. The elf wondered if he was hallucinating. Eleris did not want to disturb his leader. He debated with himself for a moment about whether to investigate the sound. If it was nothing and he responded, he would be punished. If it was something and he didn't respond, he would be punished.

Before Eleris could decide what to do, he heard Gaulcel's voice. The monster was pleading for his life. There was no doubt now whether Eleris should respond. He was in the room within seconds.

Eleris could not believe what he found there.

Gaulcel was on his knees. A woman stood behind him, holding a dagger. Her clothes were wet with refuse, her hair clumpy and matted. She was filthy. Even so, Eleris loved her. He felt Gaulcel take control of his mind and body. He felt his legs move toward the woman. Then, just as quickly, he regained control of himself. The woman had slit the monster's throat. Eleris couldn't have done anything about it even if he wanted to.

The elf wondered why Gaulcel had tried to take control of him instead of the woman. Then he realized he was free from the creature's control for the first time in ages. The woman began to make her escape. She ran right past him, and he made no attempt to stop her.

Gaulcel was now dead and lying on the floor. The revolution had begun.

III

The Outside

15

The History of Purgatory - An Introduction

Outside the cities of Purgatory, nothing ever really changes. There are lots of leaders, but none of them have much power. Government doesn't exist in any real form. There are plenty of presidents, prime ministers, kings, queens, chancellors, barons, archdukes, and other creatures who give themselves titles and claim to rule territories. Most folks who manage to live outside don't even know what supposed leader is claiming to rule them. Most don't know what territory they're in at any given time. Nor do they care. The boundaries change so often, folks don't even know where the boundaries are.

Those on the outside believe that Purgatory has a king who exerts some control over the acolyte cities. Rumor has it that this king lives in a legendary city called Moneta. According to the story, it is perfectly balanced there. The leader is strong, and the people are free. The acolytes are believed to follow this king. However, my extensive research has failed to find any evidence supporting the rumor or the existence of such a municipality. Outside of the cities, I have come across no rulers with enough reach or power to actually rule. There is no written set of laws that anyone on the outside respects.

The land in Purgatory appears to go on forever. No map contains all of it. Explorers have spent countless lifetimes looking for the edge of this world. None have found it, or if it has been found, word of it has never gotten back to the rest of us. Purgatory settlements span numerous habitats, and the topography of the land appears to repeat. Identical mountains, rivers, forests, deserts, and even oceans appear hundreds of thousands of miles apart.

The level of technology differs in the various settlements around Purgatory. In some areas, folks are not yet able to control fire, while other areas have a kind of internet, with communication possible over vast distances. In many places, technology is deliberately suppressed.

On rare occasions, motorized vehicles are found, but due to the constant fighting amongst tribes, folks are unable to maintain a standardized system for the creation and distribution of fuel. Sustained electricity has had the same issues. Space travel has been attempted but always fails. No one has been able to pierce Purgatory's dense atmosphere. Even so, nearly every invention that exists on the First Worlds exists in Purgatory in one form or another. Ranged weapons are a bizarre exception. A simple bow and arrow will break before it can ever be used. Even a thrown stone will never find its mark. This phenomenon is, to date, unexplained. Most assume it is some form of magic.

I have written extensively about the ten sentient species found in Purgatory. In my works, I separate the sentient from the nonsentient species based on whether they have a discernible and comprehensive language. In addition to the sentient ten, there are countless species of plant and animal life. These creatures do not evolve because they do not reproduce. Instead, when a plant or animal dies, it reappears the following day, just as the sentient species do. To all life on Purgatory, death is temporary.

The most notable characteristic of life outside the cities is the prevalence of what locals refer to as "ghouls." These poor creatures are afflicted with a terrible disease called Lecttum that targets and kills brain cells. The creatures are thus effectively brain dead, yet somehow their bodies remain animated. Research has confirmed that no brain activity continues, but no suitable explanation has yet been discovered as to why the creature itself does not fully die. Once infected, the host has mere minutes before its mind is lost. From there, the host body will seek out warm-blooded living creatures on which to feed. Even without an active brain, the creatures are somehow able to receive sensory data from sights, sounds, and smells.

The offending disease is incredibly contagious, spread by even slight contact with any bodily fluid from those afflicted. Though in a constant state of decay, ghouls can survive, in a sense, for decades after the infection. Infected hosts can, however, be killed with blunt trauma to the head. After a ghoul's death, the host creature will respawn as though it had died by any other means, no longer a ghoul. It will no longer carry the infection and will have no memories of the time spent in the semiliving state. Ghoul populations get out of control quickly. Entire cities have at times been lost.

Acherona – Purgatory Publishing Company

16

Talk of Revolution

Xane was excited to tell Bill about the crazy day he'd just had. It was his first moment away from Guff since his now leader made that surprise appearance at the tournament that morning. The day had been a whirlwind, and Xane was tired. Even so, he wanted to share it all.

Bill was officially Xane's best friend. He'd said as much at the tournament that morning, right before getting knocked out in the first round. When Xane got to the pizza place, Bill was behind the counter as he always was. The familiar sight lifted Xane's mood.

Bill smiled, like he'd been waiting to see Xane too, but then his face became serious.

"On the house," he said as he handed Xane an entire fresh pizza. The smell of it piqued Xane's hunger. He started eating immediately, realizing he forgot to say "thank you" only once he already had a large bite in his mouth. "Did they give you an assignment?" Bill asked.

Xane finished chewing. "Thanks. They want me to clear out a mine or something. I have to kill some creature. I think they called it an ignertia."

Bill's expression fell even further. "Oh man. Do you know what that is?" he asked rhetorically. "It's a gigantic, fire-breathing lizard that can fly. A dragon. It's a dragon. Your assignment is a suicide mission."

Xane responded with surprise but not fear. "Guess I have to kill a dragon then."

"Seriously, that's a suicide mission," Bill repeated. "They've wanted to clear that mine for centuries. I'm pretty sure the reason they would send you on a mission like that is as an ass-backward way to teach humility."

"Well, good luck with that," Xane said flippantly. "It'll backfire when I take the thing out."

Bill let out an involuntary laugh at his confidence. "You're crazy. Anyway, it's about closing time here. I want you to come with me after. I've got some stuff to show you."

Just the thought of seeing more things that day made Xane feel tired. "Hey man, I appreciate it, I really do, but I really am exhausted from everything today. Can we do it some other time?"

Bill turned stern. "No, it must be tonight. You're leaving the city tomorrow. We may not get another chance."

It suddenly occurred to Xane that Bill was being a lot more loose-lipped than usual. Normally, the man was more reticent to speak freely. It was one of the things that clued Xane in that they were being watched. Were they being watched now? "Okay. I'll go with you."

He waited with Bill until the few remaining customers left, then helped close up shop. When they were done, Bill walked him through a door behind the counter. Xane had never noticed the door before, even though he came to the shop almost every day. It led into an eight-by-eight room with cement walls. The room had no furniture except for a twin-size mattress on the floor. Cooking supplies were strewn about. "Looks familiar," Xane muttered. "Is this your quarters?"

"No." The response was matter-of-fact. Bill moved the mattress a few inches, exposing a small switch underneath. He flipped it, and Xane heard what sounded like an elevator arriving. A hidden door on the wall opened.

"Get on." Xane and Bill walked onto the elevator, and then Bill said a word in Common that Xane had never heard before. "This ride will take a few minutes."

Xane was still in awe of the secret elevator, but Bill had grown serious once more. "I want you to know, no one is listening to us right now. No one probably ever told you that everything you do and say here is being watched."

"No one had to. It's on people's faces all the time." As much as Xane trusted his friend, he became skeptical. "How do you know no one's listening? What's going on with you?"

"It's complicated, but believe me, I know." Bill said. "I've got a lot to tell you about, and we've only got a short window of time to go through all of it. We may not get another chance for a while."

Bill began to tell Xane things about the city that Xane had always thought were true but could never confirm. "Gaulcel uses the clans to keep tabs on every single person in the city. They watch and report and snitch. There is almost nowhere to hide from their gaze. He is terrified of an uprising. There's no worse crime in this city than dissidence. Freethinkers are snuffed out and tortured for lifetimes. Gaulcel thinks every citizen in the city hates him. He's mostly right about that, but no one will challenge his power as long as they fear him. Over time here, he breaks everyone's will. That's his goal."

Xane nodded his understanding.

"He's asleep right now," Bill continued. "He only needs to sleep once every few years. Only creatures close to Gaulcel know when he sleeps. Well, only those creatures, and those that they tell. If they were caught telling, they'd probably be tortured too. Gaulcel can read and take control of people's minds, but his powers may not be as strong as he wants us to believe.

"I managed to make nice with some members of the Wolf Clan. I did them favors and built their trust. They think I depend on them. I want them to think that. I did depend on them for a while, but I figured out a way to fend for myself. There's a secret resistance movement, isolated segments within the clans that are plotting revolution. I know of a few individuals, though they're unaware of each other. Most know there are others but don't know who they are. They don't want to know, yet. Their plots range from elaborate to nonexistent. All are in waiting. They need something to unite them. Someone.

"Gaulcel, of course, has his sympathizers and supporters. They act out of fear but also ambition. He generously rewards snitching. The clan hierarchies offer endless advancement, and each new level offers more material wealth and power. Once they find a dissident, Gaulcel is quickly able to learn everything that dissident knows. They fall like dominoes. This is why the resistance cannot even have a name. Did you get a chance to read that book I gave you?"

Xane was momentarily startled by the interruption in the monologue. "Yes, I had to use those glasses I won."

"Good—I knew you would win those glasses. I noticed the way you hid your face today. I think it helped."

Xane had just heard a lot of information from Bill, too much to digest at once. He stared off into space for a moment. Despite the time constraints, Bill let him stare. They rode on the elevator in silence. Xane debated with himself for a minute or so over whether to tell Bill about Comerciam. He still hadn't decided when the words fell out anyway. "That elf I fought today, I think he took a dive."

"I know he did. I paid him to."

Bill's words hit Xane like a Mack truck hitting a motorcycle. Before he could respond, the elevator door opened, and they stepped out into a huge room. The walls weren't made of cement, and they were painted a light, calming blue.

Then Xane saw it. He didn't think it could be at first. It had to be a painting made to look that way. Xane walked to Bill's window and softly tapped the glass. It was real. A real window, and the reddish-purple sky outside was real too. A full year had passed with Xane trapped inside this building. A full year, and he'd never even seen the outside. There were no lights and no stars. The color of the sky was not like home had been. Even so, it was beautiful. Xane found himself holding back tears.

"It never gets all the way dark here." Bill said.

"How can you . . . Do you live . . . What is . . ." Xane was too flabbergasted to finish a sentence.

"Like I said, there's a lot you don't know about this place. I stay here most of the time. I know the guys who are supposed to be watching me, and they don't bother me because of what I do for them."

"Pizza? Pizza pays for this?" Xane was still reeling.

"No, no." Bill laughed. "The pizza place makes no money, especially before you started coming there. I'm a bookie. I take bets on the tournaments."

"What?"

"The fights. I'm the guy clan members come to when they want to make a wager. Everywhere has its vices, especially this city. Gambling isn't technically allowed, but the higher-ups turn a blind eye because it keeps people distracted. Keeps them obedient. It's also an added layer of fear because they worry about getting caught."

"Don't you worry about getting caught?" Xane asked.

"I'm pretty sure I already have been, but most of my clients don't know how far up the ladder my business goes. The only real crime in this city is doing something Gaulcel doesn't want you to do."

"Is this how you know about those folks we talked about in the elevator?" Xane looked around the room. He was still concerned that someone might be listening to them.

"This business helps me make contacts, but I keep all that separate. It's too risky. I have a contact on the outside. I don't know all the details, but she put something in motion that started today. Specifically, it started with you winning the tournament. A lot of high-up folks lost a lot of money this morning. One of them was your new boss's boss, Talona."

"If he was going to throw the fight anyway, why was the elf such an asshole?"

"He had to make it look real. Intimidating you was part of that. That was also why you couldn't know about it beforehand. That elf, Comerciam, he's one of my contacts. He's on our side. He got wealthy today, and so did a few others."

Xane had a second wind now. They were discussing taking out Gaulcel, and that made him focus. "Wouldn't the elf want to join the clan himself? Wouldn't it be easier to start a revolution from within?"

"It's all part of her plan. Like I said, I don't know everything, but I trust her. She's our best shot, and we have to at least take a shot. I don't want to mince words here—I'm talking about starting a revolution. So, the first thing I need to know right now . . . are you in?"

Of course Xane was in. Taking out Gaulcel was all he'd thought about since arriving in this city. But the opportunity seemed too good to be true. Bill was the only person in the world Xane trusted, but those higher up must also know that. Xane realized there was a lot he didn't know about Bill. This felt like a set-up, but Xane knew his only choice was to ignore his skepticism. He had to trust.

He looked at Bill and nodded. "What do you need me to do?"

The man's expression of relief was palpable. "Just do exactly what you were going to do before. Leave with Guff tomorrow. Do your assignments as best as you can, and wait for a contact. She'll come to you directly. Her name is Maribel. That's all I know, all that I can tell you right now."

Xane had so many questions he didn't know where to begin. "Is there anyone else I know who's also in on this?"

"None I know of. I've told you everything I can. You need to get back to your quarters. Someone will notice if you're not back soon."

Xane knew that Bill was right. He also needed to rest. His friend escorted him on the elevator back to the pizza shop. They both remained silent throughout the ride. Before leaving, they hugged once more, and then as if no time had passed at all, Xane was back in his quarters.

His eight-by-eight cement room was now furnished. Xane was too tired to look at it all, though. He went straight to his new bed and concentrated his thoughts on the sky he had seen for just that brief minute until he fell asleep.

17

Beyond the City's Walls

Xane was still fast asleep when he heard a knock at his door. Guff entered before he could respond. Had he missed the announcements? "Get up. Time to go, Initiate."

Xane rolled out of bed, his eyes still groggy with sleep "I must have slept through the morning announcements."

"No announcements this morning. Don't know why," Guff said. "Now get up. We'll debrief on the way."

The word made Xane think of the military. An army recruiter had approached him in high school, but Coach Clark had talked him out of it. "Don't let anything keep you from boxing. It is what you're good at. When you find something you're good at, get better at it," Coach would say. Being in a clan was what being in the military must have been like.

Guff handed Xane a new set of clothes with the familiar wolf insignia on them. He looked around the room and noticed his new furniture for the first time. He had a couch, a table, a couple of cushioned chairs, and the bed he had slept in. Each piece had a wolf insignia. The clan must have moved it all in during his tour. It was nothing extravagant but still a significant improvement over what little he'd had before. The punching bag was still there, but they'd moved it to a different corner.

"Grab your sword," Guff told him. He was holding his scythe. "This job will pay well but only if you complete it."

Xane remembered what Bill had told him about the ignertia. His friend had said that the job was impossible and was only meant to teach him humility. Xane didn't care, though. He was game.

They boarded the elevator, bound for the outside. Xane was excited to be outdoors for the first time. He had no idea what the outside was like on this world except for what he'd seen from Bill's window the night before. The elevator went down for what seemed like an eternity. It opened into a room with nine doors, identical to what he'd seen after the tournament. The two men walked through the door with wolf symbols above it and into a long, twisting hallway. They walked around more corners than Xane remembered to count and ultimately reached another door with a push-in handle. There were two Wolf Clan guards posted outside of it. Guff scanned his wristband, and they stepped through the door. Finally, they were outside.

Feeling the fresh air was an emotional experience. It was humid but comfortable. They were on what looked like a desolate city street, but Xane didn't care, and Guff didn't seem to either. They both looked straight to the sky. It was dark red and clear. Xane felt tremendous joy and longing simultaneously. He was elated to escape the windowless cement walls of the past year, but he missed the blue sky of Earth. He would likely never see that sky again.

A tiny vehicle that looked like a golf cart pulled up. The driver, wearing Wolf Clan attire, stepped out and handed Guff a kind of key. Without a word exchanged, Guff got into the vehicle behind the steering wheel and motioned for Xane to climb in next to him. They drove for nearly a mile before passing the edge of the single building that had trapped Xane for all this time. Guff made a left, and then Xane saw the wall—a hundred stories of cement that marked the border of the city. They were leaving, even if only for a short while.

Xane thought of escape. His only escort was Guff, and he was sure he could get away from him if he tried. The man didn't even have a gun. Then Xane thought of what Bill had told him, of the coming revolution. He would have to come back after the mission to do his part. Xane didn't know what role he would play in the revolt, but he got the sense it was important.

They reached a section of the wall with a gate. It was well guarded, manned by nine total, one from each clan. One of the guards came over to Guff and scanned his wristband. "You have to leave the cart here," the guard said. Xane and Guff exited their ride, and the guard gave a sign to the others at the gate. Four of them began pulling on chains, lowering the door, which turned out to be a drawbridge. There was a moat outside the city filled with crystal-blue water. Beyond it was a field of grass—actual grass—and past that Xane saw a forest. It all felt unreal, like a hallucination, an oasis.

Once Xane and Guff had passed over the drawbridge and the door was again closed, Guff's demeanor relaxed. "Sorry about hitting you yesterday," he told Xane. "You'll learn it's important to keep up appearances. But while we're out here I don't care whether you call me Leader."

"Don't worry about it," Xane said. He was angry, but he understood. "So, what's the plan? Where are we going?"

"The mine we're going to is about ten miles east of here." Guff pulled a map from his pocket. "We go through that forest, and when we come across a river, we'll head south and we should run right into it."

"I say we take our time," Xane said. "Who knows when we'll get to be out here again?"

"I'm not going to argue with that," Guff replied.

Xane felt a breeze at his back and put his arms out, imagining he was flying. He took off his shoes and felt the dewy grass between his toes. Then he lay down in it and looked toward the sky. He was going to enjoy his freedom while he had it.

"Get up," Guff said. "They can still see us from the wall." Clearly, he knew what Xane was thinking. "They track us by our wristbands, and they'll know if we try to take them off. They don't come off easy. You'd probably have to cut off your hand before you could even get the thing loose. And it wouldn't matter anyway because once you die, you'll just wake up back in Gaulcel."

The two men had only been outdoors for fifteen minutes, and already the thought of going back was too much to bear. "Just let me lie here a few more minutes," Xane said.

"All right." Guff sat down next to him and pulled out the map again. "We can pretend we're looking at the map."

After another ten minutes had passed, Guff pulled Xane, who had fallen into a kind of trance, back to his feet. He rose reluctantly. "Let's at least get into the forest so they can't see us anymore," the man said, and Xane obliged.

The tree line was a few hundred yards away. Once they were under the trees, Xane heard birds chirping. The sound was new to him, and Guff seemed surprised as well. Xane looked up through the trees trying to find the bird. He wanted to see what color it was. Xane had never understood why some people watched birds as a hobby on Earth, but after a year stuck in Gaulcel with no view of nature, he got it.

Just then, he heard something far more sinister. It was the rustling of a man-sized creature hobbling over leaves and fallen branches. As the sound grew louder, it was accompanied by a stench of decay. A whole flock of birds flew out of the trees. Xane searched the direction of the rustling until he located the creature, a female invunt, nude from the waist down. There was something odd about her gait. Walking did not appear to come naturally, and Xane wondered whether the creature was injured.

"Hello Miss, are you okay? Can we help you?" Xane asked in Common.

The dwarf did not respond, just continued plodding toward Xane and Guff at a steady pace. Her skin was pale with shades of green. A patch of auburn hair fell from her head, leaving only a few remaining clumps. Her mouth stood open, exposing her rotting yellow teeth.

Xane turned to Guff. "Do you speak any invunt?" he asked.

By the time they realized she was hostile, it was too late. Guff's scythe was low at his side when the dwarf suddenly jumped at him. Her balding head landed face down on Guff's shoulder, mouth agape. Xane heard the crunch of teeth into Guff's deltoid and watched the creature pull out a bloody chunk of tissue.

Guff grabbed the back of the invunt's head and threw it to the ground. Then he spun his scythe around, jabbing the pointed end into where the thing's heart was supposed to be. The point pinned the dwarf to the ground, but it continued to writhe.

"What the Gonk!" Guff shouted. "Quick, cut her Gonkin' head off."

Xane had grown fairly fluent in Common, but he had never heard the word "Gonk" before. Even so, he didn't need a translation. The meaning was clear from context. Xane pulled his sword from his side and obliged Guff's request. The head separated easily, and the thing stopped writhing.

"What the hell was that? The Gonkin' thing bit me." Guff's wound was already showing signs of infection. Xane looked at the man's shoulder with wide eyes, which then moved to the headless body at his feet. It was marred with signs of decay. The former invunt's fingernails extended at least four inches from its hands.

"It looks like a . . . zombie." The word just kind of fell out of Xane's mouth.

"Zombie? What is that?"

He knew of no translation. "It's just a myth. Something people made up to scare people. They're in stories back on Earth, but they're not real."

"Well, that was sure as Gonk real!" Guff was really wound up. Xane hadn't seen him like this before.

"In the stories . . . if a zombie bites you—you turn into one." Xane said, trying to be both sympathetic and direct.

"Gonk that! You've got to cut my Gonkin' head off!"

"What? No, no, just put some pressure on it. We'll get to the river and clean it out. Then we can rest. I bet you'll be fine by morning."

"Nah, man. My whole arm is numb." Guff looked Xane right in the eyes. "I need you to kill me right now, and kill me dead. I do not want to be like that thing."

Guff was serious—and right. There were other myths Xane knew of from Earth that had turned out to be real in Purgatory. The existence of dwarves and elves and centaurs were not just legends in this world. Zombies might not be a legend either. It wasn't worth the risk of waiting to see if he turned. "All right, all right."

"Okay quick, how do you want to do this?"

"Gonk if I know! I guess I'll kneel down."

Guff got to his knees, then looked up at Xane.

"No, I can't . . . Okay, but I can't look you in the eyes." He walked around behind Guff and raised his sword.

"Wait!" Guff said. "Use my scythe!"

"I'll see you back in the city," Xane said as he took the scythe from Guff. Then he thought of something. "Should I keep going toward the mine? Is someone from the Clan going to come looking for me after you die?"

Guff thought for a moment. "I'm not sure what they'll want you to do. I think you should keep going. If I'm wrong, they may send someone to get you, but I'll tell them I told you to keep going. Now please kill me. Quick."

Xane lifted the scythe.

"Wait!" Guff took a deep breath. "Okay. Do it."

Xane took his own deep breath and then swung hard, starting high in the air to get a boost from gravity. Guff had a thick neck, and the last thing he wanted was for it to take more than one swing.

After it was done, the man fell to the ground. Xane sighed. He was on his own. Two headless bodies lay at his feet.

Taking the map off Guff's corpse, he continued toward the river. He left the scythe by its owner, choosing the simplicity of the sword over the larger weapon. Xane had almost no experience with either , but the scythe felt more clunky in his unskilled hands.

He came across another zombie dwarf about an hour later. This time, Xane knew not to wait to find out whether it was friendly. One on one, the plodding, rigor-mortis-afflicted creature was no match for him. When it fell, Xane noticed that his moneta increased slightly. His confidence increased as well.

As Xane traveled, the forest became increasingly dense. After some time, he started to hear the rush of water ahead. The map called it the Gundik River, with "Gundik" being Common word for "shine." Xane was getting hungry and he didn't know how to get food or what would be safe to eat. He was going to have to figure it out soon. The river would at least quench his thirst, he hoped.

As the Gundik's roaring water came into view, Xane took a bad step. He heard a branch snap, and before he knew it, a net made of thick rope had engulfed him. Xane found himself suspended in the air. The sudden force of the rope net caused his sword to fall to the ground. He'd sprung some kind of trap and had no means of escape. The sun was setting.

18

A Centaur Savior

Xane spent the full night in a rope net, hanging from a high branch. He closed his eyes and tried to imagine the rope net as a hammock. It didn't work. It was nearly pitch dark when a third zombie dwarf walked under him, stepping in the exact spot where Xane had sprung the trap. The zombie could have been caught in this rope net instead of him. The thing must have smelled Xane, because it looked up and spotted him. The creature leapt into the air, but he was out of reach. It kept jumping and falling back down unsuccessfully. Half an hour later, the ghoul was still trying. During that time, it managed to get close on one or two occasions. The sun was coming up, and Xane hadn't slept at all.

Sunrise in Purgatory was the one time of day where the sky looked similar to how it did on Earth. It was beautiful. Xane tried to enjoy it, but he was fixated on his hunger—and the ghoul reaching for him. He might starve in this tree. Xane looked down and saw his sword lying on the ground far beneath him. If only he could reach it.

A new sound came from downstream. It sounded like coconuts smacking together, clipping and clopping—someone traveling on horseback. This was his chance.

"Help! I'm trapped,!" Xane screamed as the galloping centaur came into view. The half-horse, half-man creature appeared, holding a long spear.

Within moments, the point of the spear pierced the dwarf zombie's head. The creature slumped to the hard dirt ground, no longer undead, just dead. Then the centaur raised its spear again. He was pointing it at Xane. "Help, I'm trapped," Xane repeated.

"It speak," the centaur said in Common. "How does it speak?"

"What do you mean, how can I speak? I can speak the same as you can speak?"

"Simple ones learning," the centaur said, speaking to himself. He poked the spear up at Xane, aiming it at his head. Xane was able to roll to the side, taking the sharp point half an inch into his shoulder instead.

"Owww! What the Gonk are you doing?"

"It feel pain. This cannot be."

"I'm not one of those things, I was trying to get to the river, and I got caught up in this trap. Please, just help me down."

The centaur gave Xane a perplexed look and poked at him again. This time, Xane managed to grab the wooden shaft just below the sharpened obsidian point of the spear. The centaur was not expecting it, and Xane pulled the weapon right out of its hands. He cut a hole in the rope net and fell all the way to the dirt, landing on his back with a thud.

The creature looked at Xane wincing on the ground. He still held the spear, and there was a falchion sword lying next to him. "That's my spear. Must give back," the centaur said.

Xane looked at the fresh blood on his shoulder. "You stabbed me. Why would I do that?"

"If do not, I trample human," the centaur said.

A good reason, he had to admit. The beast was quite large, even for a centaur, easily several times Xane's weight. Gray horns sprung from his head, which was otherwise similar to humans. The centaur had long black hair hanging loose around his shoulders and dark bronze skin. Xane tried to remember what he had read in the book that Bill gave him. The book referred to centaurs as arbanequus. They tended to be peaceful, but if they were pushed to violence, they were vicious and aggressive. Xane did not want to get into a fight. "If I give you the spear, are you going to stab me again?"

"Are you simple one? Mama told me to kill all simple one. Stab head. But human no act like simple one."

He was talking about the zombies, Xane realized. "No, I'm not a simple one. I'm just trying to get to the river for some water and then find something to eat."

"How out here by self? No worry about attack from simple one? Simple one attack, make you simple." The centaur seemed concerned for Xane.

"You're out here alone. Shouldn't you be worried too?"

"Human have two tiny legs," the arbanequus said. "Gabio run faster. Now, give spear. Mine."

Xane got to his feet and handed the creature his spear, simultaneously picking up his sword, which was still lying in the dirt. "Here. Do you know where I can find something to eat around here?"

"Mama have food. She may give some if help."

Xane was confused. As far as he knew, there were no children in Purgatory—and no parents either. "Where do I find this Mama?"

The centaur's face shifted to anger. "She no you Mama. She my Mama."

"Okay then. Where do I find this person?"

"No person. Elf. Climb on back. Gabio take you," the centaur said. He kneeled, permitting Xane to mount him.

Xane climbed on to his back. He had never ridden a horse before, let alone a centaur. He wasn't sure what he was doing. Fortunately, there was a saddle in place. Xane clearly wasn't the creature's first rider. When the arbanequus began to run, he almost fell off, but then he grabbed the saddle horn. He leaned forward to avoid the wind and any low-hanging branches.

The centaur was indeed fast. He was also agile, traveling through the woods avoiding the trees and other flora effortlessly. Before long, they reached a clearing and continued to run. A tree-covered mountain appeared in the distance. The centaur said something into the wind, which Xane didn't quite here, but he figured that the mountain was their destination.

"What human name?" the centaur asked, yelling over the wind.

"Xane."

"Me Gabio. Call me Gabio."

When they reached the foot of the giant rock, Gabio went into the Gundik River, which was about a foot deep at that section. He ran straight toward a waterfall and then through it and into a cavern. Inside the cavern was a large wooden gate built of tree trunks. Another dwarven zombie was outside.

The centaur handled the spear expertly, planting the point straight into the back of the ghoul's head before it realized they were there. The thing fell to the floor, motionless.

"Help move," Gabio said. "Put in river, or smell attract more simple one."

Xane dismounted, barely managing to keep upright. He grabbed the invunt body by the legs and dragged it back under the waterfall until he was wading in the river. The water wasn't quite deep enough to cover the dead dwarf. Once he completed the task, Xane held his hands under the falling water and drank some of it. Then he drank more.

"Hurry. More in forest. Simple one see you."

Xane heard the centaur but didn't care. He continued to drink until he quenched his thirst. The centaur made a loud and rhythmic knock on the gate with the butt of the spear. A moment later, the door opened to reveal another gate a few feet behind the first. The door had opened on a rope. The centaur went through and motioned for Xane to follow.

Xane heard a voice behind the second gate. "No visitors." The voice was distinctly female.

"Human hungry," the centaur said. "He help us. I stab him."

"All right. Close the door." The centaur shut the gate, locking it with a giant log that looked like it might have once been a small tree trunk. The second door opened, again with a rope. There was no other gate behind this one.

A striking female elf appeared in the doorway. She wasn't just the first living female Xane had seen since arriving in Purgatory, she was also the first being he'd seen who was truly elderly. Her hair was long and silver, and her eyes were almond shaped, evincing kindness and wisdom.

"Hello, I'm Nahna."

A CENTAUR SAVIOR

* * *

Xane never intended to stay with Gabio and Nahna as long as he did. They had a nice little setup in their cavern, safe from what they both called the "simple ones." Nahna used a combination of strange herbs and elven magic on the stab wound in Xane's shoulder the day he arrived. The next morning, when Xane woke up, the wound was healed. There wasn't even a scar. Nahna offered to heal the scar on Xane's face as well, but he declined. It was still a symbol and reminder for him.

Nahna called Gabio "son," and Gabio called Nahna "Mama." The elf told Xane that she'd found the centaur in the wood some thirty years prior, abandoned and alone, and she'd adopted him. They had since made a life for themselves. Gabio's sheer size made him a good bodyguard and worker, and Nahna was a wise leader. Neither of them had died in a long time.

Adjacent to the room of the cavern where they slept and spent most of their time was a cave with a seemingly endless number of batlike creatures. Gabio was quite adept with his spear, and killed them easily. Bats may not have made for the tastiest meal, but they were a meal nonetheless, and Xane was happy for it. Gabio ate something like twenty bats every day. They never ran out.

A small crack in the mountain above them allowed some light in during the day. It was enough for a single tomato plant to grow in a small pot. Nahna let Xane have a tomato fresh off the vine, and it tasted like heaven. They got their water from the waterfall right outside the gate. The centaur could carry several large buckets tied to his back, bringing in enough to last days at a time.

Nahna told Xane that not long before he arrived, an army of dwarves had come through the area. They'd discovered Gabio and Nahna's encampment and demanded taxes from them. According to the leader of these dwarves, Parth, the elf and the centaur were living in territory that he ruled, and therefore they owed him tribute. When they refused him, Parth ordered his army to ransack the farm Gabio and Nahna had set up outside the cavern.

The dwarves burned every crop they couldn't eat. The fire must have attracted zombies, because after that, the army was gone and replaced by a horde in dwarven form. As Nahna told the story, she mentioned that Parth had said something about looking for a human woman. When Xane asked her if she knew of Maribel, Nahna told him that she didn't.

Xane often worried about leading clan members from Gaulcel back to their cave, but he figured it would be okay for a few days. Then he stayed a few days more. One day, he told Nahna that he had to leave, and she insisted he stay and help them rebuild their farm. She told Xane that he at least owed them that, and she was right. Besides, Gaulcel felt like a distant dream.

Each night, Nahna prepared a potion of intoxicants for the three of them to drink. Then she told stories and shared her wisdom. Some of the stories were true, while other times she made them up. Nahna called the potion "nebreen." It made Xane feel lightheaded and lighthearted. Colors were brighter. The bats tasted better, and everything was more interesting. Though it was artificial, Xane felt happiness when they drank the nebreen.

19

Sowing the Seeds of Revolution

Eleris had only just seen Maribel, and he already loved her. With that one act, she was a superhero. He was dumbstruck, feeling a combination of admiration and awe. The body of his former boss lay dead on the floor in front of him. He would be free for at least twenty-four hours. Eleris knew instantly how he wanted to spend it. When Maribel ran past him, the elf had done nothing to stop her.

* * *

Maribel arrived as the shop opened. It was empty, and Bill was behind the counter. The grime covering her managed to conceal her gender long enough for her to get by the guards. She looked like she was straight out of Gaulcel's starving horde. Maribel approached Bill behind the counter and looked him in the eye.

It took a moment for Bill to realize that the person in front of him was a woman. Their building in the city housed only male inmates. Once Bill really saw her, he knew who she was instantly. This had to be Maribel—the woman with the plan. Bill waited for the code word the intermediary had given him.

"Do you have any anchovies?" Maribel asked. It was the signal he'd been waiting for. Bill couldn't help but laugh to himself. Of course he didn't have anchovies. He didn't even have pepperoni. With the supply chain in the city the way it was, he was lucky to get cheese.

There was no doubt this was her. The instructions Comerciam had given him were to open the door to the back of the shop. He went into the empty room for a moment and pretended to look for anchovies, and when he came back out, he left the door slightly ajar.

"We do not have any anchovies. Sorry, Ma'am." Bill caught his error. "Sorry man—I meant man, not ma'am."

As soon as the words left Bill's mouth, Maribel leapt over the counter and grabbed all of the edible stock she could carry. Then she leapt back to the other side and ran to the gate separating the inside of the pizza shop from the rest of the goppidum. She threw all the food outside the gate. Only then did the guards take notice, but by that point, it was too late. The horde was upon them. Maribel was starting a riot.

A few starving individuals saw Maribel throw the pizza over the gate and came for it like pigeons coming for breadcrumbs. While those few fought over it, more of the horde took notice, and within seconds, a full-scale mob had arrived. By that point, there were too many climbing and jumping over the gate to stop them. Starving rioters who saw this as their one shot at food stormed Bill's shop. The guards lost Maribel in the commotion, and she was able to slip through the door at the back of the shop, which she locked behind her.

Bill watched the horde tear his shop to shreds, taking and consuming all the unsold pizza and ingredients behind the counter. The guards were powerless to stop it. After that, the sheer mass of people and creatures pressing in on one another obscured his view.

Gradually, the crowd dispersed. Trampled bodies littered the floor, while survivors headed back over the fence. More guards came. Some of the horde escaped; others were apprehended. Guards led those they arrested off the floor and into a shuttle that would take them for some punishment that Bill did not want to imagine. Then it was over. A few minutes passed and it was like it had never happened, except Bill was out of pizza. He had to close the shop.

The door to the back room was locked, but Bill had the key. He opened it into a small space with four cement walls which housed only cooking supplies, some dough, and a mattress. He wasn't surprised that Maribel already knew about his secret room. He moved the mattress and flipped the switch, calling the hidden elevator.

When he entered his apartment, Maribel was staring out the window, deep in thought. She didn't notice him come in.

"You must be Maribel," Bill said. He wasn't quite sure what to think of the woman. She was the leader of the revolt, and she had started a riot in his shop. She had an uncanny knowledge of this prison city's underground. Maribel practically *was* the city's underground. No one knew where she came from or how she knew so much about the city, but she had a plan to overthrow its cruel leader, and against all odds, it seemed to be working. Bill wasn't sure if he could trust her, but it was his only real shot at freedom.

"And you're Bill," Maribel said. "Sit. Time is short, and we have much to discuss."

Bill sat on his luxury couch. "I'm all ears."

"I hope you don't mind—I took the liberty of putting on a spot of tea. It's quite difficult to get a good cup around here."

"I've got coffee too," Bill said. "Help yourself."

"Tea is fine." Maribel sat next to him on the couch. "So, I'll cut to the chase. Gaulcel is dead. I know it's true because I killed him. Right before I came to your shop."

Every muscle on Bill's face loosened. His jaw dropped to his chest. He was digging through his mind for words to say, but none came.

"This whole city hates Gaulcel, and the cruel creature knows it. He can read minds, after all. If we could get the whole city to turn on him at once, he'd be powerless to stop it. And almost everyone in the city wants to turn on him. The problem is, people are too scared to organize. They know what'll happen if they're found out."

Maribel continued, "Gaulcel capitalizes on people who live in fear, and from his perspective, that needs to be all of them. If they are given a good enough opportunity, almost all the residents are willing to take him out. Even the clans.

"His death is our opportunity. Without his fearmongering, the hierarchy of the city will gradually break down. The leaders of the clans will begin to discover that they have no leader themselves. They will break away from their duties. The inmates will go unobserved for the first time. For the next twenty-three hours and fourteen minutes, we have a chance to make real change here."

"So, what you're saying is we have twenty-three hours to win a revolution?" Bill asked.

Maribel took a sip of her tea. "No, that can't be done. We have twenty-three hours to sow the seed." Her self-assurance made Bill believe she was indomitable.

"Okay, what do we gotta do?" Bill felt like he'd been lying in wait for an eternity. He wanted to do whatever he had to. He was ready.

"We only have time for me go over the plan once. The first thing we need to do is get everyone here that we can trust. I know a few. I'm sure you do too. Mine will be arriving in a few moments. You need to go get yours, but only if you can get them quickly. The more we have, the better we are, but only if we know for certain they are trustworthy."

So Bill's apartment was going to act as the headquarters for the revolution. If any of Gaulcel's stooges found out, he would be in for lifetimes of torture, perhaps an eternity. He didn't care. He did know of several potential recruits, but he wasn't sure how to contact them quickly. Bill couldn't think of anyone that he trusted enough to let them in—well, anyone other than Xane. "I only know one, and he's not in the city right now."

"You're talking about Xane 'Reaper' Bridges." Maribel said. It was only the second time Bill had heard Xane's ring moniker. "That's a shame that he won't be here. He could have proved useful today. He still may."

Bill thought of Xane and the ignertia.

"No one will go after him," Maribel told him, "if you're worried about that. Those wristbands only have a range of a few miles outside the city. He won't come back into range, unless he's on his way back anyway."

Bill hoped he would one day learn the sources of her information.

The elevator dinged, and two elves stepped out. The first was Comerciam. The second was handcuffed and wearing a burlap hood that covered its face. Its clothes were baggy and loose. Comerciam wore a wolf emblem on his clothing. They'd let him into the Clan even though Xane beat him. They wouldn't have done the same for Xane if the roles were reversed, Bill knew.

Comerciam took the hood off the second elf, revealing that it was a she. He took off her handcuffs. The elf let down her hair, which had been hidden under her hood. This was the first female elf Bill had ever seen. She was the epitome of beauty, exuding a kind of kindness and warmth with just her eyes. One look at her face made Bill feel like everything would be okay.

"Bill, you already know Comerciam. This is Ciessa." Maribel motioned at the second elf.

"Hello," Bill said.

"Hello," Ciessa replied.

"We should have a few more arriving soon," Maribel said as the elevator chimed again. This time, two human men stepped out. They looked remarkably similar to one another ,with long brown hair and beards, each standing around five foot ten. They might have passed for twins except that one man had green eyes and the other's were brown. Their general level of filth gave the impression that they were straight out of the city's horde. The men were skinny but not emaciated. Baggy clothes hid their small yet taut muscles. Maribel introduced the pair as Tom and Tim, then introduced the rest of the group to them.

The next out of the elevator was a pair of Mantis Clan khajjine named Khane and Kurth. Bill recognized them as frequent gamblers. They almost always lost, but Bill would sometimes tell them about fixed fights. It kept them with enough money to keep betting. Khane was the larger of the two—and the more impulsive. His gray fur stood up at the sight of the room. Kurth had orange fur and striped arms. He was generally quiet but always looked angry, and now was no exception.

"There should be one more." The motley group waited a few minutes with no elevator chime before Maribel decided it would be best to continue.

She began to lay out the plan for the day. The first step would be for the group to create their own infrastructure, to enable them to pass messages back and forth unnoticed. Maribel pulled out a document that none of them had ever seen, a full map of the city. It showed the location of every building and then the layout of their interior. Each building in the city's layout was almost identical, except for one. It was the same size as the others, but it was made up exclusively of jail cells, millions of them. "That's the prison reserved for the dissenters that Gaulcel fears most, where the most severe torture takes place. It has few inmates at the moment, but it has the capacity to hold half the city if necessary," Maribel told them.

A knock came at Bill's window. Outside it, a female dwarf holding a rope appeared suspended in the air. She had short hair and a stout build. Her breasts were nearly indistinguishable from her pectoral muscles. "Ah, the last member of our fellowship." Maribel walked to the window, opened it, and let the dwarf in. She wore a Bear Clan insignia.

"Sorry I'm late," the dwarf said. "Some of our clan's leaders were out of place and acting strangely. I had to take a different route so that I wouldn't be noticed. I'm Dalthra, by the way." She looked around the room, taking in her fellow soldiers in the rebellion.

"If they are out of place, then it has already started," Maribel said. "Gaulcel is dead," the leader announced to the group. "I know because I killed him."

Bill already knew this information, but the rest of the room didn't. It was the best news that any of them could think of. There were audible gasps, and then almost in unison, the seven individuals celebrated. They cheered and hugged one another.

"We're not done yet," Maribel announced loudly, quieting the crowd.

The group listened intently as she went back to laying out the day's plan. "Gaulcel's power over the city is surface-level only. None of the city's residents follow him willingly. He inflicts so much fear that no one openly rebels, but all this city's residents would if they had a reason not to fear him anymore. The way to take him out forever is if the whole city fights back at the same time. It will take more time than we have today to rid the city of its fear. The next twenty-two hours and forty-seven minutes are the only chance we have to sow the seeds. If the seeds are sown properly, they will sprout, and sooner rather than later, Gaulcel the prison city will be no more. A free city will grow in its place."

Maribel then meticulously went over her scheme. The group would start the day by creating an infrastructure of hidden communications channels to remain in place after Gaulcel respawned. There were designated safehouses in each building deliberately hidden from most maps. These were places, like Bill's apartment, which were obscured to protect vices for clan members. The group would designate message points and meeting places in each building that would likely go unnoticed. Ciessa could get access to the station that broadcast the morning announcements. Dalthra could diagram the technology there and recreate it, so they could bypass and control the announcements at some point in the future.

Once they put the infrastructure of the plan in place, the group would move to phase two: exposing the gaps in the city's power structure left by Gaulcel's absence. Tom and Tim would go through the goppidum, doing what Maribel had done to Bill's pizza shop and doing it at as many places as they could. The horde was everywhere. Without Gaulcel's leadership, the hierarchy in the clan guards would break down. Soon, no one would even stop the food riots. The horde would get bolder, until every eatery in the city was overrun. The whole city would be in chaos.

The third phase would start after the clans had lost all control. Khane, Kurth and Dalthra would wheel in a huge supply of food to the city center. Maribel explained that she had friends on the outside who would have the food supply ready. All the khajjine needed to do was pick it up. Using Ciessa's access to the morning announcements, Maribel would create a live broadcast from the city center. She would announce to the entire population that there was enough food for everyone, and it was free.

"So, that's the plan for the day." By the time Maribel finished talking, nearly an hour had passed.

"What then?" Khane asked. "What happens when Gaulcel wakes up and takes back the city? There will be hell to pay. He'll come after all of us. He'll put us through the worst punishments he can imagine, and it will last forever." The khajjine's fur rose, and his voice became agitated.

"There's going to be so much chaos today that it will take Gaulcel and his stooges a lifetime to figure out who was involved," Maribel said. "I will be the only one on the broadcast."

"That's not good enough." Khane continued to argue. "The monster has mind control. If he catches one of us, he'll learn everything, and everyone involved with this plan. It's only a matter of time."

Maribel remained calm as she responded. "That's why we'll have the safehouses and the communication infrastructure in place. It is so we can protect one another. We must be patient. I assure you, the next time Gaulcel dies, it will be the end of his evil reign."

Khane huffed, but Maribel had assuaged his fears enough for him to stop arguing.

"There's one secret I don't know," she continued. "The location of Gaulcel's quarters. I don't know where he'll respawn. I don't know if anyone does. We need to find out." She looked at Ciessa. "Your husband is close to him—you have to figure out his respawn place. We won't be able to stop him unless we know that."

Ciessa expressed visible concern. "I almost never see my husband and I don't think he'll give up his boss like that. Even if he would, he may not know himself."

"You'll figure it out. I trust you," Maribel said, and Ciessa believed her.

"One more thing you all should know." With the tone of her voice, Maribel made clear that what she was about to say was important. "Gaulcel can't control human minds. His powers only work on the other races. Our most important mission is to make sure as many people in the city know that truth as possible."

Bill's mind began racing. Of all the self-inflicted torture he'd watched Gaulcel force others to do, he'd never seen him take over a human. From Bill's experience with the clan members, he knew that Gaulcel never did any of his own enforcement. In fact, he never appeared publicly at all. He only ever showed his face to the public on the morning announcements.

Maribel gave the group a moment to digest what she had just told them before continuing. "Once that fact is out there, the city's hierarchy will do everything in their power to discredit the truth or erase it from the population's memory."

"How do you know it's true?" Bill asked.

"How do you think I killed him?"

20

Ciessa and Eleris

For several minutes after Maribel killed Gaulcel, Eleris stood in place, stunned. The shock of that moment would take decades to digest. A huge weight had been lifted from his shoulders, but it was only a temporary reprieve. Another, even larger weight was coming to take its place. He had to come to terms with the impending uncertainty of what would come next.

Eleris knew that Gaulcel would blame him for what had happened. He hadn't responded to his calls immediately, and he had let the woman escape. Hopefully, his punishment would include a demotion. The elf had fought so hard to become Gaulcel's right-hand man. To get the position, he had played politics with all of the clans, making sure that other promising guards were made to look incompetent. He'd portrayed himself as the cruelest of them all other than Gaulcel himself. Eleris had done terrible things to get that reputation. It had been over a thousand years since he was promoted to his position as leader of the noble guard, and he regretted his actions for all that time.

With all the power and material wealth he had, Eleris was never able to enjoy any of it. He was forced to spend all of his time as Gaulcel's plaything. Now, he was free. It wasn't like the other times Gaulcel had died. Eleris had only ever known Gaulcel to die of old age. Those times, the creature was prepared for his death. Gaulcel would make arrangements so that his absolute power over the city was never in jeopardy. Those times, the exits to the city were closed, and no one could get in or out until he respawned. All of his many underlings had instructions to carry on as though nothing had happened. Most of the folks in the city never even knew the monster had died before he came back. His reemergence was met with a huge celebration of Gaulcel's life and power. They called the beginning of each of his new lives the "Reawakening." Gaulcel would come back full of youth and vigor. What the monster called a celebration was really just a chance for him to indoctrinate the population with lies of his greatness. For a week or so, the morning announcements would be propaganda instead of just torture.

The next Reawakening was supposed to be at least a hundred years away. But Gaulcel was dead. He would stay dead for a day. There was no telling what would happen in that time.

How had the mysterious woman killed him, though? Gaulcel had taken control of his body and not hers, even though she was the one with a knife to his throat. Maybe he panicked in the suddenness of the moment, didn't realize that Eleris wouldn't have time to stop it. Once the monster was dead, Eleris had regained control of himself immediately. At that point, what was done was done. He could not have saved him.

It didn't take long for Eleris to decide what to do with his newfound freedom.

* * *

Ciessa went back home following the meeting with Maribel. Comerciam had escorted her there with handcuffs and a hood over her head, so that no one in Xane's building would detect that she was a female. She wasn't able to see as they passed through the goppidum, but she heard the noises of the folks there. They were going about their day as they normally would. They had no idea what would soon happen. The idea of being able to save them from the literal and figurative chains of the city excited her. She felt hope for the first time in as long as she could remember.

When she arrived, Comerciam removed the hood and cuffs and wished her farewell. Her husband was standing and waiting by the door. She hadn't seen Eleris in ages, and she quickly realized why he was there. If she had any doubts about whether Maribel was telling the truth, they were gone at that moment.

"We're leaving now. I don't have time to explain," Eleris said.

Ciessa recognized emotion in his face, something only she was able to do. No one knew him like her. It was rare for them to see one another, but he was always on her mind, and she was always on his. For centuries, every time they were able to see each other, the first thing they did was make love. It was an explosion of pent-up longing and desire.

Ciessa barely heard his plea. She moved to kiss him, and he dodged away.

"Darling, we must go now. Grab what you need, but no more than you can carry," Eleris said.

"You're here. We're together. I don't know what's going on with you, and I don't care. We may not have much time, let's enjoy the time we have." Ciessa embraced him as she spoke. She had lied. She did know why he was so intense at that moment. His boss was dead.

She pulled his head into her breast. Ciessa didn't want her husband to see her face, so that he wouldn't know her deception.

"No, we have to leave right now. There will be time later. We will have all the time we want and more. We will have eternity together, but we must go now."

"No one is coming for you, my love. We are safe now," Ciessa told her husband.

"Gaulcel is dead." Eleris told her. His wife looked away from him, but he saw it in her eyes. "Criminy, you already know! How could you know?"

She wanted to protect Eleris from his boss. She wanted to protect Maribel's plan. If Eleris knew what she knew, then Gaulcel could find out. "It's better I don't answer that question."

Eleris knew she was right. "We can leave this city. We can escape, but we only have the day." He sensed her reluctance. "I know you hate it here as much as I do."

"That's true, but it could be better. Without Gaulcel in charge we can change the ci—" Ciessa stopped speaking abruptly.

"There's no way to stop that monster. He's too powerful. Our only option is escape."

"I'm not going. I can't say anymore." Sadness was a luxury neither of them could afford at that moment. She threw her hands under her husband's arms and pressed her chest into his, kissing him forcefully. Though Eleris knew they needed to make haste, he couldn't resist her this time. As they kissed, the elf reached down to her thighs and lifted her off the ground. Holding her firmly, he walked forward and pushed her back against the wall. Greedily, he pulled off her clothes.

The two elves made love. Then they made love again, going four times total until they collapsed on the floor, breathing in unison. They never made it to their bed. Ciessa rolled over, placing her head to his chest. It rose and fell with each heavy breath. She listened as his rapid heartbeat gradually returned to a relaxed rhythm.

Eleris clutched his wife tightly. He wanted to lie there and hold her forever, but he knew he could not let his desire get in the way of what had to be done. "I love you, but we really need to go now."

"Just a little longer," she whispered to him. Eleris obliged her, and they lay together in silence. After some time, Ciessa mounted him. This time, they made love slowly. Ciessa wanted it to last. She feared it might be their final chance.

21

Setting the Stage

Tom and Tim's plan was simple. Tom took one half of the karbero, starting all the way at the west end. Tim started all the way at the east end, and they would work their way to the middle. Once they met, or if the whole building was in chaos, they would move on to the next building in Purgatory. They both shaved at Bill's place and procured wigs for when they would have to pass as female.

For the first eatery, they entered the normal way, scanning the fingerprints to prove they had moneta. Casually, they moved past the two guards at the entrance toward the food they planned to throw into the public walkway.

At Tom's first eatery, a guard stood at his post by the food. This would happen at some of the eateries occasionally, but it was unlucky. This guard, a sturdy dwarf from the Panther Clan, could shut Tom down immediately if he happened to be paying close attention. Tom knew dwarves always did their job thoroughly, and this one was no exception. He would need a diversion.

Fortunately, the place was crowded. If the guard needed to deal with something else, it might give Tom enough time to do what he needed to do.

The plan Tom came up with was something he remembered from fourth grade. It must have happened sixty-odd years prior. He thought about how long he had been stuck in Purgatory, in this godforsaken city. It was a reminder of the importance of his mission.

Tom's first move was to buy the food. There was only one option, some kind of invunt dish he was unfamiliar with. It looked like a soup with chicken feet. The restaurant's name was written in the invunt language, which Tom didn't speak. He noticed that all the other customers were invunt. Tom stuck out as the only human there. Getting the strange food would give him at least a little credibility as a legitimate customer. After making the purchase, Tom went back into the communal area of the restaurant. All the tables were taken, so he walked toward the front fence as though he needed a little space to eat. The Panther invunt noticed him walking.

"Hey, you there—not too close to the fence," the dwarf exclaimed, scowling at Tom.

Tom nodded and walked back toward the center of the communal area. The guard watched him intently. When Tom got far enough away from the fence, he took a bite of the invunt dish, trying to blend in. It tasted awful, but Tom couldn't let that show on his face. He continued to eat. After a minute or so, the invunt went back to focusing on the line. Tom took it as an opportunity. He pulled one of the chicken feet out of the soup and threw it at an invunt a few feet away from him.

It was a direct hit to the back of the dwarf's head. Tom turned around and looked the other way.

"Hey, who threw that?" Tom heard his victim say. "Did you throw that?"

"Throw what?" said a second invunt.

Tom's plan was working. He listened as the two started arguing, then turned around again to watch it unfold. The first invunt threw a chicken foot at the second, hitting him square in the face. They approached each other in a fury, and the second invunt threw his entire bowl of soup. The liquid sprayed over several invunt in the area who'd been talking to the first. They all started throwing their soup, increasing the splash radius. Soon, the whole restaurant was engaged in a full-blown food fight.

The guards responded, knowing the thrown food might attract the horde outside the gate of the eatery. They pushed through the crowd, threatening to arrest people. The guard near the food line came forward and grabbed an invunt that had dumped his chicken-feet soup on another's head. He zip-tied that invunt's hands behind his back and then choked him with a baton. He was sending a message to everyone in the restaurant that they needed to quit throwing food or face consequences.

By this point, Tom was soaked in hot soup. He wasn't sure who'd thrown it, and he didn't care. The path to the food was obstructed, but only by patrons of the shop now, no guards. Tom pushed his way through. He picked up a hot tray of the food that looked like chicken feet and made a beeline for the fence.

"Clear a path!" Tom yelled, running with the hot tray. The dwarves in front of him were short enough that he could have dumped the whole thing on them without lifting it. In various states of surprise, the invunt parted. With a burst of speed, Tom ran through them. He emerged at the fence and dumped the tray outside in the walkway. Then he dropped it on the floor.

The horde found the mess in an instant. Many had already gathered after noticing the food fight. Tom hopped the fence out of the restaurant just before the massive horde began hopping the fence in the other direction. He had to fight his way through the swarm of starving creatures seeking their only chance at a meal. Tom was engulfed, forced to stand still, waiting for small paths to clear. A riot was forming. This was the goal. With his first stop, Tom had been successful.

In normal circumstances, guards would have already responded to the incident. They would have started busting heads and making arrests, dispersing the mob with fear tactics. This time, though, something was different. A minute passed, and the three guards at the restaurant were still on their own. There wasn't enough of a display of force to slow the horde, who still believed they could escape.

Tom finally found a bit of open space and took a deep breath. Somehow, the guard from the food line was right there. The dwarfi grabbed his arm, but Tom was too strong for him. He had been training for this moment. Tom pulled his arm so hard he nearly took the stout creature off his feet, managing to free himself from its grasp. Tom took his next step forward, but escaping had forced him off balance. He stumbled forward, tripping over his own feet. As he fell, he saw that the horde had rushed another restaurant next door. Then he was on the floor.

Tom's body tripped several sahuajin that fell directly on top of him. The sheer mass was more than anyone could take. Tom was being crushed and suffocated. He realized he would not survive this. It was not the first time he had died, but it would be the most consequential. Gaulcel would be back the next day, and Tom could do no more to help Maribel's plan.

* * *

The bright lights of the sound studio flicked on abruptly. Maribel, Bill, and Dalthra stepped into a room that they all recognized. It was where Gaulcel recorded and broadcast the morning announcements to the whole city. Dalthra looked to the back of the room, the side that was not recorded, to see the technology that made it possible. Normally, Ox Clan members would fill that area, serving as the crew, but they'd all left after Gaulcel didn't show up that morning. On the wall next to a technical board was a list of directions on how to shoot Gaulcel from different angles, always getting his "good side." Bill thought the creature was ugly every time he saw him, and now he wondered how hideous Gaulcel must have actually been without the camera tricks. Dalthra had a pad to take notes. She started disassembling one of the three rolling cameras.

"It doesn't have to be exact," Maribel said. "It just has to work."

"I'm going to need a lot of materials and some independent way to generate electricity," the dwarf said. "And substantial payment."

"Just get me a full list, and let me worry about filling it," Maribel responded. Bill and Maribel were eager to help Dalthra, but they weren't sure how. They didn't have her technical ingenuity. Maribel stared and puzzled over a technical board that had more buttons, knobs, and sliders than she could quickly count. Bill stared blankly at some color filters.

"Wait in the corner," Dalthra said. "This shouldn't take me more than a few minutes."

Bill and Maribel found their way to an empty corner of the large room. The studio lights focused on the opposite side, leaving them in relative darkness. The shadows fell from the sharp features of Maribel's face. Bill was still a bit awestruck by the woman. She had a commanding presence like he'd never known before. Despite everything that was against them, Bill believed in her. He couldn't help it.

"So, I wanted to talk to you more about Xane," Maribel said.

"I'm listening."

"When today is over, his winning streak needs to continue," she said.

"I figured as much. That's not a problem." Bill wanted to be his best self for her. "I can fix any fight."

"I know. That's why I chose you."

At Maribel's instruction, Bill had been doing everything he could to make sure Xane always won in the pit. Xane's undefeated streak was no miracle. Comerciam wasn't the first of his opponents to take a dive. Bill was a bookie, and he fixed fights. He was good at it, too. He knew how to convince folks to throw a fight, and he knew who was good enough to not get caught. With Xane, he only used the best, those he'd seen throw fights before, guys who could make it look real. Bill's position as a bookie got him so deep into the tournament booking that he often got to decide who faced who and when.

Maribel also had some strings to pull in the city. Sometimes they paid off Xane's opponents for the day. Sometimes it was the referee. Sometimes it was even the judges. The only of Xane's tournament fights that hadn't been fixed in some way were on his first day in Purgatory, the day Bill met him.

Dalthra walked toward their side of the room and found the large technical board. She opened her notepad. Her hands and fingers somehow moved with both speed and deliberation. She diagrammed the control panel down to the most minute of details. It took her less than sixty seconds. Dalthra put her head beneath the large panel to observe all the wires. Bill heard her flip a switch. Screens above their heads flashed, displaying the room in front of them. There were three screens. Two showed different angles of the torture studio where they'd seen Gaulcel commit his uncanny evil. The other screen, from the camera Dalthra disassembled, was empty.

"There's a blargafugul somewhere. We either need to find it or hack into it. It must be very high for it to reach the entire city. If we get to that, then we can broadcast from anywhere."

"It's on top of building 3489," Maribel said.

Bill assumed blargafugul to be either the Dwarven or Common word for antennae. The city broadcast the morning announcement to every nook and cranny of the city—Gaulcel made it so they were virtually impossible to miss. There were screens in every individual's quarters and screens in every segment of the goppidum in every building. Within every individual shop, there was a screen and a speaker. No matter where you were, if you were in the city, you had to watch the morning announcements. One of Bill's favorite things about his secret penthouse was that there was no screen anywhere.

Maribel must have eyes all over the city, he thought. He realized how little he knew about her. "Can I ask you something?" He turned to face their leader. "What is it about Xane? Why is he so important?"

"It's hard to explain. What makes Xane special is that he's believable. He has the skills and training to make his wins look real. Folks need someone to believe in. Xane meets that need. He genuinely believes he can beat anyone and anything. No one can fake that kind of confidence. The citizens of this city will believe in him too, as long as he keeps winning."

"He will," Bill promised. "Don't worry about that." He was silent for a moment. "But what about you? Folks believe in you too. Why can't you fill that role?"

"I've got more important things to do," Maribel said without a moment's hesitation.

Bill was perplexed by her response, but he wasn't sure how to express it. He didn't even know what role Xane was supposed to fill in Maribel's plot. After that, Bill didn't speak for some time, hoping that she would explain a bit more.

Dalthra broke the silence. "I got it. You're on in five . . . four . . . three . . ." She stopped speaking and counted off the last two numbers on her fingers as Maribel moved into the center of the recorded part of the room.

She took a deep breath and looked directly at the center camera. Dalthra pulled her last finger into her fist. A light with the words "On Air," written in Common lit up. Maribel was in front of the entire city now. She began to speak.

***

Khane and Kurth left the city for the first time but only ventured a few yards from the gate. Their instructions were to wait there. Even though it was disappointing, they agreed to follow their orders. For an hour they waited, not knowing what they were waiting for. It would be food. They knew that much, and it was supposed to be enough to feed the whole city. What kind of food, they had no idea, nor did they know how it would arrive. Kurth was not the type to be patient. Khane was even less so.

However Maribel managed to set it up, though, it worked. The gates of the city were left unattended. The guards had abandoned their posts. Something was off about the city that day. It appeared that she had been right about Gaulcel's death. Khane was still skeptical. It was his nature to doubt any good news, especially from humans. Kurth was slightly more optimistic. He was confident that something was going to show up, but he was concerned it wouldn't be enough, or maybe it would come too late. The clock was ticking on Gaulcel returning to life.

As they waited, citizens must have noticed that the gates were open. A small trickle of folks began to flow out of the city. Not many of Gaulcel's residents were allowed outside of their buildings, but there were a few who came outside to tend to city business. They would pass through the gate and then see Khane and Kurth waiting just beyond it. Then folks would turn around and go back in, figuring the two khajjine were there to stop them from leaving. Sometimes they ran back into the city, afraid the khajjine would arrest them. Of course, Khane and Kurth didn't care if anyone left.

They even contemplated leaving themselves—they might not get another opportunity this good.

Eventually, a brave soul crossed through the gate and kept going. He walked toward the cats with his eyes focused on the ground, hoping they wouldn't notice him. Kurth waved his hand, giving him the go-ahead. The man's eyes lit up in disbelief. He began to run, fearful they would change their mind. Then he was gone.

Gradually, more folks figured out that they could leave. Before long, there were groups of three or more going at a time. At some point, something must have changed. Somehow, word must have spread. All of a sudden, the number of exiters grew from a trickle to a gush, groups of ten or so, then hundreds, then thousands, all within a matter of minutes. The gate wasn't wide enough for everyone to fit through. The crowd was starting to push and shove one another. The cats just watched.

"At least there are a few less mouths to feed now," Kurth said.

"Why aren't we joining them?" Khane asked.

They both thought about that until a wagon appeared in the distance. Then a few more wagons came into view. They were covered wagons, which was good, because if the horde saw the food inside, they would have been ransacked. Each was identical, rolling forward on four crude wooden wheels attached to a long plank. A white canvas cover was tied over the top of their wooden frames, which was pulled by a single centaur. Fortunately, folks were so concerned with getting as far away from Gaulcel as possible, they didn't think to wonder what was in the wagons. More wagons started to emerge from the forest. By the time the first one reached the gate, there were hundreds behind it. The line stretched all the way back to the tree line, and still more wagons were coming into view.

The crowd that was leaving blocked the gate, and the wagons couldn't get through. The cats suddenly understood why they were there. Khane and Kurth were needed to clear a path in the crowd and allow the wagons to get to the center of the city. They were crowd control. Khane took the left side of the gate and Kurth the right, shouting for everyone to go around the wagons.

"Everyone who wants to leave the city can leave the city!" Kurth shouted. "There's no reason for anyone to get trampled in the process."

"Stay to my left!" Khane yelled to the mob.

For all their griping and skepticism, Khane and Kurth performed their jobs well. Before long, they had arranged two lanes, one for wagons entering the city and the other for the creatures leaving it. If the two khajjine had not been there, many would have died from being trampled, either by wagons or feet.

22

The Riot to End All Riots

Maribel's announcement was the turning point. Once the group took control of the morning announcement station, she went on the air and spoke to the public. Maribel was the only one to appear on-screen. This was deliberate, as there was no need to reveal anyone who was helping her—doing so would only help Gaulcel catch them and foil their plot.

Her message was short and to the point. She shared three simple statements, one after another. Each by itself was enough to turn the city upside down, and the entire city heard them.

Without even introducing herself, Maribel told the people that Gaulcel was dead and would not come back to life until the next day. Then she told the public that Gaulcel's mind control powers only worked on nonhumans. Lastly, she told everyone that in the evening, there would be enough food to fill the belly of every single creature living in the city of Gaulcel, and it would be delivered to the center of town. Then her announcements were over. The whole broadcast lasted less than two minutes.

The viewing public first responded to these revelations with disbelief, but when they saw what was happening around them, their denial could not last long. Inside the city walls, the chaos that Tom and Tim had initiated in the individual buildings gradually made its way outside. For all of the city of Gaulcel's infinite history, its streets had stayed mostly empty, but on this day, those same streets were packed tight with folks leaving, wagons coming in, and the horde rioting in search of food. The center of town was nothing special. It could have been any street corner. There were four identical skyscrapers on each side that stretched as far as the eye could see. The space in between the buildings was minimal, and the streets were narrow, typically needing only to accommodate the barest of foot traffic. Within an hour of Maribel's announcements, creatures who'd spent lifetimes in the deepest trenches of oppression filled the space shoulder to shoulder. With all their communal experience, the release of pent-up angers they shared was like nothing any of them had ever seen. It was an explosion of catharsis.

Many clan members retreated to their headquarters. The amenities that Guff had showed Xane the day prior had been dangled like carrots on sticks in front of them for too long. Upon first joining, clan members were made to believe they'd have access to everything the clan had to offer. In reality, the luxuries were withheld, and the promise of future access to them was used to keep the clan members working, to keep them loyal to the city's oppressive causes. Now that there were no leaders, they could partake as much as they wanted, and they weren't going to let the opportunity go to waste.

Other clan members removed their insignia and joined in with the mobs. They knew they were the oppressors, but the only other option available was to be among the oppressed. They made their choice, but not without guilt. Now that it seemed possible that Gaulcel's rule would end, these folks needed to be part of it. If that meant tearing the city apart, then that was what they meant to do. By early afternoon, the city was left with no guards and no police.

The residents knew the food would be in the city's center, but the center of the city was for all intents and purposes indistinguishable from every other street corner in Gaulcel. Nobody had maps except the most elite clansmen, and they were all hiding out. Everyone in the crowd followed the rest of the crowd, which was as clueless as they were. The streets became dense with wanderers, and folks grew restless.

Khane and Kurth managed to establish a path for the food wagons to enter the city, but once they were within its walls, they were again stuck in the mob. The centaurs pulling the wagons needed additional guidance to find where they were going. The line of wagons forming at the city's gate came to a standstill, with the ones ahead stuck in traffic. Kurth ran toward the front of the line to find the hold-up. The wagon leading all the others was unable to move forward because of the surging crowd searching for the city center. Kurth began yelling and motioning to the people to let the centaurs pass. The mob was unresponsive. A few individuals heard Kurth, but all that did was cause them to notice the wagon.

A sahuajin was the first one to put two and two together and realize the wagons were the source of food that Maribel spoke about. He pulled up the canvas cover and discovered the bread inside. Others saw him. Within seconds, the wagon was swarmed with the hungry horde. The centaur pulling the wagon detached himself and started throwing creatures from the horde away from the food. "Thieves!" the centaur yelled. "Someone needs to pay me."

Kurth ran to the centaur just in time to keep it from killing someone. "You will be paid. The person who'll pay you is named Maribel. Help me get the wagons in and then we'll find her together."

"No. Pay first. Then eat," the centaur said as he pulled his spear from the harness on its back. In the time it took him to say this, the horde had already gone through the bread in his wagon. The centaur grew angry as he saw the same thing beginning to happen to the wagons behind him. "You pay. Now!" He put the tip of his spear to Kurth's neck.

Miraculously, the khajjine kept his cool.

"We just need to find Maribel. She'll be in the city center soon." Kurth said.

Other centaurs pulling their wagons witnessed their leader pull his spear on Kurth. In an instant, they detached themselves from the cargo they'd been pulling and came to the leader's side. That left their wagons unguarded, but they knew there was nothing they could do to stop the horde. It was like the karbero riots. All of the centaurs' focus was on Kurth and getting compensation for the food. Khane was still back at the city gate.

Kurth said, "Help me get your caravan to the center of town. You'll get paid. These folks will get peacefully fed, and everybody wins."

"I want double," said the centaur merchant.

"I don't have the authority to promise that." Kurth didn't even know if Maribel could pay anything. "But maybe you can negotiate with Maribel when we find her."

By this point, word had spread to all the wagons behind the leader. An army of centaurs was assembling to defend its wares against the horde. Each was armed with a spear. At least five wagons had already been picked clean, but the centaurs were prepared to defend the rest of them even if it meant killing the whole city. The horde noticed them all and backed down. The smart ones, however, knew that they would outnumber the centaurs by hundreds. They started plotting.

Kurth tried to reason with the centaur merchant. "Come with me." The khajjine had memorized the path to the center of town that morning. It was supposed to be the place where he would meet up with Maribel and the others. He started through the rioting crowd while the centaur held him at spearpoint.

The walk to the city center was long, but once they got ahead of the wagons, the crowd thinned out. Most of the horde still had no idea that the wagons were even there. Kurth found Maribel exactly where she'd said she would be. Along with Comerciam and Dalthra, they'd managed to build a raised stage in the center of the intersection. Maribel noticed Kurth and the spear pointed at his neck. She tapped Comerciam on the shoulder, and he approached them.

"Is the food here?" Comerciam turned to Kurth, who nodded yes. The elf then turned to the centaur. "You're late."

"It's all here," said the centaur. "But no told bring food dangerous. My kin mobbed. Want double." He held the spear closer to Kurth's throat.

"I will pay what we agreed," Comerciam said. The elf held out his thumb to be scanned. "No more."

The merchant knew that his army, as strong as they were, were outnumbered. He had seen the hunger in the eyes of the horde. He produced a scanner, grabbed the elf's hand, and scanned the thumb. The food cost a substantial amount of moneta. He waited several seconds before it cleared. As soon as it did, the centaur jerked the scanner back and put it away with one smooth motion. Wordlessly, he turned around and headed back through the crowd toward the wagon caravan. Then he was out of sight.

Kurth glared at Comerciam. "You would have let him kill me."

"I could see in his face that he wouldn't."

"What if you were wrong?" Kurth pushed Comerciam on the shoulder, and the elf stumbled back. Then he straightened up, preparing to fight.

Maribel put her hand on Kurth's shoulder. The cat relaxed. Maribel had a mother's touch. Both creatures realized how foolish it would be for them to fight now. The city was crumbling around them. The riots could go one of two ways. If they couldn't get the food in and everyone fed before morning, Gaulcel would return and shut down their plan. Many would get trampled and killed fighting over whatever food they could find. Instead of heroes, their group would be liars. If they needed anything to come from this day, they needed the populace to believe that its terrible ruler could be overthrown. If they failed at that, then their plan failed. Their hard work was worthless.

Kurth and Comerciam gave one another a glance. They had come back to their senses. There was a mutual understanding that neither needed to say aloud. "The horde is ravaging The food wagons. Most of them can't even get past the gate. We need to find a way to get them through." Kurth said.

Then Khane arrived. "All the centaurs just up and left. They abandoned their food wagons outside the city. The ones inside are all empty and broken and blocking the path. I don't know how we'll ever get them here in time."

"Let's go," Comerciam said, understanding the gravity of the situation. "We'll do the best we can."

Maribel stayed behind. She was recognizable to the horde from her announcement earlier, and her being there would help them find the gathering point. The rest of the crew headed to the gate. On the way, they passed at least ten wagons that had been picked clean. The line of wagons outside the gate stretched for a mile or more. The ones near the city's entrance were in the process of being stripped of their contents. The centaurs who'd brought them were nowhere to be found. Much of the horde, having already eaten, were fleeing the city into the nearby woods.

Comerciam took on the role of leader in Maribel's absence. He told Khane and Kurth to take apart the wagons that were already empty and in the way. The cats reluctantly accepted the elf's orders. They knew it needed to be done. It was obvious to all—the first step was to clear a path.

Khane and Kurth headed to the front of the line while Comerciam and Dalthra went to the empty wagon that was the farthest back. The wagons were heavy, and the party did not have centaur strength. They had to take each wagon apart piece by piece just to move it out of the way. Meanwhile, thanks to the horde, the line of empty wagons continued to get longer.

A brother from the Mantis Clan stumbled upon the khajjine dismantling a wagon. He didn't know Kurth, but he recognized that they were in the same clan. They were competitors, but in a way also teammates. The stranger, a centaur himself, spoke with Khane and Kurth, learned of their effort, and decided to help. Because of his size, he was able to simply pull wagons to the side. It made the work go much faster. Before long, all of the wagons that had made it past the gate were cleared.

When the khajjine reached the city's entrance again, Comerciam and Dalthra had moved less than half of the empty wagons. However, the members of the horde nearby must have filled their bellies and taken as much as they could carry, because they were no longer attacking the immobilized caravan. With the help of the Mantis Clan centaur, the empty wagons were moved out of the way and the path was clear for the rest of the food to enter the city.

A few members of the horde who had already eaten their fill saw the crew clearing the way and wanted to help. These folks were elated to have full bellies for the first time in centuries and wanted their fellow inmates to feel the same. Comerciam called everyone over to him at the gate. A decent crowd of twenty or so creatures, including Maribel's team, responded to his instructions.

THE RIOT TO END ALL RIOTS

"If we try to bring the wagons in now, they'll just get mobbed again. We'll only be able to get a few through. I know of some back streets that lead to the center of town. If we can get them clear of creatures and keep them clear, we may be able to get the wagons through. But we'll need everyone to help."

Comerciam directed the group on which streets to clear. It took some doing, but folks started to gradually get out of the way. Dalthra made barriers out of dismantled wagon parts. Working as a team, they managed to get everyone off the designated path. The Mantis Clan members recruited a few more guards to stand behind the barricades and keep the streets clear. The clan guards were all well versed in crowd control. When Comerciam finished marking off the path and reached the city center, Ciessa and Tim had joined Maribel beside the raised stage. Eleris was not with them. The wagons began to arrive not long after Comerciam did, pulled by a consortium of Good Samaritans.

A large crowd that recognized Maribel had gathered around her. Comerciam had the crew erect another row of barricades to allow the wagons to pull up alongside the stage. Night was coming, and the plan was falling into place. Maribel climbed onto the stage. She had a megaphone with her, and she directed the first few wagons to remove their canvas covers, revealing the food inside.

They contained a centaur delicacy unknown to almost all of Gaulcel's residents. The horde loved it, though they would have loved anything edible. Kurth began handing it out to everyone, and others joined in with the effort. As each wagon was depleted another one was uncovered, and its contents dished out as well. As more folks ate, the number of volunteers grew. The additional wagons were dispatched to other locations all over the city. The riots ceased, and lines formed.

As the horde dined, Maribel directed Dalthra to record the events with a mobile camera the dwarf had found at the studio. They broadcast the feast to the whole city. Simultaneously, they shot fireworks high above to help the residents find them. More creatures came, and all of them ate. For the horde, it was a day of firsts. Because of the riots, much of the starving horde had already had a meal that day. Now the rest of them would too. Some folks would even have more than one meal for the first time in centuries, and see the sky for the first time.

The crowd shifted from rioting to celebrating. Comerciam released all of the folks in the torture prisons so that they could join in. Maribel used her megaphone to speak to the city. She spoke to the masses in front of her as well as those watching on screens. Anyone still living in the city would see the celebration and hear her.

"Congratulations on your day of reckoning," she told them all in the common tongue. "Just as I promised earlier, there is plenty of food for all. You don't need to fight for it. You don't need to risk death over something you would die without. And this could be every day. There's no shortage of food in Purgatory, but your former leader kept food supplies low for power and control. If not for him, you would all eat like this every day. In the future, you *will* all eat like this every day. We cannot reveal to you your liberator at this time, but know that he is an ardent fighter for our cause. He killed Gaulcel, and he can and will do it again. However, as great and powerful as this man is, he cannot do it alone. Each and every one of you must also be your own liberator. We all must work together to turn this city into the utopia it can be—a place where each of us can exist for all eternity in a state of bliss. Remember this night. In the infinite history of this world, tonight will be remembered for all time."

Bill took notice of what a good liar Maribel was, and it made him start to wonder if he could trust her.

Maribel removed the megaphone from her mouth and turned to him. "Time to go," she said. "Gaulcel will wake up soon. Gather the gang and get them to their hiding places."

* * *

From the forest edge, Parth looked on. His body was overtaken by the

Lecttum—he had become a ghoul. Parth's consciousness was a passive viewer of the world now, his body an animated carcass over which he had no control. Its cadaver eyes allowed him to watch, but that was all Parth could do. He saw the hordes of creatures leaving the city en masse. Then he glimpsed his own legs ambling toward them.

23

The Acolyte's Return

When Gaulcel woke up, he felt youthful. The body he had died in had been getting old. His joints had ached, his back always seemed sore and his mind wasn't as sharp. This new body had no such problems.

He took a moment to orient and allow his memory to come back. Somebody had killed him. It was a woman. He knew little of her other than that she was a spy from Gundarce. His brother, Gundarce, and his rival city of the same name, had gone to war with Gaulcel many times before. It appeared they were about to go to war again.

First, Gaulcel knew he would need to get his own house in order. He turned his attention to the screen in his quarters. They were still broadcasting the riots, which by that point looked more like a giant block party. All of his inmates were either in the middle of eating or had already had so much food they couldn't eat anymore. Gaulcel's anger overwhelmed him. It had been lifetimes since he'd felt any kind of real adversity.

This was too far, he thought, even for his brother. Among the acolytes, war was just a cure for boredom. Warriors died over and over again. No progress was ever made, and a war could go on for lifetimes, until both sides got tired of the expense. Feeding his starving inmates could embolden the city to turn against him. No, this was not Gundarce's doing. Somebody else was pulling these strings, and Gaulcel intended to find out who it was. Investigation was a special talent of his.

He was alone when he respawned. Gaulcel knew what could happen if people learned his respawn point. Humans could corner him and keep him from the other races. It was his one weak spot. Knowing this, he kept it a secret, living and sleeping elsewhere. Not even Eleris, his right-hand man, knew where he respawned. The acolyte was currently in a small, dark room in the middle of the city. The room didn't appear on any of the city's maps, even the illegal ones. Anyone who might have known that location had long since forgotten. To be sure, he'd had them tortured until they went insane.

Gaulcel would have to find a way to sneak out unseen before he took control again. With so many of his inmates out in the street, he would need to be careful. The acolyte would not take control of any other creatures until he was long clear of the hidden building that served as his respawn point. Though, he'd built a maze of underground tunnels surrounding the place that only he was aware of. Even if someone could find a way to access the tunnels, they would need to solve the maze and get to where he was. And even if they found the room, they wouldn't recognize the significance of it.

Gaulcel opened a hidden hatch, revealing a ladder that led down into the tunnels. It was the only way in or out of the room. He had his path memorized. It led to another hidden opening at the edge of the city. The exit was concealed by a large boulder. A code pad on the inside made the boulder move just enough to give Gaulcel a way out. The door faced out a few feet from the large wall of the city, so any view of him leaving the tunnel was obscured.

He emerged from behind the boulder. It was time to take his city back.

* * *

The first creature he saw was a centaur, and Gaulcel immediately took control of it. Using the centaur, he began killing any weak creatures he found—and every human. Stronger creatures were overtaken and forced to join in. It was a murder spree. A genocide. Any nonhuman creature that Gaulcel could see, either as himself or in one of the bodies he inhabited, he could take control of. As they continued, the acolyte encountered more creatures and each time he did, his army of guards grew. Within minutes, he was controlling hundreds and using their bodies and minds to kill thousands. Under the acolyte's control, the army made its way to the home of Eleris. Gaulcel was disappointed to see that his favorite inmate was not there, but he continued on without him. The elf Talona, a leader of the Wolf Clan, lived nearby; his place was Gaulcel's next stop. Elves had more powerful minds than any other type of creature, yet even so they were powerless against Gaulcel's ability. Instead, taking control of elves amplified his mind control power, which allowed him to control more of the city's creatures at greater distances.

One of Gaulcel's minions, while under the creature's control, found Talona at his home. There were many elves in the city, but none could rival Eleris's intellect. Talona came the closest. Gaulcel assumed control of the elf, directing him to come near. The closer Talona came, the more powerful the evil warden became.

His army kept killing and recruiting, killing and recruiting. Gaulcel used his unique ability to surround himself with an impenetrable army of powerful warriors, while he had the rest make their way to the city's center, where he'd seen that woman feeding the horde. As the army grew larger, there was less recruiting and more killing. On his way to the center, the acolyte left a trail of blood in the streets of his own city. He managed to do all of it from afar, never getting his own hands bloody.

When his army reached the city center, nothing short of a massacre ensued. Millions were killed within minutes. Almost all of the city's inmates were soon dead. Their bodies would disintegrate over the course of the next day.

It took Gaulcel less than an hour to regain control of the entire city. It had taken him longer to exit his tunnels.

THE ACOLYTE'S RETURN

***

Guff's living quarters were not far from the city center. Upon awakening, his first thoughts were of Xane. He wondered when and how his friend would return to the city. Hopefully Xane still considered him a friend. He'd felt so much pride for the man when he beat the elf and became a member of his clan. The guilt he felt for treating Xane as an inferior, for disrespecting his friend, still plagued him. Guff convinced himself that he'd had no other choice, and he hoped that Xane would understand. He was grateful to Xane for killing him.

Guff was so engulfed in his thoughts of Xane, he failed to notice the revolution unfolding on the screen in his room. When the bearded man finally looked up, he was in denial. Guff had no context for the rebellion that had started after he left the city with Xane the day before. To Guff, what was happening in the city center looked like chaos, except that folks were eating. Perhaps it was propaganda?

He decided that he needed to talk to someone and figure out why it was being shown. Grabbing a scythe, he went to a post where someone from the Wolf Guard was always stationed, but he found no one there. Next, he went to the building's exit and found no guards there either. A few stragglers were leaving the building. Guff wondered if he should stop them but decided against it. Instead, he wandered outside.

The sight of Purgatory's sky was still new to him. He marveled in its color and the outside air. It finally began to set in that something was very different about the city, but he still wasn't sure what it was. Guff wondered if he was losing his mind. In Purgatory, sanity was always fragile.

Not knowing what else to do with himself, he went for a walk. He wandered for a while until he reached the giant walls separating the city from the rest of Purgatory. Then he walked along the wall for a few miles. Finally, the corner came into view. In the distance, he noticed a huge boulder near the wall. Then he saw what appeared to be a large creature emerging from behind it. The creature had wings and slime-green skin. The image was far away but still unmistakable—it was Gaulcel. Or was his mind playing tricks on him again?

IV

Seeds of Reckoning

24

Eleris's Brief Escape

Eleris reached the forest edge as swiftly as he could. He was outside the city, away from his master, but he wanted to get farther. The elf was instantly recognizable to most of Gaulcel's population, and any sightings would no doubt get back to the acolyte.

The leader of Gaulcel's noble guard was agile and swift, even among the elves. His endurance would allow him to run for a considerable time and distance. The elf's plan was to run for several days without stopping to rest. All he could think was that he had to get away; he couldn't allow himself to think of his wife, who'd refused to come with him. It was too hurtful. There would be time for feelings later, but now was the time to run.

The elf reached the river in short order and realized it was the farthest he had ever been outside the city. He followed alongside it, still running, and considered quenching his thirst. *If I stop and have a drink, it will enable me to keep going for longer,* Eleris thought. To remain unencumbered, he'd packed only essentials—a dagger, a small amount of food, and a canteen. He pulled the canteen from his satchel now and took a gulp midstride.

Eleris soon noticed the waterfall. The terrain just beyond it was rocky and elevated—he would have to do some climbing. This was as good a time as any to stop for a refill, though. His body was heated from exertion, and he wanted to cool off, so the elf moved underneath the waterfall. Letting the water fall on him was refreshing. Then Eleris noticed the cave and the gate constructed past its entrance. It made him curious, but he couldn't take time to investigate.

Standing just outside that gate, four undead ghouls clawed at the wood.

Eleris had heard of and read about the Lecttum and what it did to creatures, but this was his first time encountering the afflicted. He knew better than to waste any more time. The zombies didn't take long to sniff him out, but they moved very slowly. His canteen was full, and he was on his way up the cliff long before they could reach him. As he climbed, he heard the gargling sound the ghouls made, like a death rattle on repeat. It tried his nerves, but he kept climbing. The cliff was steep but not that high—thirty feet, maybe. With his athleticism, he would be over it in minutes. The clumsy creatures would never catch up.

Then the gargling grew suddenly louder. It was no longer just coming from below—it was coming from above. Eleris looked up, and there he saw a zombie standing at the top of the cliff, as if waiting for him. And it was not just one.

He couldn't see how many there were, but the volume of their sickening sounds was thunderous. Another zombie appeared above him at the cliff's edge, then another and another. Soon, they spanned the whole edge of the cliff. Like lemmings, they inched forward. Then the pack of ghouls began falling off the lip of the cliff.

The first fell a few feet to Eleris's left. Another fell to his right. The elf wasn't sure what to do. He couldn't go down because of the zombies below him. He couldn't climb up because of those above. Another fell, almost landing on top of him. It clipped his shoulder on the way down, but Eleris held on.

The zombies continued falling. Eleris held himself as close to the cliff wall as he could, hoping gravity would force them beyond his body. Another zombie fell behind him. The thing managed to clutch at his back as it passed. He felt it graze him, but he kept his grip. *I just need to wait it out,* Eleris thought. Sooner or later, the last of them would fall past him. He stayed in place, grasping desperately at the cliff wall, pulling his body in as close as he could manage. He could no longer look up, but he felt dozens fall within inches of his torso. Still, he held on. His arms grew weary. He couldn't have known how many there were.

Eleris knew not to look down while climbing a steep cliff, and he knew he could not look up. As a result, he wasn't looking up or down. He was unaware of the sheer mass of zombies that had fallen below him. Every single one of them wanted to climb up after him and feast on his flesh. There were so many, they climbed on top of one another. The pile grew and grew until the zombies below him reached Eleris's position.

The first bite was to the elf's ankle. Feeling it, Eleris knew his trek was over. The best-case scenario now involved him dying, only to respawn in Gaulcel and answer for the crime of fleeing the city. The alternative was to become a zombie. Eleris released his grip on the cliff wall. The mob of ghouls slashed at him with their long unkempt fingernails.

He did not fall far. The disease took hold before Eleris decided whether to take his own life.

25

Nebreen

Xane's plan when he met Gabio and Nahna was only to repay them for saving him. If Gabio had not appeared at the right time, if the centaur had not killed the ghoul that was snarling and reaching for Xane while he was trapped in that net high above the ground, things would have no doubt gone very differently for him. He owed the horseman and the old elf woman. Xane recognized the risk in taking him, an unknown, into their secret cave. They'd even shared their food with him. He wanted to repay that kindness in some way. When he heard about what had happened to their farm, Xane wanted to lend Gabio and Nahna his time and his labor to help rebuild it.

A few days in, Xane and Gabio were erecting a wooden fence when a fence post as tall as Xane fell back on him. On the way down, the hulking lumber nicked his left hand. The wound wasn't serious, but the accident managed to break open his wristband—the one that Guff had given him his first day in the pit, the one the city's overlords used to track his whereabouts.

For a year, Xane had believed that wristband was indestructible. He thought if he tried to break it off, it would self-destruct and kill him or something like that. Instead, it just broke. Xane waited for an explosion, but nothing happened. They must have wanted him to believe he could never escape the wristband so that he wouldn't ever try. Gaulcel and his stooges weren't as all-powerful as they seemed.

Then he realized that he was free.

After that, Xane, Gabio, and Nahna fell into a routine. They spent their days working on the farm and dispatching any ghouls they saw. At night, the motley trio would imbibe nebreen and listen to Nahna tell her stories. The elderly elf never ventured outside their cave. The days were a far cry from what Xane thought his afterlife would be, but it felt comfortable nonetheless. He still intended to take on the dragon eventually, though that plan was becoming a distant memory.

The zombie swarm had markedly increased since he came, but with Xane helping, Gabio was able to construct a fenced-in path leading to their fenced-in farm. Along the fence was a device like a bug zapper that immobilized the undead so that Gabio could come around and kill them. In addition, Nahna knew of an herbal concoction that functioned as a sort of zombie repellant. With these safety measures, most of the swarm were kept at bay while the pair worked. They still had a few encounters every day, though, and Xane quickly became an expert in taking the ghouls out. The undead were slow and clumsy, no match for the former boxer's quick reflexes. His sword was finally getting some use. Each new encounter with a zombie was another opportunity to improve his proficiency with the weapon. Over time, Xane became a skilled swordsman.

More than anything, Xane looked forward to the evenings they spent together. Nahna had a lovely voice, and the stories she told were hypnotic. On occasion, she told tales in her elven language. Gabio couldn't speak it, but the centaur had learned to understand it from having been with Nahna as long as he had. Xane didn't understand the language, of course, but he still appreciated the sound of it. It was so musical.

Nahna would also sing songs some nights. When she did, it would give Xane goosebumps, it was so beautiful. Gabio sometimes sang as well. His low warble was nowhere near as pleasant, but when the centaur and the elf harmonized, the juxtaposition of the two vastly different voices could bring Xane to tears. Over time, he started to internalize the tunes and even sing along.

Nebreen seemed to make everything better. The drug had the three of them singing in that little cave, reverberating like a full choir, at least to Xane's ears. Their meals, mostly bats and worm soup, tasted far better than they did without the drug. The darkness of the cave, lit by a few candles, became an array of colors. When the fire flickered, it looked like a rainbow. Most of all, the nebreen brought on a sense of tranquility. It was a sensation Xane was unaccustomed to, but he welcomed it.

Nahna and Gabio were like mother and son, and she cared for him dearly. She also began to care for Xane in a way. She recognized and appreciated his intelligence. On rare occasions, their talks would venture into more complicated topics. As congenial as Nahna was, she carried a great bitterness about the world in which they lived.

"Purgatory has a long history, but the only lesson all that history managed to teach us is that we can't be taught. Folks here have had an eternity to get along, and they still can't do it." Nahna would say things like this unprovoked. "But this is where we live, with all the time we could ever want. All you can do is try to enjoy that time as best you can."

Xane often thought about those words. He decided he never wanted to go back to Gaulcel.

* * *

In seemingly no time at all, another year had passed. During that time, Xane's sense of purpose eroded. He became increasingly entranced with the nebreen and lost interest in everything else. The drug was slowly taking his mind away. When the farm Xane built with Gabio began to bear fruit, the crops needed tending to and harvesting, but Xane wasn't the worker he once had been. As the days went on, all he could think of was Nahna's potion. Xane's tolerance for the drug grew, and it no longer affected him strongly. At night, he asked for and then demanded seconds from Nahna, who had to refuse him over concerns about their supply. A small patch of the farm was designated for growing the herbs in the potion, and rather than work, Xane spent the days chewing on the small and bitter leaves. It didn't have the same effect as when Nahna prepared it, but it was enough to get him through the day.

Then it wasn't.

Xane eventually became a full-blown addict. Nahna had to hide her supply to keep him from stealing it. He demanded that she tell him how she prepared it every night, but Nahna refused. Xane even watched her make the concoction, but he wasn't able to keep up with her elven knowhow. He couldn't tell the herbs apart.

One day, he actually threatened her. It was a moment that had been gradually building. It was the middle of the day and he hadn't even bothered to go work on the farm. Xane was, as always, in some phase of withdrawal. It left him feeble and unmotivated, driven only toward his next fix. Xane waited until Gabio was clear of the cave, knowing the centaur would protect the elf he called Mama.

"Give it to me. Now!" Xane said to her.

"We're going to run out. We're almost out as it is," Nahna said with a calmness that only an elf could maintain. She recognized the restlessness in Xane's eyes.

"I don't care. You're going to give it to me now, or you'll regret it!" It was the first time he'd ever spoken the Common word for regret. The addiction was fully ahold of him now. His lizard brain had taken over.

"Xane, it's not an option right now." The elf was fearful of him, but she kept her composure. They had gotten close during their time together, but now Xane was a changed man—changed by the nebreen.

"You and that horseman, I've given you everything, and this is what you do to me!" Xane was shouting now.

His words were hurtful. Nahna and Gabio had been patient with him as his habit got worse—too patient. Neither of them was familiar with human addiction. They both saw Xane deteriorating but didn't know what to do about it. "Please, just give me a little and I'll leave it alone. I just need enough to get through the next couple of hours," Xane said pitifully.

"No." Nahna replied. Her eyes were locked with his. "I don't think you should stay with us anymore."

"You . . ." Xane searched his memory for a word in Common similar to "bitch," but he couldn't come up with anything. He got frustrated. "I know you're just being greedy. I don't want to do this, but if you don't share our nebreen right now, I'm going to have to make you." Xane placed his hand on the pommel of his sword.

That was enough for Nahna. She ran. Xane hadn't been expecting the elderly elf to flee from him. His mind was hazy from withdrawal. By the time he began chasing after her, Nahna had reached the gate that separated the cave from the outside. The elf managed to close it behind her just before Xane got through. He was unfamiliar with the latch, and it would hold him for at least a minute or two.

Xane felt a tinge of guilt, briefly recognizing that his addiction had taken over. He hadn't wanted to scare Nahna, and he would not have allowed himself to hurt her. She was a friend, but he was stuck in a dopamine cycle and couldn't control himself. Scaring her seemed the only way to get what he wanted, and the addicted man was desperate. "Come back," Xane said. "I'm not really going to hurt you."

Nahna heard him say it, but she felt she couldn't trust him anymore. She kept running. There was no way for her to outrun Xane, but if she could only make it to Gabio and the farm, he could protect her. "Help, son!" the elf cried.

Overnight, a group of fervent zombies had breached the fence by digging under it. The hole was small and easy to refill. Gabio was dealing with the small group, taking them out one by one from afar with his spear, when he heard Nahna's cry.

"Mama!" he yelled, pulling the tip of his spear from a simple one's head. The centaur rushed toward the sound. "I'm coming!" He turned his back on the ghouls, and they chased behind him. Gabio's hooves carried him faster than he had ever gone. His centaur adrenaline coursed through his veins. He managed to get to Nahna just before Xane did.

The man wasn't running but stumbling toward the pair. His body shook from the withdrawal. "Wait. I was kidding. I wasn't going to hurt you, Nahna. You're so gullible. But seriously though, I only need a little bit, especially if you make the elixir. It's stronger that way . . ." He was rambling.

Gabio recognized what was happening. At one time, he'd loved Xane like a brother. Now, he regretted leaving Nahna alone with him. The centaur had been in denial about what his friend had become. Once he saw Xane hobbling toward her, it shook him from the delusion. He pulled up between Xane and Nahna. "Xane no stay here anymore!" Gabio shouted.

He clutched the handle of his spear and faced the man with an intimidating stillness. His fear for Nahna and his anger made him forget about the simple ones coming behind. The centaur was nearly as fast as a car. Under normal circumstances, there was no way the slow-plodding undead could catch him. But now, he had stopped running. To make matters worse, the shouting was attracting more of them.

Xane, Nahna, and Gabio all stood in silence. The gravity of the moment overtook them. For a brief time, they'd been thick as thieves, a trio of friends grateful for one another's company. Nahna and Gabio looked into Xane's eyes. Xane looked toward the ground. He felt a familiar kind of shame. He had ruined their happiness, and in a world like Purgatory, happiness was rare.

They stayed like that for minutes. By the time they heard the ghoul's growls, it was too late.

A swarm was upon them. A former man, turned into something else now, let out a low, guttural bark using what was left of its vocal cords. Nahna turned to see the creature within grasping distance. "Son! Behind us!" she cried.

Xane recognized the ghoul's half-rotted face but could not place it. It was someone from Gaulcel. How could he be out here? His memory associated the face with a quivering voice, a voice that spoke in French. Then it came to him. His first day in Purgatory, Xane had watched this man die in the pit. He was brutally killed by the dwarf Xane had beaten to win his first tournament. The familiar face reminded him of other days, of who he used to be. For a brief second, he remembered his pride, his confidence.

Then Gabio's hind leg shot back and kicked the zombie's head clean off.

A horde of zombified corpses ambled right behind the dead Frenchman. Nahna came to Gabio's side, and the centaur reached out to lift her onto his strong, equine back. She wrapped her arms around his torso and held tight. Then Gabio began to run, but he made it only a few steps before he tripped. Some small animal had dug its burrow in Gabio's path. The hole was hardly noticeable, particularly in the stress of the moment. Gabio's hoof planted into the earth, and his body shot forward and down.

Xane was still in front of them, watching these events unfold. In his hazy state, none of it seemed real. Gabio fell at his feet, Nahna clutching his chest. The abrupt force flipped her over the centaur's head, and she landed hard on her back. The mass of zombies was upon them.

"Xane! Help!" Gabio cried. Xane's sword was still in its scabbard at his side. He put his hand on the smooth leather hilt. The number of zombies had multiplied, the swarm stretching as far back as he could see. There was still time, though. He could hold them off long enough for Gabio to get his bearings. Once the centaur was back on his feet, they would all escape back to the cave. Then Gabio could pick off the ghouls one by one from behind the gate with his spear.

That moment felt like an eternity. Xane imagined the three of them safe. He wanted to pull his sword. He wanted to save the day.

Instead, he ran. Xane was not Reaper anymore. His addiction made him feeble in his body and his mind. The act of cowardice sickened him even as he did it, but still he ran. He could hear the swarm feasting on his friends behind him, but he ran. Xane reached the gate easily, while Gabio and Nahna kept the zombies occupied.

Once he was safe behind the gate, Xane fell into a puddle of self-loathing. He vomited violently. His meal from the night before, half-digested bat meat, sprayed all over the dirty ground. Withdrawal had taken hold of him. Xane began to shake as he retched. He felt cold, as though his blood had turned to ice in his veins. Shivering intensely, the once-brave fighter fell to the floor, clutching his knees. He lay in a shallow pool of mud and filth, continuing to shiver. Then he passed out.

26

Xane's First Death

"**G**et up, Reaper," Xane heard a voice say. No one had called him Reaper since his first life. Back then, everyone used the nickname. It was the moniker Coach Clark had given him for his ring introductions. The coach would tell promoters, "Xane beats his opponents so bad in the ring, it's like he's harvesting their souls." It may have been a little morbid, but when the bell rang, Reaper's opponents were intimidated. "How far you've fallen," the voice said. "How could you let this happen again. You're better than this."

***

Before Xane came to Purgatory, he was in the midst of throwing his life away. He'd met Coach Clark as a teenager. The trainer saw Xane's talent right away, and Coach Clark became the father figure Xane never had. After a few bouts, there was already some buzz in the amateur boxing community. At seventeen, Xane won a golden gloves tournament. His style and his skills were unmatched among his peers. In over a hundred amateur fights, Xane went undefeated. The community believed he would be a shoo-in for the

Olympic team, and even favored him to win a gold medal.

Before the Olympic trials, Xane's family was evicted from his childhood home for not paying rent. Xane needed money, and fast. So, against Coach Clark's advice, "Reaper" turned pro early. Once he got paid for fighting the first time, he was no longer eligible to compete in the Olympics. "You are taking the easy money now and throwing away huge paydays later," Coach Clark told him. Xane knew he was right—Olympians came into the professional ranks with more notoriety. It enabled them to climb the ranks quickly. High-profile promoters would get in line to offer them lucrative contracts. When Xane took a professional fight, he forfeited the notoriety a spot on the Olympic team would have gotten him. He would have to start at the bottom.

In Xane's early professional boxing career, he fought a string of jobbers and journeymen. In each fight, Xane demolished his opponent, but because the men he beat were low in the rankings, he barely moved up. For fear of losing, well-known and well-regarded fighters refused to face him, and because Reaper was mostly unknown to boxing fans, there was no pressure for high-ranking fighters to take him on.

Four years into his pro career, Xane, still undefeated, wasn't even considered within the top twenty-five of his weight class. He barely made enough money from fighting to get by. But despite being ducked, the sheer number of victories was starting to attract some attention. One day, Coach Clark called Xane and told him of an offer to fight Bluejay Perkins, a genuine contender. The boxer that Perkins was supposed to fight had gotten injured in training, and Xane was invited to step in on short notice.

Xane immediately agreed. It was a no-brainer. Even though Perkins would receive most of the gate, a win would give him the notoriety he needed to get in line for a chance at a title. Perkins would be the most skilled opponent Xane had ever faced, but he wasn't worried.

The next day at the gym, a well-dressed stranger approached Xane. The man cornered him while he was in the locker room, alone. He offered Xane more money than he'd ever made to throw the fight. The amount the man offered would have been enough for him to live comfortably for years. But

Xane refused him outright without a moment's thought.

The strange man doubled his first offer. Xane refused him again. No amount of money was enough to buy him off. Xane had pride at the time, and lots of it.

Perkins was not known as a hard hitter. He was known for being hard to hit. The man won fights by outpointing his opponents. He would land a few scattered blows here and there and then dodge almost everything thrown at him. When his fights ended, the judges would have no choice but to give him the victory. Hit and don't get hit—that was the sport of boxing in a nutshell, and Perkins excelled at the latter in particular. Xane's plan was to swarm him, corner him against the ropes and throw so many punches that some would have to get through. He prepared by sparring against boxers in lower weight classes, guys who were fast and full of stamina. Despite taking the match on short notice, Xane felt confident.

The fight was not televised. It took place at a small venue, in the middle of a three-bout card. The crowd was sparse, but it was still the biggest Xane had ever fought in front of. They were scheduled for eight rounds, but Xane didn't intend to let it go the distance. When the opening bell rang, he came out of his corner like a lion pouncing on its prey.

Perkins was fast, but Xane was faster. In no time, Perkins was trapped in the corner. True to his reputation, he was able to elude many of Xane's punches, but not all of them. The ones that landed landed hard. Forty-five seconds into the first round, Perkins took a left hook on the chin and hit the canvas. The referee started to count, but the man got up as quickly as he'd gone down. The fight resumed.

For the rest of that round, and then the rest of the fight, Perkins ran. He circled around the ring, hardly ever throwing punches. Xane kept coming forward, trying to corner him again, but Perkins never set his feet. Xane occasionally caught the boxer with a strike, but never cleanly. The thirty or so people watching let out a collective groan from boredom. They started to trickle out of the room, figuring this would be a good moment to use the bathroom or refill their beers. Before Xane knew it, the eighth round was over. The final bell rang.

Xane knew in his bones that he had won the fight. So did everyone who watched it. In eight rounds, Perkins had barely landed eight punches. Xane had connected with ten times as many, and he was the aggressor. It may have been boring, but it would be a solid win anyway, sure to land him bigger and better bouts with bigger and better pay days. Reading the judges' scores seemed like a mere formality.

The referee, who doubled as the announcer, held up a microphone and looked at the score cards. There was a moment of audible disdain before he read them aloud. The scores sounded correct, or close to correct. Then he announced the result. "You're winner by unanimous decision, Bluejay Perkins."

The words were a knife in Xane's heart. The judges had Perkins winning every round except the first, where he'd been knocked down. The small crowd booed. Xane had been screwed. Since the stranger couldn't pay him off, he'd paid off the judges instead. Disgusted, Xane and Coach Clark stormed out of the venue.

They protested the result with the sanctioning body and the state boxing commission, but there was no proof of the fix. Maybe twelve people had watched the entire fight. Half of them probably already knew about it and had put money on Perkins. Protesting just made Xane sound like a sore loser. The fight went on the books as a loss. Xane dropped down in the rankings. It would take years for him to get another real opportunity.

After that, Xane practically lived at the gym. The injustice against him was all he thought about. It ate at him, but it also drove him to work harder. He knew he would have to get his just due the hard way. "Put that anger to use," Coach Clark would tell him. "Imagine your next opponent as one of those judges. Distill your rage into a righteous little ember, but imagine that little ember has all the energy of the burning sun. Control it. Focus it. You'll be unstoppable." Coach Clark's motivational rhetoric was working. As good a boxer as Xane was, he continued to get better, at least at first.

A new fighter named Zack started showing up soon after the Perkins fight. He offered Xane some pills. "It helps your focus," Zack said. Xane didn't want the drugs at first, but the man was persistent. They were at the gym together every day. He offered Xane the drug for free, but Xane always turned him down.

"You mind if I do a bump?" Zack asked in the locker room.

"Free country," Xane said.

Zack held a fingernail full of powder up to his nose and inhaled audibly. His pupils dilated, and he shuddered with newfound energy. "You sure you don't want any?"

Xane shook his head.

"Hey, I get it if you're scared man, no pressure—I just think it could help you, you know. I heard about that Perkins fight. Man, that was bullshit. You didn't deserve that. This stuff could get you to where you're knocking out everybody. They won't be able to ignore you anymore. I just want to help, you know, but no pressure."

Xane didn't like being thought of as scared. He acquiesced and tried the drug for the first time. He tried it again the next day, and then the day after that.

It seemed Zack was right. Xane felt like he was more focused during training. He hit the heavy bag harder and seemed to have more accuracy with the speed bag. When Coach Clark pulled out the mitts, and they trained on combination punching, Xane felt like the best boxer in the world. But it was only in his drug-addled mind. He didn't notice how the training sessions were growing shorter. He didn't notice his endurance fading. He didn't notice the strain on his heart.

In short order, Xane was taking the drug every day. Zack was always at the gym. It was free at first, but eventually Zack started charging for it. Speed was expensive, more than Xane could afford. Zack started giving it to him on credit. "I know you're good for it," he would say. "Just pay me what you can, when you can. One day, you'll be world champion."

Xane, like his biological father before him, had the addiction gene. When he devoted himself to something, he went all the way. The same devotion that made him so good at boxing now got turned towards scoring drugs. His grit and mental toughness were unshakable—until they weren't.

Coach Clark saw the change in him and wanted nothing to do with it.

Even so, he couldn't abandon Xane, who was like a son to him. So, he rode him harder. He wasn't sure how to talk to the young man about it, so he didn't. Coach Clark believed that Xane would see what it was doing to him on his own. The shortcomings in his training were so obvious, how could he not? Xane never noticed, though. The drug had its hooks in him, and he was in denial.

He lost his next fight legitimately. Rather than blame the drug, he blamed Coach Clark. Their relationship got tense. They argued constantly, and then they stopped talking to each other altogether.

After the loss, Zack called in his debt. It had grown to an amount that Xane couldn't possibly afford, and the man threatened to cut him off. Then he offered Xane a job. "Let me introduce you to a friend of mine," Zack said. "If you do some work for him, I can cut off some of what you owe."

Xane agreed. He was desperate. Zack's friend turned out to be the same well-dressed stranger who'd tried to bribe him to throw the Bluejay Perkins fight. Xane was angry at first, but the fear of being cut off from the drugs was enough to make him do anything. Addiction had overtaken any form of rational thinking.

Xane became muscle for the mob. It was his job to collect the debts owed by other addicts like himself, by any means necessary. Xane would intimidate folks so that they would do anything to come up with the money. This usually meant stealing, or worse. If, after a few chances, they still couldn't pay, Xane would hurt them. He did things that he never could have done clean. Things that he would never forgive himself for.

Zack and the well-dressed stranger liked to call their employee "Reaper," but Xane no longer felt worthy of the moniker. Eventually, he just stopped showing up at the gym all together. His boxing career was over. Xane's whole life consisted of getting high and beating up addicts. The well-dressed stranger would call Xane on a burner phone and give him jobs. Xane never learned the man's real name. When Xane asked the stranger what he should call him, the man just said, "Call me Buddy."

One day, Buddy told Xane he would need to prove his loyalty to keep his job. "Anything you need," Xane said. His self-respect was gone. He had done terrible things, and he felt like there was no turning back. Buddy had Xane get into a car with him. He said nothing about where they were going. They drove in silence for almost an hour, then parked on a curb outside of a small house in the suburbs. It was around 2 a.m. No one was outside.

"There's a man inside that house," Buddy said quietly. "He's been in jail for six months and just got out today, but here's the thing—there's no way he'd only get six months for what he did." Buddy, still a stranger to Xane, looked him straight in the eye. "He must have turned," he said. "He's a rat." There was a moment of silence. "You know what we have to do."

He handed Xane a pair of gloves, an unbranded baseball cap, and a loaded Glock Nine. He held the same three things for himself. "Do you have proof?" Xane asked.

Then Buddy slapped him. There was a time when Xane would not have tolerated that kind of treatment. Now, he just took it.

"Don't ever question me again," his boss said. "The fact that he's out is all the proof I need. We don't take risks in the business. You're going to have to learn that."

Xane realized that Buddy was grooming him for more responsibility, but he didn't want more responsibility from this man. He hated his job. Still, he said nothing. Buddy handed him some pills, and Xane took them greedily. "Let's go."

Buddy stepped out of the car, and Xane followed him. They walked to the front door, swift and nonchalant. It was locked, but somehow Buddy had a key. He opened the door, and they entered into a wide space. Buddy found a light switch and flicked it, revealing a recently cleaned living room. "Welcome home, Joe!" Buddy shouted.

Xane heard some hushed stirring from a hallway, and then a man emerged. He was skinny, with sleep still in his eyes, wearing only boxer shorts and an undershirt. "Hey Boss," the tired man said. "What's going on?"

"You're a free man. That's what. Congratulations!" Buddy said with madness in his eyes. "Let's celebrate."

"Yeah, all right. Let me get dressed." The man spoke timidly, as though he knew. He turned back toward the hallway, but before he could, Buddy stopped him with a hand on his shoulder.

"Nah, hold up a sec. Sit down, let's talk a bit."

Xane recognized that he was standing in a stranger's living room and that the stranger, named Joe apparently, was about to die. He felt a shiver in his spine. Joe sat in an easy chair and motioned to a nearby couch for Xane and Buddy to sit. Buddy remained standing, and Xane followed his lead. He was feeling the familiar high of the pills kicking in. His focus shifted.

"This here is my pal, Reaper," Buddy said. "You know why they call him that?"

Joe had fear in his eyes.

"Cause he takes souls!" Buddy exclaimed.

If Joe had any doubts as to why they were there, they disappeared at that moment. "Hey man, I don't know what you think is going on, but it's not. You know I've always been loyal. I did time for you, man."

"You're weak, you rat. I can't even listen to you. Just do it, Reaper. Get this over with."

Xane was prepared to oblige him—that was how far he had fallen. He raised the Glock and pointed it at Joe in his chair. The man closed his eyes, quaking with fear. Xane's finger found the trigger. He had never fired a gun in his life, let alone killed anyone. His hand started to shake, but he took a deep breath and steadied it. A millisecond before Xane could fire, he heard something coming from the hallway. A long, wailing, cry.

It was a baby. Joe opened his eyes again and looked back toward the sound. Xane could see the fear and melancholy in his pupils. It was enough to raise his consciousness from his intoxicated stupor.

"C'mon, what are you waiting for? Just do it and let's get out of here," Buddy said.

Xane continued to point the gun at Joe for several seconds, but the child's wail pierced his soul. He lowered the Glock. The moment felt like an eternity.

"What are you doing?" Buddy was angry. "I never took you for a pussy. Fuck it, I'll do it myself." He pulled his own Glock from his hip.

Xane felt a rush of emotion come over him. Before Buddy could fire, Xane took his lowered gun and pointed it at Buddy. This time, he didn't hesitate. He pulled the trigger, only to hear an unsatisfying click.

"You left the safety on, you stupid junkie." Buddy laughed and then shot Xane in the heart. His last memory on Earth was seeing the blood pour from his chest and crumpling to the floor.

The next thing Xane knew, he woke up in Purgatory, sober for the first time in years. In that moment, he thought about all the mistakes he ever made. In death, he finally had his moment of clarity. It was a placid feeling, almost tranquil. His sense of purpose, his consciousness, and his finely tuned anger all came back to him at once. Xane was angry at himself, but he knew that no good could come from that anger. Coach Clark had taught him how to turn self-destructive anger into something constructive instead. Xane was skilled at channeling his rage into righteousness. If he had listened to the coach and used that skill, his life would have turned out differently. But there was no sense dwelling on the past. The rage inside Xane was larger than ever. He needed somewhere to put it. Then Xane heard Gaulcel's voice.

* * *

Xane's head felt woozy as he opened his eyes. There, lying on the floor of Gabio and Nahna's cave by himself, Xane had his second moment of clarity. "Get up, Reaper. You messed up, and now you gotta fix it. You gotta save your friends." The voice was gruff and familiar. The shakes of withdrawal from the nebreen were overwhelming. "You're a fighter, dammit, so fight. Get up!" Xane lay there, shivering and sweaty. After a minute, he rolled onto his hands and knees. His head felt heavy on his shoulders.

Xane mustered more strength and pushed his body off the cave floor, but his right arm failed him, and he fell back down. His temple collided with the dirt. "So what if it hurts? Life hurts sometimes. Death hurts more. Your friends need you, and it's your fault. You need to fix it. You need to get to your feet." Xane rolled to his back, clenched his abdominals, and with every ounce of strength managed to lift his shoulders and then his lower back from the ground. He steadied himself with his hand and slowly rose to his feet. His legs were shaky, but he was standing. "That's it, Reaper. I knew you could do it." Xane raised his eyes to the voice for the first time.

It belonged to Coach Clark, and there the man was—standing in front of him.

27

A Little Redemption

"Ideas are useless without action. Talent is useless without effort. Planning is useless without execution. Action. Effort. Execution." This was the mantra Coach Clark had repeated to Xane before every fight. Now, he was saying it again. Xane knew another fight was coming. He was driven, but he wasn't ready. If he was going to fight, he'd need to regain his bearings. He had to get through the worst parts of withdrawal, or else he would be unable to defend himself.

Xane wasn't sure how long he passed out on that cave floor, but it must have been days. His appetite had returned in a big way. Gabio wasn't there to spear bats, and the farm was overrun with zombies. Fortunately, the three had created a worm farm inside the cave, which was going to have to be Xane's source of food. There was still some water in their buckets, too. Xane could only hope it would be enough to get him through. He was quitting an unfamiliar drug cold turkey, and there was no telling how long his withdrawal symptoms would last. He just needed to regain enough strength to face the zombies.

He convinced himself he could still save Gabio and Nahna. Xane had to believe that. Coach Clark was there to encourage him.

Withdrawal from the nebreen was hell. The next few days were the hardest

Xane had ever known. One moment, he felt freezing cold. The next, he felt like his whole body was on fire. At times, he wondered if withdrawal would kill him. Between the vomiting and diarrhea, it seemed like everything he ate was a waste. His muscles cramped and twitched relentlessly. Throughout all of it, Coach Clark was screaming at him. Xane would sometimes get mad and scream back. Then his stomach would hurt. Every muscle in his body felt sore. Ultimately, Xane didn't resent the coach for being hard on him. It was exactly the motivation he needed. Getting off the nebreen could have killed him, but Xane was a fighter and he fought.

Each day got a little easier. By the third day, the worms were staying put in his stomach. He felt some of his strength return. "It's time," Coach Clark said. Xane knew he was right. His long-time father figure was always right. Despite his ongoing withdrawal, he couldn't wait any longer. He grabbed his sword and headed toward the gate.

There were at least twenty zombies crowded outside. Xane saw them from above. He leaped down, over the gate, landing on one zombie's back and piercing the back of his head. *One down,* he thought. The rest of them surrounded him without hesitation. In a single motion, Xane pulled the sword out of the skull and swung it in a circle, pushing the remaining zombies backward. The unsteady ghouls fell on top of one another. While they struggled to get back up, Xane leaped over the pile. In midair, he planted his sword into one's head like a pole vaulter. When he cleared the pile, his momentum forced him into a forward roll. A ghoul came up from behind him. Xane swept its leg out from under it and placed his sword so that as the creature fell, its neck fell into the blade, severing its head.

The zombies were many, but they were slow. Xane's sword cut through their partially decayed bodies like warm butter. Some nebreen was still in his system, but it no longer controlled him like it once had. His finely tuned rage was as great a weapon as ever. He was in the zone, and nothing could stop him. Reaper was back.

Before long, a pile of half-decayed bodies lay at his feet. The entire group. His friends were not among them, so he pushed forward. More zombies came, and more zombies perished, as Xane made his way to the farm. It was there that he saw them—Nahna and Gabio, right in the middle of a swarm near the south fence. Gabio's huge horse body towered over a mass of undead, and Nahna was riding on his back. She was digging her hands into his haunches, struggling to hold on. Xane knew immediately that they were not themselves. Nahna's skin had turned a greenish shade. Gabio was slack-jawed and dead-eyed. Chunks were missing from various places in their bodies. Bite marks. Xane knew what he had to do.

He charged forward, his sword held high over his head. First, he targeted the other zombies in their swarm. He slipped one's arm as it reached for him, then took it out with a hard, downward swipe. Next, he kicked the knees of one at his side, causing it to fall forward and expose the back of its head. Xane's adrenaline coursed through him so that his ailing body could not fail. In a matter of seconds, only Nahna and Gabio were left. The undead centaur reared on its hind legs, shaking Nahna off and dislocating her shoulder. Then Xane and Gabio stood facing each other. The centaur stumbled forward, unable to run on its dead legs. With a big swing, Reaper chopped the appendages off. The zombie that used to be Gabio fell forward into the dirt, no longer able to stand. Xane slid the sword in vertically just above his eyes, and the creature stopped moving.

Nahna's body was still on the ground. It pulled itself forward with its one good arm, continuing to snarl at Xane. He looked into her eyes for a moment and saw nothing there. The lights were out. She didn't recognize Xane; she had no cognition whatsoever.

Xane mercifully ended her short reign as zombie, and then it was over. The whole area from the gate to the farm was clear. The bodies would attract more zombies, but he didn't care. He would take care of those the same way he'd taken care of these. Xane grabbed as much of the remaining fruits and vegetables in their farm as he could carry. He ignored the nebreen plants. Then he trudged back to the cave, where he collapsed.

"You did it," Coach Clark said. "They'll wake up tomorrow feeling fresh as daisies. If you hadn't killed them, they'd be stuck wandering this damn place in that god-awful state for God knows how long." Xane fell to his knees and sobbed. His adrenaline subsided, and his withdrawal symptoms returned, with them came a sense of purpose he desperately needed. "Rest up. Tomorrow, we start training for what's next." Xane thought of Gaulcel. "The folks in that city need you," Coach Clark said. "That damn monster needs to go down. But before that, we need to finish your assignment. Our next fight is against the dragon."

The words echoed in Xane's brain.

28

The Calm after the Storm

When Gaulcel regained control of his city, almost all of the residents were dead. Others had escaped outside the city walls. He let only a few members of the army he'd overtaken survive. The next day, when the dead came back, Maribel's day of reckoning seemed like it had all been a dream. Many of the folks who lived it didn't believe their own experience—it was too fantastical. It was impossible for them to imagine Gaulcel losing power, even while he was dead.

And Gaulcel was ready for their return. In the announcements that day, the creature claimed that a group of terrorists had attacked the city. Talona was by his side, and the elf claimed that Gaulcel had heroically thwarted the terrorist violence. Talona assured the public that he'd been by the ruler's side the entire day and seen firsthand his bravery and heroism. The subtext was that Gaulcel had never died at all.

Gaulcel then explained that humans were behind the terrorist plot. He said that every human in the city might be infected by a virus of the mind. The only way to ensure the safety of the city, Gaulcel claimed, was to test every single human resident. "Every human must report to a posted clan area in the industrial district of their building. This includes human clan members," he said. "This is for everyone's safety. The test for the virus is quick and painless, and even when someone's afflicted, there's a simple pill that knocks it out." The broadcast was translated into every language in the city.

Simultaneously, as the announcements aired, Gaulcel had minions begin to round up the humans in the city. Some went willingly, but most knew better. As clan members respawned, they were given new orders to join in the effort. Humans hid. They killed themselves and respawned. One small band joined forces to fight back, but Gaulcel quickly ended them. Within a matter of weeks, the city's humans had all disappeared.

In reality, there was no test. There was no virus to test for. Gaulcel's plan was simple. Humans were sent to the city's eternal torture stations, where they would be tortured to death over and over again. Extra prison cells were already in place for such a contingency. After a few centuries of anguish, the humans would be thoroughly molded into fearful and obedient citizens. Then everything Maribel had told them could be extracted from their broken minds. Once that happened, the humans present for the riots that day could be reintroduced to the city.

The clan guards reported to Talona everyday with the number of humans that were still unaccounted for. The elf's job was to get that number down to zero, and Gaulcel wasn't going to be satisfied until it was complete. Throughout the city, surveillance efforts were doubled. The fences outside every shop in the goppidum were raised several feet and covered with barbed wire. Anyone who suggested that what had happened that day had happened was sent to a "reeducation camp," which was, of course, an eternal torture station. Nonhumans in the camps were interrogated by Gaulcel himself to find out if they knew the location of any hidden humans.

As hard as Gaulcel tried, the city never went fully back to how it was before. Even the monster couldn't deny the changes. Almost half the residents escaped that day, leaving empty shops and quarters behind them. Nonhumans still in the city were taken away from other jobs to help with surveillance and defense. Many of those who fled became infected by the Lecttum. Because of the increased infected presence outside the city gates and the decreased labor supply, the food shortages worsened. More residents starved. The horde grew. Gaulcel blamed the lack of food on terrorists and humans under their control. Tournaments were temporarily suspended. Any evidence of dissidence was to be reported and dealt with immediately.

The city might not have been back to the status quo, but its leader had once again established his absolute power. Not everyone in the city approved of the riots. The powerful feared losing their power, and the promise of luxuries kept some of the clan members loyal. They had worked side by side with humans and then cast them aside out of ambition.

One day, Gaulcel brought what looked like a human onto the morning announcements and took over their body. It was actually an elf made to look human, but the ruse looked real enough to get the citizenry not to trust what Maribel told them. Over time, the public stopped thinking about the riots. They discounted what they had seen with their own eyes.

Meanwhile, the network Maribel and her followers had put in place was up and running. They had to stay mostly inactive, so as not to be discovered. Maribel herself was gone. She'd left after the Day of Reckoning on some undisclosed errand. While she was out, she put Bill in charge. From there, the group established a kind of underground railroad to rescue humans who managed to escape the eternal torture stations. Once rescued, they were given the choice to leave the city or stay and join the fight. Most left, but some wanted to stay. The army of the Reckoning was small in size, but it was growing. After a few months, the once-abundant safe houses were in short supply. People were crammed into small hidden rooms. Maribel had arranged for food deliveries, but these were often interrupted by the growing swarms of zombies outside the city.

Recruiting efforts had to stay limited to humans. If any other race were given access to their network, a rudimentary mind probe from Gaulcel could bring down the whole operation. Khane, Kurth, Ciessa, Comerciam, and Dalthra were intentionally kept ignorant of the operation, just in case. Humans, on average, were the weakest race in purgatory; when the time came to fight, they would need to be well trained. A few clan recruits were able to procure a few weapons, and they trained the group as best they could.

The group also monitored Xane's quarters. If he came back to life, that was where he would respawn, and they needed to get to him before the clan guard. Xane was integral to Maribel's plot. Fortunately, Gaulcel and his stooges didn't realize how integral. With all the commotion of the revolution, his Wolf Clan overlords had more or less forgotten about him. Talona was busy as Gaulcel's right hand. A new recruit that the elf sent to get killed by a dragon was a low priority. Xane was just another one of the unaccounted-for humans on Talona's list.

* * *

Guff managed to survive the genocide brought by Gaulcel after the Day of Reckoning. He respawned just in time to catch the end of the rioting. With his own eyes, he had seen Gaulcel come back, and he knew enough to avoid crowds. Once the monster was clear of the boulder from which he emerged, Guff went to check it out. It looked like just a boulder, but he investigated further. By knocking along the outside and listening to the sound, he found the hollow section that housed the door to the tunnels below. There was no way to gain access from the outside, so Guff left it alone.

The next day, when the morning announcements aired, Guff recognized Gaulcel's lies right away. The creature was rounding up humans. Guff didn't know why, but he knew he didn't want to find out. His first thought was of escaping the city, but he realized that was probably everybody's first thought. All exits would be well guarded. Instead, he would have to hide, and he knew where.

In the initial confusion, the former Viking procured a sledgehammer and a sack of rice cakes from Wolf Clan headquarters. Then he snuck back to the fake boulder. Guff worried that the loud banging against the door would attract attention. However, Gaulcel deliberately kept that area sparsely populated, and no one came to arrest him. It took what felt like a hundred hits before the dented tunnel door fell.

Guff disguised the entrance as best as he could by replacing the broken door. From there, he decided to get as far away from that door as possible. Guff ran into the tunnels, not knowing what to expect.

What he found was a maze of epic dimensions. Having no other choice, he wandered through the labyrinth, going around corner after corner. He wasn't sure what he was looking for, or where he would stop. An hour later, he was totally lost.

Finally, Guff rested. He stopped his roaming in an unassuming, terracotta-colored hallway that looked the same as all the other unassuming hallways he had passed through. In all his wandering, the scenery never once changed. He realized he was able to see even though there was no discernible light source. There had to be some kind of enchantment at work.

So, Guff sat in complete isolation, hearing nothing but quiet. He sat like that for at least a day, carefully rationing the rice cakes he had stolen. They could last him a week or so, he figured, and then he would need to find another food source.

Guff wanted to sleep, but his mind wouldn't let him. It raced manically on and on about the city and about Xane and about his future. Guff didn't know how the revolt against Gaulcel had started. He'd never heard Maribel's speech. He didn't know the city's warden had died, that she'd killed him, or that humans were immune to the creature's powers. Guff wondered why the creature had been in these tunnels to begin with, and hoped it was not going to come back.

Things had more or less stayed the same for Guff since he joined the Wolf Clan centuries ago. Then, in two days ,his entire world was upended. Now, he tried to quiet his mind. "Focus on the present," he told himself. "Come up with a plan." The first thing he needed to do was orient himself, to figure out these tunnels. Next, he would need to find a food source. In a year or so, he could try to slip out of the city undetected and finally be free.

Guff was never able to finish step one. He started his exploration alternating between right and left turns, expecting that moving in one cardinal direction would help him find the edge of the maze. As he traversed each new hallway, Guff used a small rock to carve a mark on its stone wall. By the hundredth identical hallway with no endpoint, Guff decided it was hopeless. He retraced his steps back to the hallway where he'd failed to sleep that first day. Hiding was suddenly less important than finding his way out of the tunnels. He had to get back to the boulder with the hidden doorway where he came from, but he had no idea what path he'd taken when he first entered the tunnels. He only knew the direction he'd first entered that hallway from.

Guff started back that way, again alternating between right and left turns and carving a mark on each new hallway he entered. After about an hour of this, Guff turned around and went back to the starting point. He remembered that he was about an hour away from the exit when he first stopped, so any longer than that and he would have gone too far. Once Guff was back in the first hallway, he headed out again, this time making left and then right turns. If his plan worked, he could gradually narrow down his original path and find the exit.

Two weeks later, Guff was still in the tunnels—and on the brink of starvation. The isolation, combined with the monotony of his task, had nearly taken his sanity. He muttered to himself as he ambled around each new hallway with hope in his eyes, only to find no door and no escape. Guff considered taking his own life. Then he could wake up the next day, back in his quarters, saving himself the seemingly inevitable anguish of dying from hunger. The thought was short-lived, however. Guff realized that as bad as his current predicament was, whatever torment Gaulcel had in store would be much worse. He had to keep trying. So, he soldiered on.

Upon rounding another corner, Guff felt a change in the air. A slight gust of wind. He had to be close. It was the first bit of encouragement since he'd started looking for the exit.

He sniffed the air, hoping to catch a whiff that he could follow. Nothing. He emphatically made his mark upon the wall, then rounded another corner. Guff stopped and felt the air. Was it closer or farther from the exit? He decided the air was worse, though he didn't know whether his instincts for such a thing were any good. If Guff went back to the start, he wasn't sure he would make it any farther. His waning body still felt heavy on his thin legs.

He went back to the previous hallway but turned the other way this time.

It had to be closer, he determined. Guff continued like that for a few more turns, and then he found it. The damaged door was still just as he had left it. For a moment, he thought it was too good to be true. Perhaps his mind was playing tricks on him.

Guff felt the door, though, and it was indeed real. His once-considerable strength had diminished so much, he was barely able to move it. Yet Guff managed to push the heavy door aside, and the thing fell to the ground with a thud. He stumbled out and collapsed.

Tom just so happened to be passing by the boulder at the time. The desolate area was a route the Reckoning were using to sneak in the food Maribel had arranged to be delivered. The entryway to the tunnels was hidden, but Tom heard the loud thud of the falling door. He snuck around, keeping a distance, to see the source of the sound. There he saw a bearded man, lying on the ground. Guff looked like a skeleton with a distended stomach. Tom had found many other humans in the same condition. To him, the sight meant a potential recruit.

Still, he approached the man with caution. When he came to Guff's side, Guff was whimpering, unaware of Tom's presence. Tom pulled out the first edible thing his hand found in his sack of rations. It was an onion. Guff bit into the raw onion with no regard for peeling the paperlike, outermost layer. It was the best thing he'd ever tasted.

29

The Reckoning in the Tunnels

When Guff was presented with the choice of joining the revolution or leaving the city, he didn't have to think long. Gaulcel had to go down. It was the only way to permanently escape the torment.

Guff's addition to the cause was invaluable. As a member of the Wolf Clan, he had inside information about the city. As a fighter, he was able to train the others in combat. Plus, Guff knew about the tunnels, which solved a major problem for the Reckoning. Now, there was ample space to house all the new recruits.

It took the man a week or so to get some strength back. When he did, Tom debriefed him on his experience.

"There's a problem with the tunnels. Gaulcel knows about them. I saw that asshole come out of there. That was how I found them," Guff explained.

"We can work around that," Tom said. "We'll keep only humans in there in case he comes back."

"If he comes back, he'll be able to learn everything. He'll wipe us all out before we can even have a chance."

Tom realized that Guff didn't believe Maribel. "It was true what Maribel said that day. Everything she said was true. Gaulcel can't control humans."

"Who's Maribel?" The rest of the information didn't register at first.

"She was the woman. On the Day of Reckoning. That's what we call it. She spoke on the broadcast. She started all of this."

"If you mean that time where all those people gathered in the streets, I was dead most of that day," Guff said.

Tom went on to explain everything that had happened. It was too much for Guff to take in at once. Tom had to slowly talk through the events of the day, but Guff struggled to get past the idea that Gaulcel had been killed. "How did she do it? How'd she kill him?" Guff asked.

"I'm not sure," Tom said, realizing he had never had a chance to ask. "But she did. That's how we took over the city. Then he came back. You know what happened then."

"There's another thing," Guff said. "A friend of mine. I want to know he's ok. His name's Xane. His quarters were in the same building as mine." He was thinking it was a long shot that Tom would know anything.

"Did you say Xane? The guy that could beat anyone in the pit. He beat an elf. That guy?" Tom asked.

Guff nodded.

"We're trying to figure out what happened to him too. How do you know him?"

"He was a friend. The Wolf Clan made him leave here to go fight a gonkin' ignertia. I figured it would have killed him be now. He never came back?"

"We've been watching closely. He never came back." Tom suddenly remembered something Guff had said. "Wait. When did you say you saw Gaulcel come out of the tunnels?"

* * *

The next human on Talona's list was named Bill Mercante. According to his file, Bill owned a pizza shop. Talona decided to find this one himself. The elf vaguely remembered hearing about a Bill's Pizza Shop that was a front for a gambling ring, and he wondered if it was the same guy.

Talona brought a small squad of three Wolf Clan elves along with him, and they checked Bill's quarters first. It was empty, and Talona could tell that no one had lived there in a long time. "No need to waste any more time here. He's likely secluded himself at his pizza place," the head elf said.

The squad went straight there, and found that the shop had been closed since the riots. They opened the door to the back and discovered a small room with some cooking supplies, moldy pizza dough, and a mattress on the floor. "This is where he stayed, even before the riots." Talona said. "Pull the surveillance footage."

There was no footage of the backroom. It was a glaring omission, which could mean only one thing. Someone had given this Bill a special clearance. There was now no doubt that this was the same shop that housed a gambling enterprise. Prior to the day of the riots, underground businesses like gambling rings were typically overlooked, intentionally ignored. After the riots, things were different. Especially now that a missing human was involved.

Catching this Bill was now a high priority. His experience away from the city's eyes may have given him valuable information about those involved in starting the riots. Talona next watched the footage from the front of the shop. He observed as what initially looked like a member of the horde started the first riot of the day, which was quickly quelled. These kinds of events were not that uncommon, even before the day of rioting. Starving inmates from the horde often got desperate. What was odd was that this member of the horde didn't take any food for themselves. They just ran from the counter and threw it over the fence.

Talona zoomed in on the individual and noticed it was a woman. This was an all-male building. He recognized her, and it didn't take long for the elf to realize where from. She was the city's most wanted fugitive, the same woman who'd broken into Gaulcel's headquarters. She was disguised in horde-like filth, but there was no doubt it was her. Talona then watched as she came back to the counter after starting the riots and went unobstructed into the back room of the pizza shop. Rewinding the video, he observed Bill making long, sustained eye contact with her. After she took his food, he deliberately unlocked the door to the room where he slept.

After seeing that, Talona handed the task of reviewing the footage off to his next-in-command. He sent one of the elves in his squad to alert the rest of the troops and Gaulcel of what he had found. Then he took what was left of his squad to the back room. They tore Bill's faux quarters upside down. It didn't take long for someone to move the mattress and find the switch beneath it. The hidden elevator came, and the elves stared at each other in disbelief. "Stay here and stand guard," Talona ordered. The turquoise-haired elf went to get reinforcements.

When he returned, twenty guardsmen from various races and clans accompanied him. They were the biggest, strongest, and most loyal creatures he could find at a moment's notice. Talona sent as many of them as could fit in the elevator, though the lead elf decided he would go on the last wave.

Waiting for the elevator to come back took an eternity. Talona finally boarded the lift and arrived in Bill's true quarters. The apartment was enormous. His soldiers were all standing around, marveling at the place.

Talona pointed at the nearest guard. "Soldier, report."

"We searched this whole place. There's no one here."

"Tear it apart for anything that could be evidence."

"Yes, leader!"

Later, Talona reviewed the remaining footage with his subordinate. The elf was shown as many others entered the back room of Bill's pizza place. Talona studied their faces. He recognized Comerciam, a new recruit in the Wolf Clan who'd been mysteriously beaten by a human in the pit. It had looked real, but with the gambling connection, Talona made a mental note to review that footage as well. Then Talona zoomed in on Comerciam's supposed prisoner. It was another face he recognized: Ciessa. Eleris's wife. The revelations were piling up.

Talona kept watching as four more individuals snuck into that back room. Two were human, and two were khajjine. "Find out who these four are," Talona ordered the elf showing him the footage. "If we don't have them in our custody by sundown tomorrow, you'll be meeting with Gaulcel."

Just then, Talona felt a tap on his shoulder. "Gaulcel wants you to meet him at the headquarters of Prison 457," a subordinate elf said to him. Talona knew better than to keep the creature waiting. When Talona arrived at the prison, Gaulcel probed the elf's mind and learned everything Talona learned that morning. When he was finished, he cackled menacingly. The mysteries of the Reckoning were unraveling.

***

Tom put two and two together at the end of his conversation with Guff. Wherever Gaulcel respawned, it could be accessed from those tunnels.

"I never want to be down there again," Guff told him. "It's gonkin' huge." What the Viking described sounded unfathomable. The network of tunnels would have to be bigger than the city itself. Much bigger. "And its enchanted somehow. There's light everywhere even though there's no torches and no electricity."

Tom listened to Guff intently, but he knew his compatriots needed that space. If this was all true about the tunnels, they had ample space. And if Gaulcel respawned there, they could block the creature's exit. Tom didn't say anything to Guff, but he took what he'd learned straight up the ladder. When Bill heard about the tunnels, he instructed the network to house as many humans there as possible.

Within a week, more recruits were living in the tunnels than outside of them. Their entrance's proximity to the food supply line made the arrangement very convenient. Their instructions were to explore until they had a full map. To ensure everyone's safety, Bill moved there himself. "Look for anything out of the ordinary," he said. "We need to find somewhere that looks like a living space."

The task proved just as difficult as Guff had explained. Even with twenty people looking for weeks, it seemed like they weren't making any progress. People searched in small groups, marking each new hallway and carrying string that led back to the main settlement. Before long, they ran out of string.

Bill's army was starting to question his leadership.

"Why are we making this harder than it needs to be? We only need to block the exit. He'll never escape, and when he dies, he'll just keep respawning in the same place."

Bill was speaking with one of his recruits, Naplana. She had been one of the earliest humans they found after the Day of Reckoning. Since then, she had proven herself smart and capable. Bill trusted her. He liked that she wasn't afraid to question authority, even though it was his authority she was questioning now.

"There may be exits we don't know about," Bill said. "If he escapes, he'll take over everyone in the city again and wipe us all out." Despite the Reckoning's growing numbers, there was still no official hierarchy in place. Everyone just understood that Maribel was in charge, and Bill took the reins while she was gone. It was a nice system in thought, but in practice it didn't work. The recruits had taken to squabbling amongst themselves. There were more things that needed doing than Bill had time to oversee. If he tried to delegate tasks to a group, that group would often devolve to useless bickering before making any progress. Bill had no military or clan experience, and he often wondered why Maribel had put him in charge. He needed her back.

Naplana often questioned Bill's orders, but she never failed to do exactly what he asked. She understood the importance of chain of command better than he did. Bill learned that she was a natural leader and started giving her more responsibility. She had been a member of the Bear Clan before the day of reckoning. A tall brunette with a stern demeanor you couldn't help but listen to, she became Bill's right hand. At times, he wanted to put her in charge, but he didn't. He had to trust Maribel. Nonetheless, he always appreciated Naplana's counsel.

One day, a group came back with news of one hallway ending in a wall instead of more hallways. Finally, they had found an edge to the endless space. It was only a three-day hike to get there. Once they found that edge, they found the path to other edges. Suddenly, what had seemed impossible was possible. It took several months and several groups of explorers, but eventually they managed to map out the full network of tunnels.

The map just showed a giant maze. The entrance was the boulder, and there was no known exit. Nothing significant separated one part of the map from any other. The center of the whole thing was in the middle of another indistinguishable hallway. They searched and searched, but nothing came close to resembling a creature's quarters.

30

Romance and Zombie Bats

Xane had been training with Coach Clark when Maribel found him. Coach made him run laps around the farm every day, killing zombies all along the way. Then it was farm work, followed by whatever strength and conditioning reps his coach assigned. Through all the running, Coach Clark never left Xane's side.

After killing the undead versions of his former friends, Xane had destroyed the remaining nebreen plants. He wasn't sure whether he would be able to maintain his willpower to avoid them for long. Despite the torment the plant had caused him, he still craved the stuff from time to time. Xane had to make sure that going back on the nebreen wasn't an option. Instead, all of Xane's focus was on the ignertia. All he knew about the creature was what Bill had told him. "A giant fire-breathing lizard that can fly."

Xane laughed at the description—Reaper had no fear. He had faced other powerful creatures in this world and had always come out on top. Once the dragon was dead, he would return to Gaulcel triumphant. The Wolf Clan would have no choice but to give him more responsibility and more authority. He would use the responsibility and authority to work his way up the clan ladder until he was in a position to take out Gaulcel. That was his plan, anyway.

In his brain, taking on a giant fire-breathing dragon and a creature that could control other's minds seemed logical. Like all his battles in the pit, Xane decided he would not use the sword against the beast. He would do as he always did in a fight, strategize and execute. After all, when he was focused, that approach had never failed him. "Ideas are useless without action. Talent is useless without effort. Planning is useless without execution. Action. Effort. Execution," Coach Clark said. The words washed over Xane like the waterfall outside of their cave. He had heard them so many times before, they were engrained in his brain, designed to activate the parts of it that kept him motivated.

From this relentless training, Xane's proficiency with his sword went from good, to great, to masterful. Every day, he killed more ghouls. It had almost become too easy. Xane felt like he could take out a whole group in his sleep. He'd nearly forgotten that a single bite or scratch could turn him into one of them. At times, Xane wished he kept count of how many of the things he killed. It had to be in the hundreds by now, maybe thousands.

Of course, Xane didn't know anything about the Day of Reckoning. He didn't know that Gaulcel had died on that day. He didn't know there was a growing army of revolutionaries waiting for his return. All he knew about Maribel was what Bill had told him. Her name.

Then he found her one evening in his garden. She was nibbling on some fruit.

It was the most beautiful sight he could ever remember seeing. A woman. A real, honest-to-God, human woman—a sight for Xane's sore eyes. With breasts and hips and long hair and high cheek bones. Her face was stern and splendid. In all his time in Purgatory, the only female Xane had ever seen was Nahna, an elf whose body was centuries old. Maribel was like seeing an oasis in the desert. Xane didn't trust his own eyes.

He took her by surprise. When she looked up at him, her expression betrayed her excitement. It had taken many months to find him, and now here he was. He was all the specimen she had hoped for. "Hi," she said in Xane's language.

The former boxer just stood there, literally slack-jawed. He couldn't find a word for a simple reply greeting. His mind failed him.

"I'm Maribel. What's your name?" she asked, even though she already knew the answer.

Xane remembered what Bill had said. He was supposed to be on the lookout for her this whole time. With the nebreen, he had forgotten. Now, as luck would have it, she'd found his farm. "Hi." Xane barely managed to get the word out. Even though he'd been talking with Coach Clark every day, his actual voice was sore from disuse.

"Well, hi . . . Hi." Maribel thought the joke would break the ice. Xane was still silent. He had one of those faces that made him look angry, even when he wasn't. Maribel had never considered that he might be anything other than happy to see her. She was a bit worried. "I found this fruit here. It looked yummy, and I was hungry. Is this your farm? I'm sorry—I didn't think anyone would mind."

The word "yummy" almost made Xane cry from wistfulness. It was the kind of word a mother would use with children. Xane's own mother had used it with him. "Xane. My name is Xane."

With that, he confirmed that he was stunned but not angry. Maribel was grateful. "I have some rabbit meat that I hunted. I'm happy to share it with you. I can even light the fire to cook it."

"It's no problem." Xane was still catching up with the conversation. "There's plenty of food here. Help yourself." He was finally snapping out of his initial bewilderment. "Rabbit sounds great. I have a place we can cook it that's safe from the zombies." The word "zombie" felt silly coming out of his mouth, but speaking with a human woman in his own language almost took Xane out of the hellish world he'd been living in for years.

"Where did you find rabbit around here?"

"They have little burrows. They're hidden under logs and stuff. Maybe I can show you how to spot one later." Maribel noticed that her general disposition had changed. Xane's presence was having an effect on her. "Then you set a snare with some sticks and rope. Just need to be careful so the zombies don't get to the rabbit before you do."

"That sounds great." Xane smiled at her. He hadn't used those muscles for a while, and it hurt his face a little. "Why don't we pick some of this fruit and then we'll go sit by the fire and cook?"

To Maribel, the sight of Xane's dimples was disarming. It was like the rest of the world melted away. "Sure!"

Xane took her to the area outside the cave. They passed under the waterfall, and their hair and clothes got wet. He focused on starting the fire, trying not to stare at the wet cloth clinging to Maribel's curves.

Soon they sat by the flames together, cooking and eating and chatting for over an hour. Neither Xane nor Maribel even acknowledged that they had heard of one another before. They were enjoying each other's company and the moment they were in. The constant threat of the undead and the evil dictator they had separately conspired against were out of mind. Instead, they chatted about how good the meat tasted and how warm the fire felt and how nice the moon looked. They went back and forth telling jokes and laughing together.

Suddenly, a swarm of bats flew out of the cave. Xane immediately noticed that their flight pattern was strange. Typically, the bats in Purgatory never flew anywhere near people, but these were coming straight for them. The flying black rats had somehow been turned.

Xane launched himself onto his feet and pulled his sword from the scabbard. He jumped in front of Maribel, putting himself between her and the bats. "Get down!" he yelled. His blade swung through the air. Xane had a sense for where each bat was. One swipe took out three of them. He spun around. His steel cut the air with a whistling sound. More dead bats fell. The last few were spread out. He swiped in a triangular shape until nothing was left in the air.

Some of the undead bats lay on the ground, still screeching and crawling, their wings injured from the blade. "Are you okay?" Xane asked Maribel as he finished them off.

Maribel had a small dagger on her. She had been ready to take care of herself, but Xane dispatched the creatures so quickly that she didn't have time.

"I'm fine," she said, feeling the pounding of her heart and the adrenaline in her bloodstream gradually dissipate. The pair stood in silence for a moment, looking at each other in disbelief of the danger they'd survived. The light of the fire twinkled in Maribel's eyes.

Despite his heroism, Xane felt sheepish. "I'm sorry about that. I knew there were some bats in the cave. One must have gotten infected somehow."

Maribel couldn't help but laugh at him. "You should be sorry! How dare you save us from a swarm of zombie bats!" The sentence sounded so ridiculous, she struggled to get it out. She gave him a playful punch in the arm. After another silent moment, the tension broke, and they were giggling like teenagers. Hours before, they'd been perfect strangers. The frightening experience had heightened their sudden closeness. Their courtship felt like destiny.

Maribel looked at Xane. She knew that he wanted her now. She wanted him too. "Well, we're going to need showers after that. Race you to the waterfall!" In a flash, Maribel stripped off all her clothes and ran away giggling.

Xane was in disbelief and awe of the brazen act. His jaw dropped, and he stared as her ass jiggled with each step she took away from him. Then he realized he was staring, and he averted his eyes to the ground, embarrassed. By the time it sank in that she wanted him to follow, she was already at the waterfall.

"I guess I lose," Xane said as he approached her. Maribel was still stark-naked and unashamed. His eyes darted nervously between the ground and her wet body. He stepped underneath the water, but she reached out and stopped him.

"No fair," she said as she looked him up and down.

Xane caught her meaning and stripped down himself. For an instant, they both stood naked together in the moonlight, unabashedly admiring each other's bodies. Maribel, with one finger, made a motion for him to come to her. Xane obliged, placing his hands under her wet hair. He softly put his lips against hers, then pulled back to examine her expression. She grabbed him by his arms and pulled him back into her. Maribel held her breast against his chest, and they held a long kiss into the night.

***

When Xane woke the next morning, Maribel was gone. It was as though she'd never been there at all. He figured he must have hallucinated the whole encounter. "Women weaken legs!" Coach Clark shouted suddenly. "Now, get up, Reaper. It's time for training!"

As Xane was doing his usual laps around the farm that day, he pondered his night with Maribel. He checked the place by the waterfall where she'd left her clothes, but there was nothing there. Even if it wasn't real, it had been a nice dream, he decided. He hoped to dream about her again.

Just then, Xane's pleasant thoughts were interrupted. A gigantic, red, flying, lizard-like creature passed overhead. It was as high in the sky as an airplane, but it appeared to be coming in for a landing. Xane followed the dragon's descent. It gave him a rough idea of how to find the mine the creature called home. "Well, I'll be," Coach Clark said. "It's a sign. You're ready. Tomorrow, we fight!"

31

The Coming Battle

Gaulcel had gone to great lengths to shroud the truth about humans from most of his inmates, but to the clan guards close to him, there was no doubt about what was true. Every creature sent to the reeducation camps after the riots was personally interrogated by Gaulcel, so that he could read their minds. But he never interrogated the humans. They were housed in separate prisons, far away. No matter how well guarded they were, Gaulcel never went near that building.

After Talona discovered Bill Mercante's quarters, he discovered all of Maribel's team. The discovery kept leading to more new information. Talona had seen the security footage as each of the individuals entered Bill's quarters, where they met with the woman who'd killed Gaulcel. The meeting happened within an hour of Gaulcel's death.

Talona figured out their identities. He watched the footage from the Day of Reckoning. All surveillance cameras had gone down that afternoon, but there was enough footage to see how each of them participated in making that day happen. Talona was convinced he knew everything there was to know about them—except where they were hiding.

The more new facts Talona discovered, the more it seemed that all paths led to Xane. The fighter had met with Bill every day at his pizza shop. The shop was a front for a gambling ring, and that gambling ring was a front for the Reckoning. Talona noted how Bill had gone to Xane's quarters a couple days before the coup. The day after, the elf Comerciam threw his fight against Xane, allowing him entrance into the Wolf Clan and making all the other dissidents rich in the process. That same night, Xane went back to the pizza shop and then into the back room that housed the elevator to Bill's actual quarters. They must have been planning the events that occurred the next day. Xane had to be pulling the strings, Talona decided.

Talona himself had also met with Xane that day, of course. It was Xane's first day as a Wolf, and Talona was his superior. The elf had believed the undefeated prospect had become overconfident, so he sent him toward what was supposed to be certain death. Afterward, he'd barely thought of Xane at all. He saw the rage in the man but didn't see his maneuvering.

If only I had seen it then, Talona thought. He recognized that Guff, Xane's direct superior, was missing too. Guff had left the city with Xane, so Talona had to believe he was in on it too. Guff was one of Talona's direct reports—how much had he known? It seemed the whole rebellion was planned right in front of his face.

***

Everything Talona knew, Gaulcel knew as well. The ruler probed Talona's mind daily. Because Talona had given Xane the assignment to leave the city, Gaulcel was suspicious of the elf. He knew that his former right hand's wife, Ciessa, had been involved in the plot against him. Eleris could have been as well, though Gaulcel didn't see how that was possible. He knew every single thought Eleris ever had. Still, there was doubt in the acolyte's mind. Eleris was still missing. Had the elves figured out a way to hide their thoughts?

The simple ones on the outside had surrounded the city. Getting food in and out had become so challenging that more than half the city was starving. Gaulcel worried about feeding his own guards. Food had become so expensive, even the powerful could barely afford to eat. Taking out the ghouls required a delicate balance. Gaulcel didn't want to send too many guards and risk losing them all, but at the same time, if he sent too few, there was a greater risk of the group being overwhelmed.

Gaulcel blamed the shortages on his second-in-command. Talona should have prevented the mass exodus from the city that had led to the creation of so many zombies, as he would tell anyone within earshot. While the elf held authority over everyone in the city besides Gaulcel himself, Gaulcel made him look and feel small. Ambitious clan guards conspired against Talona, in hopes that they could take his job. Gaulcel recognized what they were doing and encouraged it.

He was not used to being in a situation, where he couldn't trust his main subordinate. He could read minds. But now the acolyte was worried that he could not trust his power. If Talona were somehow involved, it would be better to keep him close, Gaulcel decided. He needed to break him. The monster plotted by himself, keeping his right hand in the dark about his plans.

The last time, they'd caught him while he was sleeping. Gaulcel was not going to let that happen again.

Talona hated working for Gaulcel. The job afforded him boundless luxury and authority, but he was unable to enjoy it. Under Gaulcel's watchful eyes, he had no privacy, autonomy, or freedom. He felt powerless. Did Eleris feel like this? Talona felt ridiculous for once being jealous of him. His subordinates were jealous of him in the same way he was jealous of Eleris. *They have no idea how terrible it is,* the turquoise-haired elf thought. The lure of power has made fools of us.

In the chaos of the insurrection, clan guards lost some respect for Gaulcel's power. They openly discussed keeping him away from humans, and by doing so openly acknowledged their ruler's weakness. There was an increase in minor acts of rebellion. Guards were complaining, making jokes at their superiors' expense, and shirking duties more often. When these acts were discovered, they were swiftly punished, but the punishments were not as severe as they once had been. Gaulcel needed the manpower too much to take guards off their post for long. Many acts of insubordination no doubt went undiscovered. Small cracks were forming in the city's once-robust hierarchy.

Despite the challenges, Talona had done his job well. If the elf hadn't used all his talent for investigation, Gaulcel would know. Talona studied the architecture of every building in the city, which led them to find several resistance safe houses. Most were empty, but some were not. They were able to apprehend hundreds of rebels and confiscate their weapons. The elf also had the idea to put double agents in place, fake rebels to fool the real rebels into giving up more information. Each discovery led to more information, which led to more discoveries. Talona's investigative skill led him to all the major players involved. They were getting close to finding them.

Even with the progress, nothing was ever good enough for his boss. Gaulcel regularly punished Talona for not finding them sooner. The punishments were arduous. Of course the creature knew the elf hated his job. Everyone who'd ever held that job hated it. Gaulcel took over his mind and his body and degraded him. Talona knew his boss wanted to break him, but he also knew the tactics were working.

* * *

The Reckoning had been damaged by Talona's ceaseless investigation, but it was not enough to cause any serious harm. Bill sent trained guerilla units to leave the city for food, and they had become adept at killing ghouls. Those zombies would then respawn alive and inside the city, which led to an influx of new recruits. The tunnels offered ample living space for everyone coming in. Supply operations were getting more efficient. Numbers were growing.

With guidance from former clan members, Bill had turned the tunnels into a defensive stronghold. New recruits were trained in guerilla warfare. There were many hiding places in the tunnels, places where forces could catch an enemy by surprise. Troops were trained on how to use them. If they were attacked, they could put up some resistance. Bill hoped it would be enough to at least escape and survive.

As Talona was learning about them, Bill was trying to learn about the workings of Gaulcel's inner circle. Most new recruits knew nothing, but some held jobs or had been in clans, so they knew a little. By putting together their knowledge, the Reckoning was getting closer. When Maribel came back, Bill wanted to be ready. The longer they went without taking over, the more likely Talona would find them and terminate their cause. Bill knew it was a matter of time. With enough of it, Talona would end them. They had to make a move before then. They had to beat him to the punch.

The recruits talked to one another. They knew they couldn't hold on forever either. Xane had somehow become a figure of legend. Rumors hailed him as a coming savior. Bill wasn't sure how the rumors got started, but he figured Maribel was behind it. Her plans were still a mystery, but Bill knew that she intended to use Xane as a kind of figurehead. It was no coincidence that these rumors were furthering that end. Bill knew Xane as a friend, and it always felt strange to him to hear people talk about the fighter like a deity. Xane was just a man. He was good at what he did, but certainly no god.

Bill was one of a handful of folks who knew his fights had been fixed, of course. Even Xane hadn't known. Bill did not want to dispel the rumors, though. He saw how the people believed in Xane. They needed something to believe in, something to give hope to a situation that otherwise felt hopeless.

The most important goal was finding Gaulcel's spawning quarters as soon as possible. If they didn't do that, it really would be hopeless. They mapped the tunnels and searched nonstop, but so far there was nothing. Bill started to wonder if Guff had hallucinated the creature emerging. But if that were true, what were the tunnels for? Gaulcel might not know they were in there, but the monster had to know the tunnels existed.

Bill wanted to have a spy on the inside with Talona's forces, but since all the humans had been purged from the clans, it seemed impossible. Nonhumans were too much of a liability. Bill still had contacts within the clans from his days as a bookie, but approaching them would be too dangerous. Still, they needed to know what the enemy was up to. Dalthra explained to Bill how to hack into their surveillance system, but the dwarf couldn't come out of hiding to do the job herself. So, Bill sent the soldier he trusted most: Naplana.

She met with Dalthra, who drew her a diagram and wrote out a set of instructions to follow. They went over it hundreds of times until Naplana believed she could complete the hack blindfolded. The problem was getting to the mainframe. Naplana had to figure out that part herself.

32

Infiltration

Naplana got inside the ventilation system of the principal surveillance building. Compared to the other buildings in the city, the principal building was small. Three stories. Naplana grappled up to the roof and removed the grate from the ventilation system, then carefully slid down until she was above the large, single room that made up the top floor. The cold air rushed through her body, and she shivered. The air ducts were barely wide enough for her to fit through. She could hear clacking on keyboards below her and monitors buzzing.

Dalthra had explained to her how the surveillance system was set up. All of the city's cameras went through a single mainframe so that the view from any device could be accessed from anywhere. The visual signals were then transmitted all over through an antenna. If the Reckoning could access the signal, they could see everything happening in the city. To do that, Naplana would need to hack into the mainframe.

That large computer was directly below her now. She couldn't see what was happening through the air duct, so she had to use her ears. Based on the volume of keyboards clacking, Naplana figured there were at least three individuals in the room. She crawled farther into the duct, until she discovered a grate. She peered through the pierced screen, but nothing was visible from her angle. At least she would be able to remove the lattice and get in through the opening. That would have to wait until the coast was clear.

Naplana crawled back a few feet from the grate and waited. She could hear talking below. The individuals were khajjine by the sound of it.

"This job is ridiculous," one khajjine said.

"Quiet," whispered a second. "They could be listening." He sounded anxious.

"I don't care. I haven't had a break in days. I'm through with this gonk."

"Shut up. Seriously. I can't hear this."

"He's right," said a third voice. "There's hardly anyone left to listen, anyway. Why would they waste other guards on us? The bureaucracy is so broken, they'd probably assign us to watch ourselves"

The first khajjine laughed. "What are we even looking for, anyway? They don't tell us anything anymore."

"Anything suspicious," said the anxious khajjine.

"Here, I found a sahuajin from the horde taking a shit in a bag. Is that suspicious?" All three khajjine laughed at that. "Woah, he just sniffed the bag." The khajjine laughed again.

"You're kidding?"

"Nope. Watch this."

Naplana heard the keyboard clacking again, then a few seconds of silence.

"Uhhh." The khajjine groaned in unison, then laughed again, the type of laughter only shared among tired coworkers.

"I'm going to mark this for my leader to review," the first khajjine said. "Just so he has to watch it too." Naplana could hear the vindictive smirk in his voice.

"Okay, that's enough. Seriously, if we keep this up, I'll have to report you. If they hear us, and I don't, they'll punish me."

"If you report us, then I'll report you."

"For what?" asked the anxious khajjine.

"For having a stick up your ass," said the third one. The tension broke with boisterous laughter. "It's conduct unbecoming of the Bear Clan." They laughed again.

"Guys, please," the anxious khajjine pleaded.

"All right. All right," said the first. Then the keyboards went back to their erratic clacking.

The clacking continued. Meanwhile, Naplana waited. The khajjine didn't speak again for hours. Naplana started getting tired. She had been running through the hack in her mind over and over again, the step-by-step instructions Dalthra had given her. If nothing else, it kept her mind active. Still, she felt the weight of her eyelids. How long had she been there? Eight hours, maybe longer. She knew she couldn't stay awake too much longer. The erratic clacking of the keyboards below her was hypnotic. As uncomfortable as the air ducts were, she was in a prone position, and there was very little light.

She couldn't fight it any longer—she fell asleep.

* * *

Naplana awoke to the feeling of something crawling on her body. She opened her eyes and saw a flash of coarse black hair on her chest. Eight spindly legs rushed over her shoulder and past her face. She let out a small welp from the shock before remembering that she had to keep quiet. The keyboards were still clacking below her.

"Did you hear something?" the anxious khajjine said. The keyboards stopped clacking. "Shhh." A long moment of silence followed. Naplana held her breath.

The third khajjine finally broke the silence. "I don't hear anything." The keyboards resumed their clacking, and Naplana felt relieved. The spider must have gone. More time passed. Naplana no longer felt sleepy. The spider had brought a jolt of adrenaline.

The khajjine had to take a break eventually. She started thinking about surprising them. Taking out all three would be tough, but Naplana convinced herself she could do it if she had to. It wasn't worth the risk for now, though, she decided. She continued to wait.

Suddenly, a mass of coarse black fur appeared at her feet. It wasn't just one spider this time. Then Naplana realized, they weren't spiders at all. She could see their tiny chests and faces rising from their arachnid bodies. They were arak, newly hatched. Individually, they were so small that they were barely visible, but now there were hundreds of them.

Naplana's heart raced as a cluster of newborn spiders with acolyte torsos marched over her legs, her abdomen, her chest, and her face. She had to keep her eyes and mouth closed to avoid tasting the creatures. At least one crawled up her nose and then back out again. Still, Naplana kept silent. She felt like she was about to throw up, but she managed to force it back down. Naplana tried to imagine that she was somewhere else, anywhere else. *This will pass,* she thought, and tried to imagine her world without Gaulcel. The minutes felt like eternity, but eventually, the infernal creatures were gone.

She couldn't stay in the air ducts any longer, she decided. It would be risky to take the khajjine on but riskier to wait to be discovered. Naplana squirmed her body forward, back to the grate. As quiet as possible, she yanked at the metal vent. It came off with surprising ease. She lay there a little longer, holding the grate, in case the khajjine heard something. The clacking of the keyboards continued uninterrupted.

Naplana poked her head out of the vent, just enough to get the layout of the room. There were countless desks and large terminals to hide behind. The three cat creatures were about fifty feet away. One of them was facing her, but his eyes were glued to his monitor. Naplana brought herself back up, took a deep breath, and prepared to descend.

The linoleum floor was about ten feet below her. Holding the edges of the vent, she slowly lowered herself into the room until her arms were fully extended. Then she dropped down, landing in a squat position to muffle the sound of the impact. The smack of her feet on the floor was audible but soft. She knew they had heard it, but by the time they looked up, she was behind a computer terminal.

"Hey, what was that?" The first khajjine spoke this time. Naplana heard his feet shuffle toward her position. This confrontation was going to happen fast. As soon as the khajjine came around the terminal, she kicked his knee, hard. She intended to sweep him off his feet, but the creature was well balanced. He stumbled a bit but didn't lose his footing. Then Naplana leaped up, climbing to the top of the terminal. From there, she kicked the khajjine again. Her foot landed stiff on his chin. That was enough to knock the diminutive thing to the floor, and as soon as he hit, Naplana was on him. She restrained his hands and feet with the zip ties that she'd brought.

The other two watched this unfold, too surprised to move at first. "Sound the alarm!" the first khajjine cried from his prone position. Naplana shot her elbow into the back of his head, rendering him unconscious, but it was too late. She looked up just in time to watch the second press a button at his desk. An earsplitting siren played over an unseen intercom.. *'VROMP... .VROMP.....VROMP.'*

"Gonk!" Naplana said. She was back on her feet in an instant, scanning the room for a door to escape through. There was only one, and the other two khajjine were in the way. Naplana galloped toward them and sprang on top of the mainframe that she was meant to hack. Using all her weight, she launched herself at one of them. With one step back, the feline caught her midflight and wrapped her body in a strong bearhug. Naplana swung her knee up and found the creature's knackers. The khajjine let out a cry of pain, and his grip loosened. Naplana's knee joint was bent so that she wasn't able to get that foot underneath her. When the khajjine released her, she fell, landing hard on her ass.

Naplana was back to her feet swiftly, but by that time, the third khajjine was behind her. He reached around her stomach and lifted her off her feet before powerfully slamming her right shoulder onto the linoleum. The siren was still blaring. *VROMP... VROMP... VROMP*. The khajjine dug his knee into her back as his coworker restrained Naplana using her own zip ties. Her wrists were clasped, but she wasn't going to give up yet.

The khajjine whose knee was in her back stood up, thinking he'd subdued the woman. Naplana pushed her toes into the linoleum, sliding herself forward and putting some space between her and the khajjine. She rocked her torso backward, up to her knees, then brought each foot under her one at a time, until she was again on her feet. She turned to face the two remaining khajjine. They stood between her and the door, gathering themselves for the next exchange of blows. *'VROMP....VROMP...VROMP.'* The rhythmic blasting of the siren loomed in the background. "Come and get me," Naplana said menacingly.

Suddenly, the door behind them opened. Reinforcements had arrived. An entire squad of clan elves flooded into the room. There was nothing she could do now. Naplana was caught.

33

Face-to-Face with a Dragon

Xane stepped out of the cave the next morning with Maribel in his thoughts. He still believed her to be a hallucination and tried to conjure her again, but it wasn't the same. Xane imagined her smile, tried to think of a clever, playful remark like one she would have made. He couldn't. Coach Clark took her place in his head. "Women weaken legs!" the man said, as though reading Xane's mind. It was a familiar refrain. Xane could not be distracted today. Yesterday, he'd learned the location of the mine where the dragon lived. Today was the day he would finally kill the beast.

He ate a big breakfast that morning and skipped his usual aerobics—he would need all his available energy for the coming showdown. Xane estimated the mine to be about three miles away. He brought only his sword with him. The freshness of the farm crops entered his nostrils. Xane had worked hard, and the farm had done well that season. There would be plenty of food to spare if Nahna or Gabio came back. He hoped they would find their way back, even though he wasn't sure if he would ever return to the cave himself.

Xane climbed up and over the fence surrounding the farm. Then he hopped outside. It was the only time he had been outside that fence since his friends died. He scanned the surroundings for dangers. The coast was clear.

A shrill howling suddenly crashed into his eardrums. Xane turned to discover the source of the sound. He craned his neck to look up at the top of the cliff. Standing there was some kind of wolf. It was unlike any wolf on Earth. Its fur was longer, and its large eyes were dark yellow and deeply set. Its expression was almost human. Xane somehow knew it meant no harm. The creature just wanted Xane's attention. Now it had it. Xane and the animal sustained eye contact for a time. Then without any notice the wolf turned and ran, disappearing behind the cliff wall. Just like that, it was gone.

Xane clutched the wolf emblem around his neck. He remembered his time in the city of Gaulcel. His thoughts drifted to Guff and the day he got into the Wolf Clan. Then he thought of Bill and his pizza place. He remembered his friends in the city that he was determined to protect. Determined to save. With these thoughts, he began his journey.

* * *

About an hour later, the mine came into view. It had been obscured by an outgrowth of hickory trees. When Xane walked into the cluster of foliage, he saw that it surrounded a small pond. Behind that was a raised rock wall with a gigantic opening. Xane peered in. It was clear even from a ways outside that the cave floor sloped downward, leading deep underground.

Xane savored the short walk to the mine's entrance. His heart was beating as though he were walking into a boxing ring before a cheering crowd. He grasped the hard, smooth pommel of his sword as he walked around the edges of the pond. Clusters of bubbles showed on the surface, meaning there were fish swimming below. A pond skater glided along the top of the water. The bug could have made great bait, Xane thought, wishing he'd learned to fish during his first life. He looked up and found himself outside the cave. He'd set out for this place over a year ago, and it was only a few miles away the whole time.

Just then, Xane heard an otherworldly voice coming from behind him. "Looking for me?" the voice said. It sounded husky and jovial. Xane turned and was surprised to see his foe, the dragon, just across the pond. The creature was seated on its hind legs, relaxing. Its gigantic teeth showed a kind of twisted smile. "Come here. Sit beside me and I'll teach you how to fish." A fishing pole jutted from in between its claws. The pole was dwarfed by its huge talons. A second fishing pole rested next to the dragon, leaning against a rock. It seemed it was meant for Xane.

"Hey, I got a bite." The dragon yanked on the line, and the fish on the other end flew out of the water straight into its mouth.

It couldn't have been there a minute ago. Where had it come from? The dragon, even seated on its hind legs, was almost as tall as the hickory trees around them. Up close, it was the most imposing thing that Xane had ever seen. "Oh, that. It's nothing. I made myself invisible before you walked in. I didn't want to spook the fish.". It was now clear that the beast was hearing Xane's thoughts. "Here, watch." In a flash, the immense creature was gone. A second later, it reappeared in the same place it had been before.

"Look, I know you've got some business here. We might as well relax a bit before we get down to it. Let me show you how to bait a hook."

"I don't come in peace," Xane finally said.

"I'm sorry to hear that. I'd really rather not kill you. I mean . . . I will if I have to, but it'll be too easy. No fun. So why don't we just hang out instead." Xane couldn't believe what he was hearing. "You know, fishing is the perfect activity for hanging out." The dragon picked up the other fishing rod and held it out for Xane to take. He didn't know how to respond. "Ooh! And I've got a little something special for you too."

Nebreen plants began to grow all around Xane's feet. A month's worth of growth shot out of the ground in seconds, like footage from a time-lapse camera. Xane did not believe they were real. He reached over and felt the familiar texture of the nebreen leaf. They were ready to be picked and prepared for Nahna's tea. Xane was surrounded by his biggest weakness. The familiar scent of the plant alone was intoxicating. "I can show you how to make the tea you like?"

Xane heard the voice of Coach Clark in his ear. "It's messing with you, Reaper. Now put an end to it, once and for all."

"I think eating all those bats made you batshit," the dragon said, laughing to itself. It was speaking in Xane's native language now.

Xane felt the lure of the nebreen. He yearned to chew on the tiny rough leaf he held in his hand. Temptation was upon him. "No!" Xane yelled aloud. He dropped the leaf to the ground, took out his sword, and chopped down the nebreen plants around him. "I don't care how many powers you have. I came here to fight you, and that's what I intend to do." Xane's face was bright red with anger.

"In that case, we better take this inside." The dragon disappeared again. The trees between it and the cave entrance appeared to pull themselves apart. Giant footprints appeared in sequence, leading into the mine. The wind picked up, and Xane heard the beast descending into the cave. With no hesitation, he started in after it.

As he made his way to the entrance, more nebreen plants grew around him. Their vines reached out, wrapping him up. Xane kicked the vines off his legs, but the plants continued to grow. Vines wrapped around his waist, then his chest, and then the nebreen leaves were tickling underneath his nose. Their hold on Xane wasn't that strong physically; it was Xane's mental addiction that was the problem. The scent of the nebreen was engulfing his prefrontal cortex. He wanted the high badly. All he would have to do was open his mouth and take a nibble.

Instead, Xane pulled his sword from its scabbard and cut through the vines trying to strangle him. They fell limply to his feet. More vines grew around him, but Xane trudged forward until he reached the thick rock of the mine floor, where the plants could not grow. The vines were gone, and so were their addictive leaves. The fighter had finally reached his destination, but there was no time to appreciate the accomplishment. He ran forward, after the dragon, deep down into the mine.

The slope of the floor grew steeper as Xane moved after his target. A few minutes in, he realized that there may still be a long journey to the dragon's lair, but he kept running anyway. It served to warm up his body for the coming fight. About fifteen minutes later, he came upon a large room. Shiny coins littered its floor, along with ancient weapons set with precious gemstones. The treasure was piled high, taller than Xane, a dragon's lifetime worth of loot. Then the creature spoke.

"My name's Tanager, by the way. Not that you were going to ask . . . Xane!" The dragon enunciated his name mockingly. "Can I give you some advice?" he asked rhetorically. "Always play the long game. It's the only way you ever really win. Also, you shouldn't fuck with a dragon."

The creature continued, "I bet they never even told you why they want this mine. It's sitting on a vein of monet ore, the metal used to make moneta coins. You can't do anything else with it. Those bastards you're working for just want to get richer." Tanager paused to let Xane respond, but he stayed silent. "I know. I know. You're only pretending to work for them. Somehow, you think doing exactly what they want you to do is going to help bring them down. Buddy, you got your priorities all backwards. By the way, do you know who else joined up with a clan because they thought it would help them take down Gaulcel? Pretty much everyone who joined up with a clan!"

"I'm different," Xane said.

"You're overconfident," Tanager replied. "Way too confident in your abilities. That kind of confidence can get you to the top of a mountain, and then it'll push you over the cliff. In time, you would have turned just as greedy and ambitious as the others."

Would have? Xane thought. For a moment, an image of Maribel flashed in Xane's mind. He wondered if the dragon was responsible.

"You'll see," Tanager said. "I suppose it doesn't matter much to me. I've only got a short time left anyway, and unlike your kind, I don't come back." Xane was stunned by the admission, but the dragon continued before he could say anything. "It won't be by your hand though. You can be sure of that. That sword on your hip has given you a false sense of confidence. It's enchanted, you see. There's a name for a sword like that. The Slayer of the Simple, it's called. It helps you kill zombies. When you hold it, it links you to them, so that you sense their movements. It gives you a connection with the disease. All the afflicted have a kind of collective consciousness. Hive mind isn't the right term, but it is as close as that silly language of yours can get. Stupid hive mind, maybe. Anyway, it's a subtle but powerful effect. Your human brain can't grasp it. You just feel it."

Xane heard the dragon's words, but he didn't care. His focus was singular.

"But, you see, son, I'm not a zombie. That thing won't do a lick of good against me."

Xane pulled the sword from the scabbard and dropped it on the floor. It was his prefight ritual, like a batter stepping up to the plate. Releasing the sword was how he got his mind in the right place to fight.

"I must admit, I'm impressed. Many have faced me, but none have been so stupid as to seek a fair fight," the dragon said.

Xane was Reaper now. He locked eyes with Tanager. Then he took his fighting stance, lifting his arms to guard his face.

"Last chance, buddy. Just let it go. You really don't have to do this. If I were you, I'd get high and go fishing with me. I may be old, but I can still make for pretty good company. I'd really rather enjoy what's left of my time. Waddya say?"

"That's enough talk."

Xane heard the voice of Coach Clark in his head. "Get him!"

He pushed forward. He had a strategy in mind for defeating the large beast, but it didn't matter. Tanager opened its mouth, and a cone of flame shot out. The fire was on Xane instantly, covering him from head to toe. His death was instantaneous. Xane had just enough time to remember the last time he'd died.

* * *

After killing Xane, Tanager took a nap. The old ignertia had been sleeping more lately. It knew its days were numbered. The dragon pushed aside a pile of coins, opening the path to its nest. Tanager felt relieved to see that the egg was still there. The small embryo inside that fragile shell was Tanager's only chance at offspring. It was time to move out of the mine. The ignertia had already scouted a safe place to bury the egg. It should not wait any longer. She would not be alive when her progeny hatched.

V

A New Gaulcel

34

The Coming War

Naplana was already sore from having slept inside of the air ducts, and the cold metal table she now lay on wasn't helping matters. It didn't take long for Talona to figure out that she was involved with the rebels somehow. The elf decided to interrogate her himself.

Naplana's arms were stretched out over her head, and her legs were spread wide. All four limbs were tied to posts at the edges of the table. It was an uncomfortable position, but Naplana was tough, and she could take it. The fact that it was some elf interrogating her and not Gaulcel himself confirmed for her that no one could read her mind, which only strengthened her resolve. She wasn't talking.

"We need to know where your compatriots are hiding," Talona said. He produced a glass jar filled to the brim with fire ants.

"What compatriots?" Naplana said.

Talona unscrewed the lid and pulled a single ant from the jar with tweezers. Then he placed the insect on Naplana's stomach, just below her breast. "Most humans die after about a hundred stings, but you look to be in fairly good shape. I bet you could survive more than that." The elf looked at the entourage of clan guards behind him. "Place your bets, gentlemen."

The ant stung Naplana above her ribcage. She winced a little. It hurt, but not too bad. It was like a bad itch that she couldn't scratch.

"Let's try this again. Where are your compatriots hiding?" He positioned his tweezers above the ant jar. The elf's disposition was stonelike.

In that moment, Naplana realized two things. First, Talona wasn't going to let her die. Her compatriots, as the elf called them, would have virtually no chance to rescue her in the heavily guarded prison where they were. But they could be watching her quarters, where it could be possible to mount a rescue operation. Talona would not take that chance.

Second, she realized that there was no reason for her not to lie her ass off. If it worked, Talona might stop torturing her, and she might even take his investigation off the scent for a while. "Okay . . . okay, I'll tell you everything I know." Naplana feigned her best damsel-in-distress impression. "There's a base outside the city."

"Where?" Talona said.

Naplana searched her mind to come up with some bullshit. "It's about a mile outside the wall. East of the city I think. Hidden in a forest. There are scouts hidden high up in the trees."

Talona sensed that she might be lying, but he also knew that sometimes nuggets of truth slipped out inadvertently. He wanted her to keep talking. "Where is the one they call Xane?"

The ant stung Naplana again, a few centimeters from the first spot. "Ouch! Can you get this thing off me, please?"

Talona reached toward the ant with his tweezers. Then he pulled back. "First, where is Xane?"

"I was going to tell you. Please. Please. He's at the base I told you about. In the forest. If you show me a map, I can point to where it is." Naplana had never seen a map of the outside.

"What else do you know about him?" Talona pulled the ant off Naplana with the tweezers. Then he dangled the insect above her crotch.

"Xane's the leader. Everything goes through him. They call him 'elf slayer' cause he beat that elf in the pit. He's crazy strong and smart, like far beyond anyone else. He's got some kind of magic powers or something." Naplana was doing her best to sound scared.

Talona put the ant back in the jar. "What is he planning?" the elf asked.

"They don't care about Gaulcel. They only want to get the people out of here. To find somewhere else to live."

Suddenly, the door to the interrogation room swung open. Another elf guard clambered in. He wore a stunned expression. It was unlike an elf to ever show any emotion detectable to other races, but even Naplana could tell this guard was shaken up. "Leader, sir. We've returned from the mine. There's no one there."

Talona turned, frustrated with the interruption. "Your sergeant will debrief you downstairs. Now please, leave us."

"B-but Leader, sir," the elf stuttered. "The ignertia wasn't there either. The mine was empty sir."

"What do you mean empty?"

"Empty, sir. We searched the whole mine. There was nothing there but some fishing rods."

Had Xane actually done it? Killed a dragon? Talona wasn't sure what to think. Either way, he would need to tell Gaulcel posthaste. His boss had dreamed of access to that mine forever. If he didn't report this as soon as possible, the elf would have to feel Gaulcel's wrath. He turned back to Naplana. "We'll have to continue this conversation later." Then he turned to his elf subordinate. "Walk with me, Sub. Tell me everything."

* * *

When Gaulcel's meeting with Talona ended, the creature was despondent. Gaulcel had searched the elf's mind as soon as he saw his face. Talona hated the feeling of having his mind searched, but Gaulcel reveled in it. Exercising his ability made the acolyte feel powerful. In a matter of seconds, Gaulcel could probe into every memory, emotion, and experience Talona had ever lived. Every thought. When it was over, the elf would mourn the loss of his privacy, which delighted Gaulcel as well.

This time, however, he was not delighted. Talona had expected his boss to be overjoyed upon learning of the empty mine. Instead, Gaulcel was angry and fearful. Even though he knew everything there was to know about the elf, Gaulcel still didn't trust Talona. His most-relied-upon inmate was not broken yet. Not like Eleris. To Gaulcel, it didn't matter that Talona thought Naplana was lying. The creature believed Talona's skill for detecting deception was pretext. Some way to justify not pursuing leads, allowing the revolution to carry on.

Worse yet, Gaulcel was convinced that Xane had killed the dragon. How could a mere human accomplish such a miraculous feat? However he'd done it, Gaulcel feared that this was no ordinary human. He also believed that Xane had led the woman who killed him. And this man, his adversary, wanted to release every human from his city. That was what Naplana had said.

Gaulcel needed his humans. Keep your friends close but your enemies closer, the monster understood. Gaulcel had no friends, but the creatures he could control were much less concerning than the ones he couldn't. Plus, having humans in the city was the perfect cover. It allowed him to maintain the ruse that his powers worked on them.

Worst of all, the mine was clear. This meant war, he knew. When word got back to his brother, his army would come. Gaulcel needed to ready his troops, but the city was still recovering from the day of his abrupt death. His guards were stretched thin as it was. He would have to recruit from the horde, folks who were either weak or inept or both. Also, if he needed to control troops at the mine, he might even need to go near there with them, which was dangerous with a revolution going on. Gaulcel had found the perfect hiding place. Only Talona and a few others knew where it was. Hiding may not be a forever option.

Before their meeting was over, Gaulcel slapped Talona in the face. It had nothing to do with anything the elf had done, it was just an act of cruel, personal catharsis. Shooting the messenger. The acolyte felt the elf stew in his mind. Talona was not yet broken. Such things took time.

THE COMING WAR

* * *

Meanwhile, outside the gate, in the forest east of the city, an army had begun to rendezvous. Elves and dwarves and centaurs and the other sentient races of Purgatory were its soldiers. Each one was equipped with weapons and armor crafted by the most skilled smiths in Gundarce. Soon, the invasion of Gaulcel would commence.

Gaulcel's brother was with them. Gundarce was guarded by the greatest elven warriors from his city of millions, sycophants who wanted to please their leader, believing that doing so would increase their own wealth and power.

Another squad of soldiers was on its way to capture the mine. This attack was about holding it as long as possible, securing as much monet ore as possible. Gundarce would not enter the city himself, of course. That could prove dangerous. Instead, he would control his forces from nearby, which meant he needed a leader on the ground, in case his mental connection was lost. Someone he could trust completely. Someone who had studied the city and learned its secrets. The invading army would be led by his best spy. A woman named Maribel.

Within the hour Gundarce's troops were on the march. The war for the mine had begun. Unlike the everlasting wars of the past, Maribel was determined that this one would be short-lived.

35

Prison Break

Before Gundarce attacked, Maribel went into Gaulcel to scout out the place one last time. Sources had already reported to her about the tunnels where her rebels were hiding. She went there first.

When she found Bill, he was happy but surprised to see her. "You're here!" Bill said. He had long been waiting for her to return. His army needed her leadership—*he* needed her leadership. "It's good to have you back. W-welcome back." Bill stuttered.

"Have you found the respawn point?" Maribel wasted no time getting down to business.

"Um . . . it's somewhere in these tunnels, or at least we think it is." Bill replied. "One of our recruits—Guff's his name—he said he saw Gaulcel coming out of these tunnels the day after you killed him."

"Guff from the Wolf Clan?" Maribel asked.

"Yeah, I think so." Bill was surprised that she knew of him.

"He was Xane's leader. He helped train him and teach him the language. I trust him," Maribel said.

"Well, we looked everywhere in this damn place. I mean, it's big. Really big. It took a long time, but we mapped the whole space, and nothing sticks out. Then again, none of us knows what his respawn point looks like. Best we can figure, it's in a random hallway somewhere. But the boulder is the only exit, so if he comes back, he'll be trapped."

"Good. Cause we need to move now."

"Okay. Um. I can have our forces ready in a few days I think."

"We can't wait that long. What can you get together in a few hours?"

"Huh?"

Maribel continued to look at Bill, waiting for an answer.

"I honestly don't know. I'll do the best I can, but we're not ready. Why does it have to be so soon?" Bill thought for a second. "Holy shit. You killed him again, didn't you?"

"No. Gaulcel's alive," Maribel said. "But there's an army outside the city about to invade. Before that happens, we need to break all the humans out of their prison and get them into the tunnels."

"Wait . . . what?" Bill was perplexed. "I'm sorry, what? There's another army? Okay, who are you?"

Maribel recognized that she could not keep Bill in the dark any longer. "I'll explain everything. Give the order. Get the troops ready. This'll take a while."

"Xane never came back," Bill said suddenly. "It's been so long. I don't think he's coming back. At least not anytime soon."

"He'll be back."

Bill stood blank-faced for a moment. How did she know so much? Then he called in one of the early recruits, a leader among the others. Bill told her to prepare the best fighters. "Tell them we move tonight."

The recruit looked stunned but knew not to question him, especially with Maribel there. "Yes, sir," she said and marched off to tell the others.

Then Bill turned to Maribel. "Okay, start talking."

* * *

Maribel had always been gifted, going back to her first life. From an early age, she understood people. She understood the kinds of weakness to which every mind was susceptible. Insecurity, bias, fear, greed, anger, tribalism, overconfidence, and raw emotion. Unlike most people, however, Maribel understood that she was susceptible to the same weaknesses, and that she had a knack for recognizing them. On Earth, Maribel had tried to use her gifts for good. Because of her gender, and the prejudices during the time she lived, she was often stifled. She had to learn to work around that. From that experience, Maribel developed a mind for understanding the systems that made up a society. She became skillful at manipulating those systems.

When Maribel arrived in Purgatory, she spawned in Gundarce. The city of Gundarce was exactly like Gaulcel in all but two ways: its name and its leader. Gundarce was led by Gaulcel's brother, who of course named his city after himself. Gundarce the creature was exactly like Gaulcel, in all but one way: Gundarce was dumber.

The two brothers fought, as all siblings sometimes do. They were competitive with one another. But unlike other siblings, they commanded armies. Armies of soldiers that only died for one day at a time. The thing they always fought about was the monet mine. Both wanted exclusive access to its valuable ore. That, and boredom. The wars were as much about the brothers' boredom as anything else.

The wars between the two cities lasted lifetimes. Neither brother would nor could win. Respite would finally come when an ignertia took over the mine. Ignertia were attracted to such places by nature. A single dragon could take out both armies with no difficulty. Once that started happening, the brothers would decide their quest was futile. Only then would the war end. The cycle repeated every few thousand years.

Gaulcel had countless brothers in Purgatory, and each one was more or less the same as the others. They all controlled their own prison cities, which they always named after themselves. The evil creatures coveted command over others and used their exceptional power to get it. They were both egotistical and insecure. Maribel knew that Purgatory's acolytes had the kind of minds that were the easiest to manipulate.

Maribel managed to learn about all the acolytes in a relatively short time. She feigned loyalty to Gundarce, took advantage of the creature's insecurity, of his loneliness. They weren't that different, after all. Maribel also had authoritarian tendencies, except she recognized them in herself. By cozying up to the monster, she gradually gained his trust. He recognized her vast intellect and saw how that could be useful, so he made her his spy. Her assignment was to spy on Gaulcel.

Maribel's gifts made her an excellent spy. She learned almost everything about Gaulcel. She developed contacts in the city and figured out how to avoid detection by its omnipotent leader. Maribel spent so much time in Gaulcel, it became like a second home. As she reported her findings to Gundarce, she gained more of his trust.

The acolyte gave Maribel a long leash. Meanwhile, she plotted revolution.

* * *

A few hours after their talk began, Bill and Maribel were outside the human prison. Maribel knew the full layout of the building and the assignments of their guards, which numbered in the thousands. She also came up with the plan of attack. It was a large building, and there were a dozen ways in. They would be coming through all of them.

This was the first ever military operation by the Army of the Reckoning. It was clear many would die—perhaps most. They could lose as many people as they gained, and the ones they'd lose would be their most valuable. All the recruits knew this and agreed to participate anyway. They were true believers. However, Bill's trust was fading. He understood why Maribel hadn't told him the full story, but now he knew she was a spy. Maribel had worked for an enemy of the city where they lived. Her boss was just as evil as the one the Reckoning wanted to take down.

It was a lot to take in at once, and Bill was used to taking in a lot at a time from her. "My loyalty to Gundarce is a ruse," she had told him. "I want to take both leaders down. I want people to be free." That was enough for Bill to keep his commitment to the group. The Reckoning was bigger than her now. It was bigger than any one person.

Maribel's plan involved splitting their soldiers into small groups. They were to act independently from one another. Using stealth, the groups would stay undetected as long as possible. One group would create a distraction at the main entrance, attracting all the guards away from their posts to defend against the attack. Then the rest would enter the prison from every other entrance and take advantage of the unguarded areas, freeing every human they could find. The operation had a simple goal. Free as many humans as possible and get them to the tunnels. One final group was to wait outside the prison. These soldiers were there to lead the freed people to safety. They were the most important in the operation. Guff was with them.

The first group began their assault at the main entrance. A slaughter ensued. There were three or four guards posted outside, and a lone soldier managed to sneak up on them. He took the first guard out from behind with a sharp rapier through the neck. The guard fell to the ground, loudly gasping for his last breaths. Before the others could react, the soldier pierced a second guard through the heart.

Two guards remained outside the main entrance, and they were fully aware that their lives were in danger. The rest of the group ran toward them but couldn't get there in time. Both guards swung their broadswords at the first soldier simultaneously, the one who'd killed their comrades. They both hit—one blade on the shoulder, where it got stuck in sinew and muscle a few inches into the body. The other blade hit the neck. The force of the shoulder blow pushed the soldier into the second sword, separating him from his head. The soldier's body fell limply to the ground.

The remaining members of the Reckoning group swarmed the two remaining guards. One guard opened the entrance and took off down the hallway, while the second stood his ground. His bravery earned him a battle axe through the skull. The revolutionaries held the door that the guard had opened and followed him in.

'VROMP...VROMP....VROMP.' The alarm sounded. It was the signal. At the same time, a voice came over the loudspeaker. "We're under attack. All hands to the main entrance immediately." The Reckoning waited exactly two minutes, and then, all at once, thousands of them began to enter the prison from every direction.

The group at the back entrance entered quietly, first making sure the coast was clear. The prison had a security room equipped with monitors showing live feeds of the rest of the prison. This squad's first stop was to empty that room, so that no one was watching those monitors. They had studied the building and knew the most direct route. The group stealthily made their way to the security room, facing no resistance along the way. The plan was working, at least for now.

The security room was staffed with ten khajjine guards. The khajjine fought hard—the Reckoning squad lost half their members in the scuffle. When the dust cleared, a slew of bodies littered the floor of the security room, but no one was watching the monitors.

From there, what was left of the group headed toward the nearest cells, just as every other group was doing the same thing.

Once Maribel knew her plan was in action, she snuck away from the battle. She returned to Gundarce, outside the gates. Her boss would be anxiously waiting for her. Another battle was about to commence.

Maribel told Bill to hang back outside the building, but he refused. He was supposed to be a leader. Bill didn't know much about military strategy, but he knew that soldiers follow leaders who lead. He wasn't much of a fighter, but he had to be brave if he expected his recruits to be. The group Bill joined was assigned an entrance on the side of the building. There were no guards around when they entered, so they headed straight to the nearest hallway of cells.

The doors in the hallways were made of solid cement, and the air smelled of burnt hair. Each door was locked, but Maribel told them how to find the key. Every cell in the prison used the same design for its lock, and a skeleton key was hidden in the ceiling of every hallway.

Bill retrieved the key and opened the first door to find a decomposed body on the floor. The group moved on. Each door held a new horrific surprise.

Several of the inmates were recently dead, and those still living often had some kind of gruesome injury. If the prisoner could walk, Bill released them from their chains and instructed them on how to find a soldier outside who would lead them to the tunnels. The group had to move fast. There were hundreds of thousands of prisoners to free, and they could only open one door at a time.

Twenty or thirty doors in, Bill found Naplana. She was tied up with her limbs stretched to the corners of a solid steel table. When she saw Bill enter her cell, she got angry. "What are you doing here? You didn't need to rescue me, it's too dangerous. Our cover is totally blown now—they'll find us, you idiot!"

Bill wordlessly untied her from the table. She stretched her arms and gathered herself. Naplana was nude, but she didn't seem to notice. Bill couldn't help but see, but he tried to ignore her body and maintain his composure. There was more important business. "Shut up. We need to keep it down," Bill whispered. "There's someone waiting outside. Help them escort people to the tunnels."

"Fuck that!" Naplana said. "If we're here anyway, we need to save as many as we can."

"Which is why you need to get them to the tunnels." Bill said.

"Don't be stupid. If you're doing this, you're going to need fighters here. Now give me a weapon."

Bill handed her the short sword strapped to his back. She was right that they needed her, and she could do more with it than he could.

* * *

Meanwhile, in the hallway of the front entrance, bodies were piled to the ceiling. The first squad fought valiantly, but the guards kept coming. They never stood a chance. Unaware of the other squads in the building, leaders ordered the guards to clean up the mess. A few guards trickled back into the prison to resume their post.

The first squad's goal was to buy time, and they bought as much of it as they could. The rest of the Reckoning used that time well. Thousands of humans escaped through other exits, but many more remained. There were too many people running to freedom now. The strategy of silence and stealth could not be maintained. Every prison hallway was crowded with Reckoning soldiers and freed prisoners. The first guards to come back were overwhelmed. Swarms of men and women rushed by them. They couldn't tell who was doing the freeing. Maribel's troops disguised themselves in the swarm, killing the guards as they returned. All the while, their compatriots freed more prisoners.

Eventually, word got back to the front entrance that the battle was not over. New guards assumed posts in the security room and discovered the anarchy going on. They alerted their leaders. Then their leaders assembled the guards, and they systematically worked their way through each hallway of cells, killing every human they saw. To ensure victory, the army cleared one hallway at a time. Gradually, they regained control of the prison. By that time, almost every cell door was open, and nearly every human in the city was either dead or free.

* * *

The alarm alerted Talona of the attack. He was on his way back from his meeting with Gaulcel. His face still stung from his boss's senseless strike.

He rushed to defend the prison, but before he could get there, he received word that the attack was over. The Reckoning soldiers had all been killed. A few minutes later, however, word came that more were attacking and freeing prisoners.

Talona arrived to see huge crowds of men and women running as a group in the same direction. The elf wanted to know who was leading them. He told his entourage to protect the prison, and he followed the group by himself.

He stayed hidden as he trailed the group to the edge of the city, then watched them go toward the wall and disappear behind a large boulder. One human stood outside that boulder, waving the group on, telling them where to go. Talona recognized the bearded man immediately. He used to be his subordinate. Now he was a traitor.

Guff.

Talona snuck up along the side of the wall for a better view. The swarm of humans wasn't escaping from behind the boulder, somehow—they were going inside it. The sight confirmed his intuitions about the honesty of Naplana. The Reckoning's base was not outside the city. It was right here in front of him.

The elf thought of Gaulcel. Now that he had discovered the headquarters of the revolution, ending it would be easy. Gaulcel would gather his guards and take control of their minds. They would mount a full-fledged attack at anyone and everyone behind that boulder. Every rebel would be killed.

Talona realized that he didn't want that to happen. It was a painful epiphany. The elf found himself in tears. There was no way for him to stop it now. Gaulcel would read his mind, and that would be that. He could not hide this knowledge.

Talona put his hand to the sensitive spot on his face where the acolyte had slapped him.

The elf approached Guff. There was no cover concealing the former Viking. Talona tried to disguise himself among the swarm of humans rushing the boulder. The tall elf crouched low as he ran with them, but his turquoise hair stuck out. Guff saw him from a mile away.

"Oh Gonk." Surprised by seeing his former leader, Guff spoke his thoughts out loud. He pulled his scythe, convinced that he was about to die.

Talona came out of the crowd with his hands up. He dropped his elven sword to the ground. When the crowd noticed him, they scattered away from the boulder. The flood of humans was gone. The man and the elf were alone.

Tears poured from Talona's eyes as he approached. His face was red with emotion. Such a display was unheard of from an elf. "I come in peace." Talona's voice quivered as he spoke.

Guff backed away with his scythe still pointed in his former boss's direction. There was no trust. In his mind, this had to be a gambit.

"I'm sick of him too. That prick slapped me today, for no reason. It's horrible. He's horrible. I'd rather join the horde than work for him another day." Speaking ill of his boss for the first time was exhilarating. Talona couldn't stop. "Do you know what he makes me do? You couldn't possibly understand how much I hate Gaulcel."

Guff had to interrupt him. "On your knees. Hands behind your back." The man was stunned when Talona complied. Guff carried zip-tie handcuffs, which he attached to Talona's wrists with no struggle.

"Now do you believe me?" the elf said.

"No," Guff said matter-of-factly. "But you're coming with me until we get to the bottom of this."

"You don't understand. It must be now." Talona was pleading for more than just his life. If Gaulcel discovered his actions, it meant lifetimes of torture. It meant the Reckoning was done for. "Once he knows I'm missing, he'll piece it all together. If not him, then another guard. We have a day at most."

Guff shook him off, still wary, trying to figure out what to do with the elf. It was too risky to take Talona back to the tunnels.

"Gaulcel must die. It must be you. You must kill him, and you must do it now."

36

A Battle of Brothers

Bellowing war cries, the Gundarce army stormed the gates of Gaulcel. Guards posted above could not believe what they were seeing. An armored sahuajin infantry made up the first line. Directly behind them, dwarves holding long spears prepared to jab in between the lumbering lizard bodies. Waves of diverse soldiers followed the dwarves. Then the cavalry came, a squad of agile elves and khajjine riding on centaurs. There was no time for Gaulcel to prepare a defense. The gates were open.

After Maribel snuck away from the operation at the human prison, she tricked the guards into opening the gates for her. A delivery of fresh produce served as the trojan horse. The centaur who pulled the wagon diplomatically entered the gate. As soon as he was inside, a squad of elven assassins jumped out of his covered cart and killed the guards below. The guards high in the posts above, the lookouts, were all that was left. They couldn't close the gate themselves, so they watched helplessly as the Gundarce military emerged from behind the cover of trees.

The streets were almost empty when the foreign army entered the city. Most of Gaulcel's guards were still back at the human prison. Maribel led the army straight to them. Gundarce took control of the surprised guards outside the prison. Then they broke up into squads. Some charged into the prison, while others broke off to attack the other buildings in the city.

The newly assigned watchmen in the security room stood in amazement at the rushing tide of soldiers coming in from every entrance. They sounded the alarm, but they didn't know how to use the intercom. Even if they had, where would they have told the guards to go? The enemy was everywhere.

When the guards heard the alarm, they collectively sighed. Another false ending, it seemed.

The huge prison was cleaned out in minutes. Gundarce was controlling the brunt of Gaulcel's forces. The invaders' casualties numbered in the single digits. The city of Gaulcel was being decimated, and most residents didn't even know it. They would soon.

Thanks to Maribel, Gundarce knew the layout of every resident building. The forces under his control easily broke in and headed straight for the most crowded area, the gopiddum. Every creature they found was either killed or taken over by Gundarce.

As the battle raged inside the walls of the city, another large company of killers emerged from the forest outside. The scent of death had attracted the undead. Hordes of ghouls lumbered forward toward the open gate. Lecttum was no ordinary disease. Those afflicted lost control over their own bodies. Their consciousness was replaced by the collective consciousness of the disease, like puppets on strings. The Lecttum smelled the chaos of the city and saw an opportunity. Slowly, its army of diseased and dying bodies ambled into the corners of the city. The streets were desolate at first. The resident buildings were not guarded.

* * *

Lastoya stood behind the register at his bookstore, dreaming of one day reading new books. He had gone through everything on these shelves countless times. As usual, the store was empty of customers. It seemed its only purpose was as a place to bring potential clan recruits. The elf was grateful to have it nonetheless.

Suddenly, Lastoya heard a cacophony of footsteps, the sounds of a crowd approaching. It was accompanied by loud, terrified screams. Peeking his head out of the store entrance, the elf found the source of the noise. The horde, and all its mass, was running from something. They were running fast, and they were scared.

Then Lastoya noticed the guards running too, right alongside them.

It took a few seconds to process. Lastoya didn't know why they were running, but he decided he didn't want to wait around to find out. The clumsy elf took off ahead of the crowd. Unlike others of his race, Lastoya had always lacked agility; he was just not the athletic type. His short legs—and his tendency to gain weight rather than burn it off—had steered him toward intellectual pursuits. Through sheer luck, he had managed to survive the tournaments for several decades. He'd even survived Gaulcel's tirade after the Day of Reckoning by hiding in his quarters, his only injury a bum knee that never quite healed.

Lastoya hobbled away as quick as he could, but he was old and slower than ever now, and the stampeding horde soon overtook him. The nimble elves and khajjine rushed by him until he was enveloped in the crowd. He could feel the imminence of the unknown danger approaching. More creatures rushed past him, and soon, he was near the back of the herd.

A sahuajin pushed him down. "Out of the way!" the creature yelled as Lastoya fell to his knees.

The impact weakened his already injured joint. As he tried to regain his feet, a second sahuajin stepped on his leg. The immense weight of its reptilian body shattered a bone there. There was no way the old elf would be able to stand. He lay on the floor, pulling himself with his arms, scooting forward at a snail's pace. The mass of creatures hurried past him. Then he was alone.

Behind him, the danger appeared—the reason the horde was running. He had to blink to confirm, but then he was certain—that was an army marching toward him. Gaulcel's clan guards were leading the way, and an armored battalion followed. All the warriors had the same hollow look in their eyes. Lastoya recognized the look. It was the same one he saw after the Day of Reckoning. The day Gaulcel murdered almost everyone in this city.

He lay on his back, waiting to accept his fate.

Then, all of a sudden, the marching stopped. He glanced back and saw that the hollow look had disappeared. The guards and soldiers awakened in their own consciousness. They looked around, confused for a moment. Then, with their minds returned, the clan guards turned and began to fight the armored soldiers behind them. Somehow, the link with their master had been broken.

All Lastoya could do was watch and listen to the clashing of their weapons. There were enough clan guards to make a fight of it, but nowhere near enough to win that fight. Blood splattered. Death filled the air. War cries echoed through the building. Then it was over. Every clan guard was either dead or wounded and the soldiers were making quick work of the latter.

Finally, their gaze turned to Lastoya.

The bookstore owner sat up and stuck his neck out, hoping his death would be quick. But then something caught his eye—an animated body, appearing from a side entrance. The creature looked to be dead, but somehow it was moving.

One of the soldiers jabbed a spear into the head of a wounded clan guard. He looked up from his kill just in time to see the dead creature as it bit into his cheek. The walking cadaver ripped off a chunk of skin, and the soldier screamed as he brought up his spear and stabbed the animated corpse where its heart should have been.

The ghoul was unfazed. It ambled forward and bit another confused soldier. Instinctively, the zombie's second victim swung his mace into the dead creature's shoulder, knocking it to the ground, where it proceeded, undeterred, to bite a third soldier on the leg.

At last, one of the soldiers crushed the zombie's head, and it stopped moving. But by that time, its victims were turning. The newly undead proceeded to bite more of Gundarce's confused soldiers. Lastoya looked on in horror as the disease worked its way through their entire force.

Then a new noise, a strident gurgling, filled the room. It was coming from the direction in which Lastoya had been crawling before he saw the army. The elf looked toward the noise. The horde that had run past moments ago was coming back in his direction—and they were moving very slowly.

* * *

Bill and Naplana returned to the tunnels. It was just the two of them. The rest of their squad had died in the prison. Naplana had proven herself to be invaluable. If not for her, Bill would surely have been dead as well. Before fleeing, their squad had managed to free hundreds.

The two leaders of the Reckoning lowered themselves into their headquarters and looked around. They saw a sea of people, standing shoulder to shoulder and stretching down into every corridor. There was barely enough room for the pair to fit. The space had a sort of buzz to it, as though a concert were about to start. Maribel's plan had worked.

Bill said his first thought out loud. "How are we going to feed all these people?" He looked at Naplana and let out a joyous laugh.

She smiled back, proud of their accomplishment. "How the fuck should I know?" She shrugged and then slapped him on the back playfully. She was wearing his shirt.

One of the Reckoning recruits, a soldier who had also survived the mission at the prison, saw Bill and came up to him. She carried a megaphone. "They are waiting, sir. Someone has to tell them what to do now."

Bill took the megaphone and held it down at his hip while he pondered what to say. Reluctantly, he brought the megaphone to his mouth and hit the button to turn it on. The folks nearest to him heard it buzz and turned around. Others followed suit, until everyone was looking at him. "Um . . . hello," Bill said. "Welcome." He cleared his throat. "There's plenty of room here in these tunnels for you all to stay. For those of you who want to leave, we can help escort you out of the city. Um . . . we're the source of the revolution."

A woman in the back started clapping. Almost in unison, the rest of the crowd joined her. The sound of applause was thunderous. Bill had to stop talking and wait for the noise to die down.

Above him, the tunnel entrance opened, and Maribel appeared. She climbed down into the room, looking around just as Bill and Naplana had. Then she saw Bill.

He looked back at her with wide eyes. Holding his hands out in front of him, Bill shrugged his shoulders, as though asking her what to say.

She waved her hand forward, motioning for him to keep going. *You're doing great,* Maribel mouthed.

Bill looked back at the crowd, who were now silent again. He spoke once more. "Please, everyone—move back into the nearest hallway a little farther until everyone has some personal space and can get comfortable. Our leaders will be around to help you set up sleeping areas and give you further instructions." Bill lowered the megaphone, then thought of something else. "Again. Welcome. We're glad to have you here."

Another round of applause broke out. Then the crowd followed Bill's instructions and dispersed deeper into the tunnels.

Maribel walked over to him. As usual, she wasted no time getting down to business. "Where are Dalthra, Ciessa, Comerciam, Khane, and Kurth?"

"Nice to see you too," Bill said.

Maribel stared at him. She was not amused.

"They're holed up in different safehouses around the city," he added.

"Get them back here as soon as possible."

"What about Gaulcel? What if he figures out where we are?"

"We don't need to worry about that right now," Maribel said.

It was another comment from her that left Bill flummoxed. She had a way of always doing that to him. He rolled his eyes. "Okay, no more secrets. What's going on?"

"The whole city is in chaos right now. We've got to get them out of danger ASAP," Maribel said.

"Okay, we'll get them. Can you please just tell me why?"

"Gundarce has taken over. And now there are zombies. Everyone out there is either dead or will be soon."

"Did you just say zombies?"

* * *

Despite his millennium of combat experience, Guff was scared. Gaulcel was huge. Talona was helping get the creature alone, but Guff would have to take him out by himself.

The bearded man did not trust his former leader, and he never could. But this chance was worth the risk, he decided. Talona already knew where the tunnels were, and that people were hiding there. If he were lying to Guff, Gaulcel would find out about the tunnels anyway.

"Can you free my hands please. I can't talk to the guards handcuffed, or they'll catch on," Talona explained. His composure had returned.

"Shut up." Guff thought about changing his mind and killing the elf right where he stood. "What if you're lying?" he muttered.

"What if I'm not?" Talona responded.

If Talona was lying, killing him would only buy the Reckoning one day. It was enough to convince Guff to give him a chance. He cut the zip-tie on the elf's hands, then held up the scythe, just in case Talona was about to attack him.

A pair of elves stood hidden outside Gaulcel's hiding spot, another boulder against the city wall. Guff glared at Talona, but the elf averted his gaze to the two elves by the boulder.

"Ok. Here's the plan. I'll get rid of the guards. Then you go in," Talona said.

"Simple enough." Guff tried to push aside his mounting doubts.

"Stay here. I'll let you know when the coast is clear." Talona came out of the hiding spot and walked straight to the guards. When they recognized their leader, they straightened up and puffed out their chests.

"Where have you been?" the first guard asked. "We're under attack!"

Talona slapped him hard on the chin. "You will address me as Leader, worm. I'm aware of the attack at the prison. It has been handled."

"Yes, Leader!"

Talona remembered the slap Gaulcel had given him and regretted hitting the guard, but he couldn't allow himself to show it.

"But Leader," the same guard continued, "there's another attack. An enemy, armored soldiers, have invaded the city."

"I know," Talona said. The elf had no idea what he was talking about. "That's why I'm here. You two are relieved of your guard duties. You are needed in the fight. Report to the battlefield. I will assume this post and protect our great leader myself. Now, are there any guards inside with him?"

"Yes, Leader. Elerea is inside."

"Well, go get her and take her with you," Talona ordered.

"Do you mean to guard him all by yourself?" the guard asked.

Talona raised his hand as if to slap the elf again but then stopped himself. "Do not question my orders! Worm!"

"We need to move him—and none of us can know where," the second guard said to the first.

"Stop bickering and go get Elerea," Talona ordered again.

"Yes, Leader!" The elf disappeared inside the boulder and soon reemerged with the one they were looking for.

"Sergeant Elerea. Get to the front line and take these worms with you."

"Yes, Leader!" Elerea said. The three elves sprinted toward the center of the city. Guff, still hidden from view, watched them go by, stunned. Still, he didn't trust Talona. Guff believed certain death was inside that boulder, and not for Gaulcel. This was all some elaborate ruse. Even so, for the sake of the Reckoning, he was going to find out. It was a risk he had to take.

Once the elves were out of sight, Talona waved for Guff to come join him. The man jogged over. "He's inside by himself," Talona said. "I must leave here now in case you fail. Try to take him by surprise. Good luck." After his pep talk, the elf ran away.

Guff took a deep breath. His adrenaline was going, and his palms were sweaty. He felt the handle of the scythe slipping and gripped the weapon tight. Then he passed through the entrance.

There he was. Gaulcel. All by himself, as promised. The huge creature stood with his back to the entrance. Guff was able to recognize him from the wings and the green skin. Gaulcel towered over even the large, bearded man. Guff's heart thumped hard in his chest. Then the monster turned around.

As soon as Gaulcel saw Guff, he shrieked and fell to his knees in fear.

The monster looked around frantically for his elven guards. They were nowhere to be found.

Guff didn't want to waste time. He brought his scythe straight down between the kneeling creature's panicky eyes with a *thwack*. Green blood gushed over Gaulcel's face, creating an olive-colored mask. The creature hunched over, collapsing on the floor. Dead.

Guff was in disbelief. Was it really that easy?

37

Lecttum in the City

When Xane woke, the physical withdrawal effects of the nebreen were gone. Xane had gotten so used to the feeling, he didn't realize they were still with him until they weren't. He reached up and felt for the scar on his face. It was gone as well. He'd kept it as long as he could. The whole encounter with the dragon seemed like a weird dream.

Xane's quarters appeared as though he never left. He knew he had to come back to the city eventually, but he was not happy to be there. Soon, Gaulcel would appear on the morning announcements. He hated the sight of the ugly monster, so he prepared to ignore him and train with his heavy bag.

The giant screen wall clicked on. Xane looked away, but then he heard a familiar voice. It did not belong to the evil creature. He turned, and there was Maribel. Xane thought he must be hallucinating.

"Good morning." Maribel said. "Now that you see me, you know the Reckoning is back. We believe it will be for good this time. If you are hearing this, you probably just woke up from a death. The city has changed a lot in the past day.

"First, Gaulcel is missing. We are trying to locate him so that he can be brought to justice. If you missed it the first time I spoke, know that his powers only work on nonhumans. Even so, he is still extremely dangerous and could reappear at any time. The good news is that, in its current state, he will not be able to retake the city like he did last time.

Here's the bad news. The reason Gaulcel will not be able to take back the city so easily is that we have been overrun by creatures called simple ones. Simple ones cannot be controlled by Gaulcel, because they are not alive. They are dead, decaying corpses, able to move around. The disease they are infected with is called Lecttum. It is very contagious. And they bite. If one bites you, you will die and become simple yourself."

Xane was so shocked and enamored to be seeing her, he barely processed what she was saying. But he knew that she was talking about zombies. Lots of them, apparently, and he'd left his sword in the dragon's mine.

"It is imperative to avoid these creatures," Maribel continued. "We are trying to clear the city, but it will take time. The more of you that turn simple, the longer that process will take. In the meantime, please try to stay in your quarters and away from large groups of people. If you do find yourself in trouble, the way to put one down for good is with a hard blow to the head. I'll be back tomorrow morning with more information. Please take care of yourselves."

The screen shut off, and Maribel was gone. Xane was as confused as ever about the state of the city. He decided not to ruminate on the source of his confusion, though. Instead, he focused on the next step. It was clear what he needed to do now. Get another weapon.

Xane stepped onto the elevator and commanded it to take him to the pit. There would be no tournaments that morning. He stepped into the large cement room. The stench was palpable. Clusters of zombies were scattered around the makeshift arena, wandering aimlessly. They didn't notice Xane, and he wanted to keep it that way. He crawled on his hands and knees over to the fighting hollow, then lowered himself onto the sand floor, keeping his landing as silent as possible.

One of the dead creatures was down in the pit with him—a sahuajin with no legs. The creature wore Mantis Clan garb. Xane crouched and made his way around the pit's curved wall. He was about to climb out, but then he heard a low, guttural growl.

The legless sahuajin pulled itself toward Xane through the yellow sand, its dead eyes fixed on its living prey. The deceased creature let out another loud snarl, alerting the rest of the undead that filled the large cement room. A few of the creatures in the viewing deck tumbled forward, falling prone into the powdery sand a few feet from Xane. These ghouls righted themselves, readying their attack. Then more came, from every direction, falling in bunches and landing with Xane in the pit. The fighter was surrounded and unarmed. A dozen or more zombies stood between him and the rope ladder that he needed to escape.

Xane entered the pit as a shortcut, figuring he could cut across and get to the side door that led to clan headquarters undetected. Instead, he'd alerted every zombie in the room and trapped himself with them in the sand pit.

As the simple ones approached from his sides, Xane strode through the center of them. He leaped forward, planting one foot on the head of the prone sahuajin, using its dome to propel himself forward. Xane landed on his knees. He tucked his head and used the momentum from the jump to roll forward, away from the undead. While he was in midair, the zombies reached for him. One of the creatures managed to lay a few fingers on Xane's arm. The feel of its cold and clammy fingers gave him a shiver. He checked his arm. It was a close call, but the touch hadn't broken the skin.

Xane had no time to be relieved. The zombies turned and plodded after him, again trapping the fighter against the wall. Xane noticed that the crawling sahuajin was not moving. His weight on the creature's skull did him in. The other zombies continued their slow steady march. Xane ran around the circular wall of the pit, narrowly avoiding the ghoul's grasp. The creatures followed. They huddled together in a swarm as they moved.

Xane waited for them to get close, then took off along the wall again. He reached the other side, and the rope ladder. The dead walkers were still heading toward him. Xane vaulted up the ladder, fast, leaping onto the edge and looking around. The room was clear. Every single zombie had fallen with him into the pit. He looked down to find the creatures clawing up at him. They weren't strong enough to climb the rope ladder. Xane had inadvertently forced them into a trap. He was safe, at least for the moment.

He took a moment to catch his breath. Bent over at the waist, he clutched at his chest and felt the rapid beating of his heart. Xane sighed a sigh of relief, in awe of his luck. Then he strolled to the side door and looked at the piffum plaque next to it. He suddenly remembered—he had no wristband. The door would not open.

Xane thought for a moment, then turned back toward the pit. He looked down, where the living dead were still reaching up toward him, snarling. Behind them lay the dead sahuajin, still in its Mantis garb. Xane looked at the creature's hands. It wore a wristband.

"Fuck!" Xane said aloud.

He ran around to the opposite side of the circular hollow, and the undead followed, but they moved through the center. By the time he got to the other side, the creatures were traveling over the dead sahuajin. Xane felt his frustration rise, overtaking his fear. He waited until all the undead were pressing up against the pit wall. He walked back a ways from the edge to get a running start. Then he ran forward as fast as he could, leaping over the mass of zombies beneath. He tucked his body as he landed and rolled forward, taking some of the impact on his shoulders. His weight coming down was hard on his legs. He would feel it later, but adrenaline would not let his body acknowledge the pain now.

Xane came up from the roll a foot from the body of the dead sahuajin. He pulled at the wristband and realized it wasn't going to come off easily. Standing, Xane stomped on the dead creature's hand, breaking the bones in its fingers. By then, the zombies were almost upon him. There wasn't time to reach down and try to pull the wristband off again.

He sprinted back to the cliff wall, where he waited for the huddled swarm to get close again. Then he ran along the circular wall, and the creatures followed. He was herding the zombies like they were cattle. Xane took the herd to the farthest point from the sahuajin, then made his way around them and back to the center. After a few hard yanks, the wristband came off. As it came free, Xane felt a clammy hand on his shoulder. He turned to see a zombie's face inches away. The creature was reaching toward him with its mouth open.

Nimbly, Xane pulled away from the creature and again made for the wall, where he waited for the ghouls to get close again. Then he ran around the side. The rough feel of the frayed rope ladder felt good in Xane's grasp. He launched himself up the side of the pit and back to safety.

* * *

Xane had believed that the clan headquarters would be clear of zombies. He was wrong.

Somehow, the dead creatures had gotten past the locked doors. There seemed to be clusters of fiends in every room. Xane relied on his stealth and agility to avoid confrontations, careful to keep his distance. The Mantis headquarters was remarkably similar to the Wolf Clan's. The indoor park smelled like rot. Inside, the zombies' own putrid scent seemed to mute their sense of smell.

The butterflies were gone, but the foliage remained. It was useful for Xane to hide behind.

He had no difficulty finding the weapons room. Every wall was decorated with sharp steel. Some of the weapons had been taken, but many remained. Xane looked around to take it all in and then realized he was not alone. There were around a dozen zombies scattered throughout. Most of them wore Mantis insignia. Fortunately, the room was warehouse-huge, and the dead creatures didn't notice him right away.

The spot on the wall closest to the entrance was adorned in greatswords. These were larger than the falchion Xane was used to, but he decided it'd be better to get whatever he could. He shot a glance across the room and saw a group of falchion-style swords with familiar markings hanging on the wall. A crowd of zombies were hunched over in front of them. The creatures looked to be asleep.

Xane pulled the greatsword off the wall. It was too large to wield with one hand.

He crouched low as he made his way toward the falchion wall, but he didn't get far before one of the creatures sniffed him out. The room offered little cover. As soon as one of the fiends saw him, they all did. Their stiff legs lumbered toward him in the center of the room.

Xane had a weapon this time. He ran toward the falchion wall. Three zombies stood in between him and his favored sword, and ten more closed in on him from other directions. Rather than go around, Xane decided to run straight into them. He lifted the greatsword over his head as he ran, swinging it down toward the head of the first zombie. The blade whizzed by the front of the zombie's nose. Xane had missed.

His momentum kept him running until he collided with the creature. For a moment, they were shoulder to shoulder. The force of the impact knocked the ghoul over. Then Xane sensed something on his shoulder that felt like teeth. He looked down, and it looked like teeth. For a moment, Xane thought his shoulder had somehow pulled the creature's teeth out of its gums. The things were still in his shoulder.

Xane continued toward the falchion wall and side-stepped the second zombie, slipping under its grasp like he used to slip punches in the ring. For the third, Xane juked to the right and then spun to the left. He expected to fake the zombie out of its Mantis boots, but the simple one was not fooled. The zombie fell into Xane, tackling him to the floor. He managed to scoot backward in time to avoid the creature's bite.

Something felt off. Killing the dead creatures had been so easy back at the farm. He looked down at the teeth still attached to his shoulder. Dentures. Luckily, they were dull from grinding. Xane pulled the dentures off and threw them to the floor. Then he turned his eyes to the creatures lumbering toward him. He had just enough time to grab a falchion sword from the wall.

"That's better," Xane said aloud to no one, feeling the familiar weight in his hands. The blade was still in its leather scabbard, so Xane ripped it from its sheath. He moved toward the first zombie and prepared to fling his weapon at its skull. But before he could get to it, he tripped and almost lost his footing. The fighter had to lower his hands to regain his footing.

The zombie that had taken him down was still on the ground. Its long arms stretched out, grasping Xane's ankle. He kicked the ghoul off to free his leg. Another close call.

Xane glanced at the blade in his hand. It was different from his old sword in one way. The symbols on the blade, the ones Xane never had been able to translate, were not the same. Xane remembered what the dragon, Tanager, told him. His old sword had a name—"Slayer of Simple Ones," it was called, or something like that. It carried a special enchantment.

The ghouls were close now. Xane ran toward the nearest open space. Zombies lumbered toward him from different angles. Anywhere he went, they followed in a straight line. He ran toward one corner of the room, side-stepping two of the undead on the way.

As the zombies neared, they began to come together and form a cluster. Xane ran the four corners of the room, waiting each time for the dead to get close. It was an exercise in timing. Soon, every zombie in the room was in a tightly packed swarm. He went around the group and returned to the falchion wall. As he arrived, he noticed more zombies trickling in from the entrance. He figured he had about twenty seconds before the slow-moving dead would catch up to him.

There were about twenty falchion-style swords hanging on the wall. Xane pulled swords off, yanking each one out of its scabbard, and looking at the markings on the blade. He went through three before finding the right one. As soon as Xane held the sword, he felt it. There was no need to look at the symbols. He had never noticed the feeling before, but he did now. The sword in his hands carried the same enchantment.

Xane turned towards the mass of zombies plodding toward him, and his confidence returned. These ghouls didn't stand a chance.

* * *

After Xane gathered the swords, he made his way to Bill's place, hoping to find his old friend. The pizza place looked abandoned, like no one had been there in years. Xane made his way into the back room, where he took the elevator up to Bill's hidden quarters. The place had been ransacked, and still no Bill. Where was his friend?

Over the next few weeks, Xane stayed at Bill's place, hoping he would come back. Bill had a fridge and other luxuries. The place was well stocked with canned foods, so that Xane didn't need to leave often on food runs. And Bill had a window, something Xane had never seen anywhere else in the entire building.

At times, the luxuries of Bill's place made Xane feel out of place. In Purgatory, Xane had slept in an eight-by-eight cement cell and then on a grungy cave floor. Now, he was sleeping in a massive apartment with a view, and he didn't want to leave. Something about that made him feel guilty and awkward. He combated the feeling by maintaining his focus. Xane kept up his daily training and killed time shadowboxing with a mental image of Gaulcel. The thought of taking him out still gave Xane the sense of purpose he needed.

There was no screen in Bill's quarters, so Xane would come down to the shop for the morning announcements. It was the best part of each day, hearing Maribel. They seldom lasted longer than ten minutes, but Xane relished those ten minutes. The situation in the city was getting more dire. Even still, Xane liked the sound of Maribel's voice. The fighter had never been in love in his first life. He was too focused on survival, and then boxing, and then drugs. His feelings for Maribel, a woman he'd only met once, were confusing. He still wasn't sure if that night had even been real.

Reading between the lines of Maribel's daily broadcast, Xane knew the Reckoning was not getting anywhere with the zombie problem. She tried to sound optimistic, but the facts were the facts. Xane wanted to help, but he wasn't sure how. According to Maribel, the best thing to do was sit tight and not get bitten. Which was what he'd been doing for weeks. He thought of trying to visit Guff but didn't know where the man was. He thought of going on a zombie killing spree, but even with his special sword, Xane couldn't take out an entire city by himself. There'd been several close calls that first day. He wanted to go to Maribel, but she never revealed her location. So he waited.

The waiting was driving him even crazier than he already had been. Xane needed a next step. He needed a plan to follow.

One morning, Maribel finally spoke the words Xane had been longing to hear. "I am pleased to announce that we have a place where we can provide food and safety for humans. If you are hearing this and you are human, there is a system of tunnels underneath the city. It can be accessed from a large boulder against the Eastern city wall. Unfortunately, we can only take humans at this time, but we are clearing out other areas and hope to be able to invite nonhumans soon."

As soon as the announcements were over, Xane grabbed his sword and stepped onto the elevator.

38

Spring Cleaning

Naplana was acting as bait in the karbero, thinking about the last few weeks. She had never seen anyone like him. She'd witnessed him do things that seemed impossible. The hero that single-handedly turned around the war on the undead. Before he came to the tunnels, they were losing. There was little hope the Reckoning could ever get rid of the simple ones. Most folks were trying to escape the city, but they'd get bitten before they could get out. Those who stayed could barely keep themselves safe.

Then Xane showed up and changed everything.

Naplana had helped build the fence around the boulder outside the tunnels. It was a little makeshift, but it seemed sturdy enough. The truth was, they were desperate. When Maribel had made the announcement inviting humans, they expected a trickle of folks. Instead, it seemed like the whole city came, nonhumans included. The other residents were just as desperate as they were. The crowd coming in naturally attracted the simple ones. Within a matter of minutes, all the hopefuls at the gate had turned. The guards spearing them in their heads could not work fast enough. Naplana had been one of those guards. Before her eyes, a mass of living dead pressed against the makeshift fence and toppled it, leaving the whole of the Reckoning exposed.

SPRING CLEANING

If one of the ghouls ever got into the tunnels, it was over. The Day of Reckoning, getting captured, the battle at the prison, killing Gaulcel twice—all of it would be for nothing.

Suddenly, a mysterious figure appeared in the distance. The hero. He whistled with two fingers, and some of the simple ones turned toward him. With no fear, the hero barreled into the swarm. He disappeared into the teeming mass of death and somehow emerged on the other side. Unscathed. From there, Naplana watched the hero's sword and fists and feet effortlessly land on the heads of undead creatures. They fell faster than she could count them. The numbers thinned, and the guards resumed their spearing. Soon, they had created enough space to retreat into the boulder.

The hero introduced himself as Xane. Bill and Maribel knew him, and once they saw him, they embraced. Since that day, Xane had been no less heroic. Naplana felt grateful to be chosen for his squad of zombie slayers. She felt grateful to be close to him, and she admired him. So did everyone else, it seemed.

Xane picked a crew of good fighters to help him clear out sections of the city. The squad was limited to five members. He kept that number low deliberately. The smaller the group, the easier it would be to escape danger without losing anyone. He chose Naplana, Talona, Kurth, and Tom.

On their first excursion, Xane insisted they raid the weapons room of every clan headquarters in every building in the city. It sounded crazy at first—the Reckoning already had plenty of weapons—but their leader insisted. Every clan stocked a few falchion-style swords, but few carried the enchantment. They managed to find four more, enough for every member of the squad to have one.

Kurth complained. He was used to carrying a scimitar and didn't want any other kind of weapon. Xane threatened to toss him off the team, and Kurth acquiesced. They also carried a spear for its range and wore quilted leather over their arms, legs, and shoulders, the places most vulnerable to a surprise bite or scratch. Unless he was giving instructions, Xane almost never spoke. Outside the presence of close friends, Xane had always been a man of few words. The loss of Gabio and Nahna had only exacerbated his insular nature.

Once they were outfitted with weapons and armor, the squad began clearing the city's farms. They escorted a separate crew to build a fence and stand guard over the precious food. When the farms were clear, they created traps in heavy-traffic areas around the city, large holes for the simple ones to fall in and trap themselves. Put a little bait in the hole, and the brain-dead creatures would keep walking until they fell over the edge. Soldiers from the Reckoning were standing by, ready to spear them.

Clearing out the buildings was the hardest part. There was no way to get herds of zombies into the elevator and down to the exits. "Here they come!" Tom yelled, bringing Naplana out of her daze. A herd of undead ambled toward her. Tom was leading them. She prepared to run. The squad had their method down to a science now. Tom had done his job by bringing the herd to her. He ran to the side through the bathroom door, where Kurth, Talona, and Xane were waiting. The herd followed Tom, but the doorway was too narrow for more than a couple of zombies to pass through at a time. While the rest of the herd tried to push their way inside, Naplana distracted them until they started chasing her.

Naplana started her lap around the food court. While she ran, the other members of the team moved the bodies out of the bathroom. When Naplana returned, she would do what Tom had done and lead a manageable number into the bathroom. Talona would be waiting to distract the rest of the herd. Everyone in the group took turns being the runner, including Xane.

In the middle of her route, a zombified barool wandered out in front of her. She glided around the huge beast and continued running. About ten minutes later, she was nearing the bathroom trap. Talona stood in front of her. "Big Pig!" Naplana yelled.

"Big Pig!" Talona repeated.

Xane heard them and came out of the bathroom. Barool were slower than the other zombies. They couldn't keep up with the rest of the herd, and stragglers were dangerous. Xane climbed up the fence of the kabloaf restaurant next to the bathroom.

As Naplana approached, Talona trained his eyes on a single zombie near the front of the herd. It was someone he recognized. A fellow elf. The elf's body had gone through many stages of decay, but the face was unmistakable.

"I'm doing this one myself!" Talona yelled. The turquoise-haired elf stopped waiting and ran toward the herd. He lifted his spear and planted it in the dead elf's right temple. The lifeless body of Eleris, the former leader of the noble guard, fell onto the karbero floor. Talona left his spear in his predecessor's head and took off in the other direction while Naplana headed into the bathroom. "Please grab my spear while I'm gone!" Talona yelled as he ran.

"Don't ever pull any shit like that again!" Xane yelled at the elf. He was perched on top of the fence, waiting for the barool to hobble past. The giant bipedal hog passed underneath the tall fence, and Xane leapt off. He pointed his sword downward, and the point pierced the top of the barool's head. Xane landed on the hulk's shoulders and rode its colossal body as it crashed to the floor. It took all four of them to move the barool's body out of the way. Then Xane took his position as the next runner and waited for Talona to make his way around.

***

Thanks in large part to Xane and his squad, every morning more residents of the city came back to life, and every morning Maribel let them know what was going on. The group had saved tens of thousands from the disease in a matter of weeks. While Xane and his group did their thing, soldiers escorted the newly living to the tunnels.

"If you are just waking, please be advised that this city is still infested with simple ones," Maribel said to the camera. She went on to describe the zombies and how to kill them again. Then she moved to the next part of her planned speech.

"We have set up safe communities large enough to provide food and shelter for every individual in the city. To access a safe community, first go to one of the large pits located outside every building. Several soldiers from the Army of Reckoning will be hiding nearby to escort you to safety. If you are followed by simple ones, run near the edge of the pit. The simple ones following you will be unable to stop themselves from falling in. Our soldiers can assist you.

"Next, I would like to recognize Xane 'Reaper' Bridges and his squad of zombie slayers for all their fine work in clearing out residential buildings. Many of you may even be hearing this from a building that has been cleared. Without Xane and his crew, that would never have been possible.

"And there's one more order of business. The Reckoning will be holding the first ever democratic elections in the known history of Gaulcel. Candidates for four cabinet positions will be announced next week. Elections will take place one month from today. Keep watching these morning announcements for more information.

Thank you everyone. Hang in there, and stay safe."

* * *

Once Maribel was done speaking, Dalthra turned off the camera. The clever dwarf had set up a makeshift broadcast studio in the tunnels by running a wire to an antenna located above ground. No other nonhumans were allowed in the tunnels, but Maribel needed Dalthra's technical know-how. Bill was standing by, waiting for the broadcast to finish. He stepped up to Maribel.

"What are we going to do if too many show up?" Bill said.

"We'll figure it out," Maribel replied.

"We'll figure it out? That's your plan?"

"Some residential buildings are practically safe. Folks won't want to leave their homes if they don't have to." Maribel sounded self-assured as always, but Bill wasn't buying it.

"You need to consult with me before you say something like that."

"It's my planning that got us this far," Maribel said.

"The city is overrun with zombies!"

"Walk with me," she said as she moved around a corner. "No one could plan for every contingency. Gaulcel's out of power, isn't he?"

Bill followed behind her. The hallways of the tunnels were all buzzing with activity. Over the weeks, the tunnels had become a city unto themselves. "What about your old boss? What if he comes back and brings his army? We could get overrun again."

"Gundarce just wants the mine. When he left, the city was in chaos."

"It still is!" Bill interrupted.

"As I was saying . . . the city was in chaos. Gundarce is not expecting Gaulcel to mount a counterattack for a while."

"What'll he do if he finds out we're leading his brother's city?"

"Tough to say," Maribel said.

Bill felt exasperated. "I liked you better when you had all the answers."

"I still do," Maribel said. She turned down another corridor. Each hallway carried a colored marking to help folks find their way. "So, what did you want to talk to me about?"

"You need to reach out to your centaur friends again. Someone needs to pay them for all the food they've been bringing."

"I'll handle them." Maribel stopped at the end of another hallway. She looked around for a minute, then motioned for a soldier to come over to her.

"Yes, ma'am?" the soldier said.

"Where's Guff?" Maribel asked.

"He's training new recruits. Down that hall, ma'am."

"Thank you, soldier," Maribel said. Then she turned to Bill. "Looks like this is my stop." She headed off down the corridor, leaving Bill to ponder their conversation. After a few steps, she turned to him again. "Oh Bill, by the way, just so you know, you're running for secretary of the treasury."

* * *

As promised, Maribel found Guff in the training area. He was with a squad of new recruits, trying to teach them how to use a spear. "Like this." Guff said. "Hyah!" Guff pushed the spear forward in a straight line.

"Hyah!" the recruits cried in unison as they awkwardly tried to imitate Guff's move.

Maribel approached their trainer. "Guff. Can I talk to you for a second?"

"Yes, ma'am?"

"How's the search going?" she asked.

The recruits suddenly noticed who Maribel was. "That's her. From the screen," one of them whispered to another.

"Are we going to meet Xane too?" the second whispered back.

Guff ignored them and turned to Maribel. "If he's in the tunnels, there must be a secret passageway somewhere. I have a squad doing tap tests throughout the halls as we speak. But it could take a while. There's a lot of tunnel to check. We are also trying to map the land in the city above the tunnels to see if anything sticks out as suspicious. Then again, he could be down below. We just don't know, ma'am."

"Can we get a couple more recruits on the tap tests?" Maribel asked.

"Yes, ma'am," Guff replied. He motioned to the two recruits who had been talking, and they stepped toward him. "You two. I'm going to need you to work doing tap tests. Talk to Scott, and he'll assign you specific corridors."

"What's a tap test?" the first recruit asked

"It's simple. You walk down the hallway and tap the bottom of your spear against the walls. Listen to see if a spot sounds hollow. You need to cover every foot, and don't forget to check the floor and ceiling too."

The recruits gave Guff a dumb look.

"Like this," he said and tapped the bottom of his wooden spear against the ceiling, making a knocking sound. "Then you try again one foot from the spot and see if it sounds different." Guff took a step and tapped his spear on the ceiling again. It sounded different, more of a thump.

Guff gave Maribel a look of disbelief. He tapped his spear on the same spot, thumping it twice. Then he tapped harder. A section of the tunnel's ceiling rose slightly, and a cloud of sediment fell to the floor. Then he thrust the spear into the ceiling with all his might. A metal panel abruptly dropped, and a mass of green skin and feathers fell to the tunnel floor.

Gaulcel had been listening in on the Reckoning since the day after his most recent death, waiting for an opportunity to make an escape. Now, he covered the exit to his quarters with his body, trying to dull the hollow sound of Guff's jabbing. But the exit flew open, and the acolyte fell from the ceiling and landed right at Guff's feet. Gaulcel looked haggard and starving, lying there prone, staring up at the humans surrounding him and their spears.

39

Maribel's Speech

"Good morning." Maribel said, and cleared her throat. "Today is a special day. I'm pleased to announce that the city of New Gaulcel is under control and the infestation is all but eradicated. To the extent any simple ones remain, they are few in number and can be dealt with. Even so, please stay vigilant. If you do encounter a simple one, get away and report it to your building chief immediately. If you cannot escape, remember to target the head."

Maribel was speaking in front of a large crowd at the city center instead of the studio where she usually made her announcements. She had been planning this speech for weeks, and she'd brought half the population of the tunnels with her for support and applause.

"Within the coming weeks, those living in our safe communities will be moving back to their old quarters in the residential buildings of the city. Business owners can reopen their restaurants and shops. The butterfly gardens located within the old clan headquarters, and which used to be exclusively accessible by elite clan guards, are now available to be enjoyed by all."

Maribel paused for a second. The supportive crowd read her cue and applauded. Once the applause died down, Maribel continued. "Tournaments will continue to take place, but they are no longer mandatory or necessary for income. In the coming weeks, we will be announcing several infrastructure projects that will improve our city and ensure everyone has a job and can afford to feed themselves." More applause.

"Furthermore, surveillance operations are suspended permanently. Everyone, you get to have your privacy!" The crowd exploded again. Dalthra panned the camera to show the enthusiastic throngs. This broadcast had been planned out beat by beat in advance. She'd heard Maribel practice this speech so many times, she had it memorized. *Here comes the crescendo*, the dwarf thought.

"Now," Maribel continued, "for the best news of all. Your newly elected cabinet of New Gaulcel is pleased to announce that the Friends of the Reckoning have captured the evil monster Gaulcel!" The applause at this line was thunderous. Gaulcel had been captured over a month earlier, and everyone in the crowd at the city center already knew it. This speech was dramaturgy, meant to convince the city's residents to accept the new order. Even if it was for the best, Maribel was about to embark on drastic change, and she needed the population on her side.

The applause continued for a full minute before Maribel spoke again. "Gaulcel is being held in his quarters, guarded by a full squad of armed and armored human soldiers." She enunciated the next seven words loud and slow. "We. Will. Never. Suffer. His. Evils. Again." She pounded on her podium with each new syllable.

This time, the applause wasn't just for show. The crowd's catharsis was real. They were not just clapping but shouting and screaming with emotion. Dalthra panned the masses again. Several folks had tears of joy in their eyes.

"I do not fear that monster. His horrific reign as this city's leader is over for good. What I fear"—Maribel paused for effect as the applause continued—"is another leader like him taking his place." A hush fell over the crowd. "We are at a crossroads right now, and we must choose which path we will take, each and every one of us. And the choice of path is a collective one. Leaders, no matter how great, no matter how respected or powerful, cannot choose for us. You, each and every one of you, must choose for yourself. If you do not, your actions will choose for you.

"Gaulcel created a place where the only law was his whim, and the only justice was his vengeance. But he wasn't as powerful as he seemed. The tyrant kept his power as long as he did by turning us against ourselves. He scared us into submission. He took away our power to control our own lives. He manufactured ignorance and mistrust so that we could never discover his weakness.

"That monster created a society where the only skill worth any merit was the skill to hurt and control your fellow man. A place where the only means of survival was fear. Your own fear, and the fear you instilled in others. But a free society cannot exist in a state of constant fear. In a world of every man for himself, every man is by himself, unable to enjoy the fruits of community, unable to fulfill the power of collective action. In New Gaulcel, the power of our leaders will not depend upon our fear. It will depend upon their ability to lead.

"Gaulcel denied us the right to decide the course of our own life. He forced us to live in service to his will, to his desires. He had us fighting for his scraps, gaining his favor by oppressing our neighbors. To his lackies, he offered the illusion of power, but power dependent upon compliance with his will was never really power at all. In New Gaulcel, every individual will have the freedom to pursue their own happiness, the freedom to use their mind to enrich themselves and their community. We must celebrate the great minds among us. We must allow their owners the freedom to use them. That said, great minds do not always think alike. Disagreement will occur, and it will occur often. Know that some of the world's deepest truths can only be discovered from contemplating two conflicting points of view. We must let reason, and not ego, be the arbiter of these conflicts.

"Our former leader created a wall to keep out knowledge. The only kinds of information allowed in the old Gaulcel were lies and propaganda. He hid the truth behind a cloud of falsehoods, so no one ever knew what to believe. In New Gaulcel, we must learn the lessons of our past. History must be recorded and unedited. Speech critical of those in power is a right of the public. Only then can the public trust and believe in their leaders, as well as each other. No one individual should ever have absolute power."

As Bill listened to the last line, he couldn't help but marvel at how powerful Maribel was. If someone was going to have that much power, it might as well be her.

She continued. "Purgatory could be a genuine utopia, a land of everlasting life. If we came together, if we put our fear aside and replaced our longing for power with a quest for knowledge, this god-awful hellscape could be like heaven. We have dwelled in violence and squalor for much too long. Now, we finally have a choice. If we have eternity, why should we not choose to enjoy it? Let us choose peace and freedom and happiness." The crowd let out another long round of applause.

"With that, I am pleased to introduce the first democratically elected cabinet of New Gaulcel." Three empty chairs sat stage left. Dalthra zoomed out so that the chairs appeared on the screen. "Each of these individuals holds the well-being of this city as a top priority. I know them all well, and I can assure you that they care deeply about the welfare and happiness of each and every one of you." Maribel introduced Ciessa as secretary of education and community, Naplana as secretary of justice and defense and Bill as secretary of commerce. They were each applauded as they walked on stage. "And finally, I am both humbled and proud that you selected me to oversee the other three departments as the chief of administration."

Less than 1 percent of the population had voted in the election, and every candidate had run unopposed. Most of the population had never even heard of democracy or voting. The ones who did vote were almost all leaders in the Reckoning army, the same folks who were now in the crowd. They continued applauding their friends and leaders.

"And now, we have one final announcement." Maribel paused for dramatic effect. "You all know this next individual as a strong leader, a zealous supporter, and an incredible fighter. He will fight for this city. It brings me great pleasure to announce that your democratically elected cabinet has consulted, and we unanimously agreed to nominate Xane 'Reaper' Bridges to serve as New Gaulcel's first king." The Reckoning assemblage responded in a sound like roaring thunder.

"As is customary, your new leader must first defeat the old leader in the fighting pits before taking their place at the throne." The crowd audibly gasped in unison. "We have arranged for this fight to take place immediately. Our cameras are standing by in the pit, and we take you there now. Thank you, everyone. Stay safe." Maribel wore a large, friendly, and fake smile. The camera turned off.

Bill sat in his seat, barely able to maintain his phony politician's grin. As soon as the red light on the camera turned off, he went over to Maribel. "Are you fucking crazy?" Bill whispered so that the crowd wouldn't hear. "A fight. With Gaulcel. Why the hell would we want to do that?"

"What'd you think of the speech?" Maribel asked, ignoring his vexation.

"A little preachy, and way too wordy," he whispered back in a caustic tone. "And you really should have cut out that last part." Bill glared at her as he spoke.

Maribel met his look and equaled its intensity. "This was a culture of violence. That won't change overnight. The people need to see Gaulcel beaten for themselves."

"But what if he loses?"

40

Fist Fight for a Crown

Xane stood on the familiar sandy floor of the fighting pit. His archenemy stood across from him. The viewing floor was packed with humans, eager with anticipation. Gaulcel was covered from shoulder to toe in steel chains, and a muzzle encased his jaws. The monster's muscles protruded through the hard metal. Tom and Tim stood on opposite sides of the creature, holding spears pointed at his head. Gaulcel towered over them.

Guff was in the center of the ring to referee the bout. His scythe glistened from the pit's harsh lighting, which reflected off the khaki-colored sand. Guff held a megaphone in his other hand. Three cameras, set on mobile tripods, were positioned around the edge to capture the action.

Comerciam was in the security room of the human prison building, watching the live feed from each camera. Dalthra had taught him to operate the switcher just for this occasion. Once Maribel wrapped her speech, Comerciam switched the broadcast from the city center to the pit. The live camera focused on Guff, and its operator gave him the signal.

The whole of the city was watching, including Bill and Maribel. A giant screen had been constructed in the city center. Bill's palms were sweating profusely. This fight was not fixed—Xane was on his own.

Guff raised both of his hands, and the crowd raised their voices. They had arrived at the scene with no warning about what to expect. Xane and Gaulcel had been brought to the ring during Maribel's speech. Most of the audience were just discovering the identities of the combatants, just now recognizing the magnitude of what they were about to witness firsthand.

Guff spoke into the megaphone. "The prize for winning the contest today is this crown." He dropped his scythe and pulled a circlet from his front pocket. It was made of solid monet and adorned with jewels. "This crown bestows upon its wearer the right to rule the city of New Gaulcel. Now, to introduce the fighters. To my right is the human, Xane 'Reaper' Bridges."

The crowd erupted, repeating his name in unison. "Xane! Xane! Xane!"

"And to my left the acolyte, Gaulcel," Guff continued over the chants. As his name was announced, Tom and Tim removed Gaulcel's chains and muzzle. The creature stretched, showing his immense size. "Both of them have a recognized right to compete for the honor of wearing this crown, but only one can win. Please give a round of applause for today's combatants."

When Guff finished, he tucked the circlet back into his pocket and raised his scythe.

The "Xane" chants from the audience resumed, but they ended abruptly once the red light above the pit flashed on. Xane pulled his sword from its scabbard and dropped it in the sand. His ritual.

Watching on the monitors, Bill rolled his eyes and clenched his fists. Maribel extended her fingers and placed them on her knees. She was giddy with excitement.

Maribel and Xane had known all along that Gaulcel was not a fighter. He never had been, because he'd never needed to be. The monster had never had to do anything for himself, especially fight; he'd rarely dealt with adversity. He lacked the capacity to handle it.

Gaulcel was bigger and stronger than Xane, though. He had wings that allowed flight, horns he could impale Xane with, and sharp talons that could shred Xane to bits. Yet none of that mattered, because Gaulcel was a coward, down to the core. This would be the easiest fight of Xane's career.

As Xane approached the former warden of the prison city, he recognized the look in Gaulcel's eyes. He'd seen the same look when he faced Joe, the man Buddy had tried to make Xane kill. Gaulcel puffed his pectorals to look intimidating. Xane just smirked at him.

The monster leaped up from the sand and extended his wings. He took flight up above the pit and then flew outside of it. Gaulcel did not want to fight. He was trying to escape. The acolyte landed in front of the elevator used to enter and exit the pit.

When Gaulcel opened the door, a swarm of simple ones met him. Zombies rushed into the room, blocking his exit. He flew up toward the ceiling. The audience screamed and crowded to one side of the room, trying to get away from the ghouls. For their own safety, the cameramen left their post.

All three cameras hung loosely on their tripods, pointing toward the sand, where Xane and Guff were still visible. Xane picked up his sword. Comerciam didn't know what was happening in the rest of the arena, but he heard the screams. The elf tried some controls and managed to access a live feed from an old security camera. It showed an overhead view of the zombies attacking the audience. Comerciam patched the feed into the live broadcast.

Bill and Maribel looked on in shock and horror. "Tell me this is part of the plan." Bill said emphatically.

Maribel sat silent next to him, avoiding eye contact, keeping herself from showing emotion.

Bill knew what that meant. His heartbeat became rapid and erratic. He wanted to scream, but his voice refused him. He gasped for air in a rapid staccato rhythm. No matter how hard he tried, it seemed no breath would come. New Gaulcel's first secretary of commerce was having a panic attack.

Gaulcel flew in front of the camera so that all the viewing audience could see was his hefty wings flapping in a hurried rhythm, struggling to hold up the creature's immense weight. A moment later, the airborne monster moved out of the way, revealing Xane going to work with his sword.

Xane cut through the undead with incredible efficiency. Within minutes, all the simple ones who'd breached the door had been immobilized. Meanwhile, their first victims were beginning to turn. "If you haven't been bit, get behind me!" Xane screamed. Everyone able to walk of their own accord ran behind Xane while he went to work on the other side of the room.

A cluster of newly created zombies wandered over the edge of the pit and fell to the sandy floor below. One zombified member of the audience clutched at Gaulcel's leg as he fell. The ghoul managed to pull the acolyte down with him. Gaulcel landed hard in the packed sand, lying prone. The simple ones in the pit were on him in an instant, biting and clawing at his wings and legs.

Meanwhile, Xane finished off every undead creature on the main floor. Then he turned his attention to the pit. Guff clearly needed no assistance defending himself. Three motionless bodies lay at his friend's feet. Gaulcel, on the other hand, was getting eaten alive. Xane lowered himself down and ran to Gaulcel's aid. His sword slid through the back of one zombie's skull, spilling its brains onto the monster's lap. The head of a second rolled across Gaulcel's chest.

Thanks to Xane, Gaulcel was soon freed from the zombie attack. "Get up!" he yelled at the beast.

Gaulcel stood to his feet and opened his wings. The simple ones had ripped holes in the flaps, keeping the monster from taking flight.

There was one more in the pit with them still. It had been part of the cluster that Guff was slaying, but then it noticed Xane and his opponent and stumbled toward them. Gaulcel ran behind the hungry fiend and pushed it toward Xane. He side-stepped the clumsy attack, then finished the last zombie in the room with an intense downward slash from his falchion blade.

The red light was still on. Xane advanced and threw his first punch of the bout, a hard right to Gaulcel's gut. The blow took the wind from the monster's lungs, and he fell to his knees. From there, he landed his signature left hook and put Gaulcel on his back.

Xane observed the copious bite wounds all over the monster's legs. The Lecttum was beginning to work its way through Gaulcel's veins. He had to die. *"Finish him, Reaper!"* Coach Clark screamed in Xane's head.

He pushed his knees down into Gaulcel's shoulder and launched his fists at his head. Left and rights landed like bombs dropping on the monster's temple, over and over again, unimpeded. The violent, thwacking sound rang out through the arena.

One of the surviving camera operators returned to shoot the fight's conclusion. Comerciam switched over the live feed. The whole city witnessed as Xane beat their former leader to a pulp with his bare hands. An onslaught of strikes, all directly on target. Xane felt pain in his hands, but Coach Clark continued to yell words of encouragement, spurring the Reaper on. Gaulcel's face was covered by a mask of dark green blood. His brains leaked from the cracks in his skull before being scattered through the air by fresh blows. It was over.

Guff ran to the scene and pulled Xane off Gaulcel. He was still in a state of bloodlust when Guff raised his hand.

Xane had ensured the disease never took hold. The acolyte was dead before he could turn.

41

Epilogue

After killing the acolyte Gaulcel, Xane was named king of New Gaulcel. Purgatory's common tongue had no literal translation of words like "president" or "prime minister." The closest alternative was king. However, under Maribel's scheme of governance, the title was meaningless. Xane held no actual authority.

Instead, he aimed his focus outside the city. His new enemy was Lecttum, and his goal was to eradicate the disease from all of Purgatory. On occasion, Bill would send word asking Xane to come back for a public appearance. He remained popular with the citizens, and that popularity was useful for selling the new government's agenda. As soon as an event was over, Xane would head straight for the city gates to resume his hunt for the undead. He often thought of Gabio and Nahna and hoped to find them someday, if only to apologize.

Likewise, Maribel was seldom in the city of New Gaulcel. She was busy working her influence in Gundarce, doing her best to keep their army from attacking, all the while plotting to remove Gaulcel's brother from power. It was rare for Xane and Maribel to cross paths, but they remained fond of each other and spent time together when their quests allowed.

Bill spent most of his days fundraising for the city. There was no system of taxation at first; the government relied on volunteers and donations. Bill

EPILOGUE

solicited funds by offering gambling tips. Khane, Kurth, Tom, and Tim were all big donors. It was not a fair system, and it wouldn't be sustainable in the long term, but it was easy to implement and necessary during the city's infancy. Bill also worked closely with Comerciam to establish trade routes with outsiders, which led to an abundance of food and other resources. He kept his pizza place open, though he had to hire someone else to run it.

Bill and Naplana tried dating but decided they were both too busy. Naplana was using her new position to install and oversee a police force and court system. Most police were former clan guards. Much to the guards' chagrin, the accused were always entitled to a fair trial.

Ciessa opened a school in every residential building to teach residents how to speak, read, and write in the common tongue. They also offered classes in various trades. The most popular was window building and installation, as taught by Dalthra. Ciessa did not teach herself. She spent most of her time with her husband, Eleris. They rarely ever left their house.

Guff first took the position of police chief, under Naplana. But after a short time, the bearded Viking decided policing was not for him. He started teaching courses in combat in Ciessa's schools and continued to referee in what remained of the daily tournaments.

Talona chose to get out of his old profession and open a bookstore. Comerciam helped him track down new books from outside the city, and the elf did quite a bit of writing himself. He released a "tell-all" disclosing all the gritty details from his time as leader of the noble guard. It quickly became a bestseller. Eleris reached out to him after reading it, and the two elves became friends.

Most of the city were grateful for the new way of life, though some detractors endured. A few former clan guards missed their positions of power and used their newly acquired free speech rights to undermine the new government. Mostly, they just hated sharing the butterfly gardens. In addition, because the leaders in the Reckoning were overwhelmingly human, the humans of New Gaulcel held a disproportionate share of wealth and power. This created several problems around race relations. Some humans felt and acted superior to the other races, and the nonhuman races harbored resentment.

When Gaulcel respawned after the bout with Xane, his quarters became his prison. Armed humans stood guard in the tunnels at all hours. The acolyte was reportedly writing a memoir, wanting to bear his soul. At first, the public called for Gaulcel to be tortured to death for lifetimes, the punishment he had inflicted on many others. Constituents wanted not only for him to be tortured, but for the torture to be broadcast to the whole city every morning.

Bill and other leaders of New Gaulcel refused the demand and faced a harsh backlash for their principles. Detractors seized on the issue, using it to drum up resistance to the new government. Bill had to call in Xane, who helped assuage the public's anger. The king's first public speech consisted of only four words: "We're better than that."

* * *

After the fight that earned Xane his crown. Bill and Maribel spoke again. They sat together at the side of the stage. Bill was still in a state of shock. He was angry at Maribel, but he also loved her for what they had accomplished.

"We actually did it." Bill said with disbelief. "It's over. The revolution succeeded."

"Now comes the hard part," she replied, pulling her hair out her face. It was a rare moment where she let her guard down.

"Yep," Bill said. They stared into space for a few minutes, and then he thought of something. "I still don't understand one thing. Why Xane? The people in this city love you too. Everyone would back you as queen, and as much as I hate to say it, you would probably be pretty good at it."

"I don't want to be the queen of Gaulcel. I want to be the queen of Purgatory," Maribel said with a sly grin. She thought of the future as she held her hand to her stomach. The quickening life inside her womb was kicking.

EPILOGUE

✷ ✷ ✷

About the Author

Art Quarry can typically be found in or around Philadelphia, Pennsylvania. When not writing, Art spends his time fiddling with a guitar, practicing law, and gazing out windows.

Printed in Great Britain
by Amazon